MW01196574

IN MY FATHER'S BASEMENT

A serial killer novel

T. J. Payne

In My Father's Basement: a serial killer novel
Copyright © 2018 T.J. Payne
All rights reserved.

This book or any portion thereof may not be reproduced or used in any manner whatsoever without the express written permission of the publisher except for the use of brief quotations in a book review.

This book is a work of fiction. Names, characters, and places are products of the author's imagination. Any resemblance to actual events or persons, living or dead, is entirely coincidental.

ISBN: 978-1-954503-03-8

PROLOGUE

It was 4:32 a.m.

Officer Cornett was the first responder.

When he exited his vehicle he initially thought it was a prank call. He didn't *hear* any gunshots. He didn't *see* any signs of mass panic. The campus was silent, and the dorm—from the outside, at least—looked as though most of the residents were still sleeping. It did not appear that an attack was in progress.

Then he heard a rustling.

Several first-floor residents opened their windows and dropped down into the bushes. They silently crept away from the building until they got some distance, then they broke into panicked sprints across the parking lot. They were barefoot and still in their sleep-clothes.

For the first time in his career, Officer Cornett drew his weapon.

He approached the building. He was still confused as to why he couldn't hear gunshots. Maybe the attacker had finished his spree and already committed suicide.

As he neared the entrance, he glanced up at the five-story dorm. Many students on the upper floors stood at their windows, waving and gesturing wildly. They were trying to relay information to him. Some had typed up messages on their devices that they now held to the glass. Others had scrawled their messages on sheets of paper.

Officer Cornett couldn't read any of it. It was all visual noise. Five floors of terrified students who knew a madman was loose in their building. They gesticulated wildly but made no sense.

He approached the Smith Hall entrance.

It was there that he found Body #1.

***

Janice Holgate. Sophomore from Hood River.

Electrical Engineering major.

Janice's best friend, Moira, was leaving on Monday to study abroad in London and that night had been a surprise going-away party in the lounge of Moira's dorm.

Everyone got wasted.

Janice woke up on the couch in Moira's dorm's lounge at 3:30 a.m. She had a dry mouth and a splitting headache. All she wanted was a shower, a toothbrush, and to sleep in her own bed.

So, she walked across the campus back to her room.

She fumbled with her key at the front door, struggling to fit it into the lock.

That fumble, that delay, that distraction... *that* was the opening he needed to walk up behind her and bash in the backside of her skull.

Janice died instantly. On the front step of her dorm.

The killer used her key and entered the building.

***

Officer Cornett saw that Janice's key still hung in the door lock. He stepped over her body and turned the key, pushing open the front door.

He advanced down the first-floor hallway. All the doors were colorfully decorated with the names of each room's occupant. They were all closed.

Except for one.

The door to Room 113 hung wide open.

Officer Cornett crept forward. He shined his light into the room.

Inside were Bodies #2 and #3.

***

Sasha Hernandez. Junior from Portland. Biology major.

David Wong. Junior from Medford. Psychology major.

Sasha had been excited for this weekend.

Her roommate had gone home to do laundry and get a home-cooked meal, meaning that Sasha and David—whom she had been dating for three months—had the rare opportunity to have a dorm room all to themselves.

They had sex.

Got high.

Had sex again.

Watched a movie.

Had sex one more time.

Then fell asleep in each other's arms.

At some point that night, David awoke and went to the men's bathroom down the hall. He didn't have a room key, so he left the door to Sasha's unlocked. When he returned to the room and crawled back into bed with Sasha, he forgot to lock the door behind him.

Sasha awoke to the sound of David's head cracking open under repeated blunt force blows. His blood splattered on her in the dark. She managed to get out a single terrified scream before her temple was struck with such force that her eye socket collapsed.

Eight people reported hearing that scream.

Three of the eight checked to make sure their door was locked. None of them called 911 at that time. Instead, they sat in their beds and listened for any other strange sounds. But there was silence and they went back to sleep.

***

Officer Cornett scanned his light over David and Sasha's bodies.

Someone screamed on the *third* floor.

He bolted out of the room and raced toward the sound.

There was a stairwell at the end of the hall. He advanced upward, his gun held ready.

When he reached the second floor, he saw Body #4.

***

Tristan Peterson. Sophomore from Beaverton. Undeclared.

That night, Tristan consumed two 40s and half a Mad Dog. He wasn't a social drinker or a party drinker. He was an alcoholic. He fell asleep in his bed but awoke a few minutes later. He covered his mouth as he vomited, which only resulted in the alcohol-and-stomach-bile-scented chunks of pizza spraying out at awkward angles.

His roommate, with whom he already had an unpleasant relationship, demanded that he go to the bathroom and clean himself off. Tristan was very susceptible to orders when he was drunk, and so, he obeyed.

He dragged himself out of the room and into the hallway. He walked into the wall twice and smacked his hip into a drinking fountain along the route to the bathroom.

As he turned around the corner in the hallway, a claw hammer cracked into his forehead. It burst the blood vessels in his eyes. He stumbled around. He propped his back against the wall and slid to the ground. Tristan died in a sitting position with his bloody eyes open and staring toward the stairwell.

***

Despite his efforts to stay calm, Officer Cornett audibly gasped when he saw Tristan. The body slouched on the floor, blood framing its face as its red eyes glared toward the officer.

Officer Cornett quickly pushed the gruesome tableau from his mind.

The screams had stopped, and Officer Cornett needed to locate the assailant. He raced up the stairs to the third floor.

Four bodies would be discovered on this floor. Two males. Two females.

***

Ritesh Rhat. Sophomore from Bend. Political Science.
Justin Yamazaka. Junior from Wailuku. Electrical Engineering.

Ritesh and Justin never locked their door. They didn't drink, but they did own a futon. Their room had come to be called "The Oasis," a haven where dorm mates could crash for the night if they got locked out of their room. As two self-proclaimed "good kids," Ritesh and Justin enjoyed serving as sober guardians of the dorm. That's why they barely stirred when their door opened. They assumed it was another friend in need of a place to sleep.

Ritesh died quickly from a single blow to the head.

Justin awoke to the sound of his roommate convulsing. He realized that someone was in the room with him. The door was open and the light from the hallway backlit the man.

All Justin could think to do was to stay quiet and pretend to be asleep. Perhaps the man would leave.

Justin died from a single blow to the head a few seconds later.

The attacker left the room and closed the door behind him. He would find his next victim three doors down the hall.

***

Maddie Rector. Junior from Boise. Undeclared.

Maddie lived in the floor's only single-room.

She was a light sleeper.

Her eyes popped open the moment she heard her doorknob rattle. An ex-boyfriend had jammed gum in the strike plate three months ago, preventing the door from sealing shut. Maddie intended to report it to Facilities, but it always nibbled at the back of her mind that she would have to pay for the repair. And so, she ignored the problem, hoping it would fix itself.

She saw the figure in the dark approach her.

As it raised the hammer above her head, she was too terrified to scream, but she had the wherewithal to block the blow with her arms. The hammer shattered her forearm.

She rolled out of bed and tried to run away, but she got clipped with a strike to the back of her head. She kept her legs moving, but she was woozy and disoriented. She stumbled out into the hallway. She never looked behind her. Never noticed that it wasn't so much that she was outrunning her attacker, as that he was intentionally hanging back, waiting to see how her escape developed.

In her dazed, confused state, the best plan Maddie could manage was to throw herself against the door across the hall. She clawed at it while weakly gasping for help.

The room belonged to Body #8.

**

Katie Hale. Sophomore from Portland. Latin American Studies.

Katie was the second-string shooting guard on the women's basketball team. The team was traveling to Los Angeles for the conference tournament the next week and Katie wanted to enjoy the trip without any homework hanging over her head. Always a planner, Katie designated *this* weekend as the one where she would stay up all night and crank out her mid-term essays.

Around 3 a.m., the caffeine started to upset her stomach, and so, she kept herself awake by taking long walks around the dorm.

She hiked up and down the stairs, from one floor to the other, for 15 minutes.

But as she did her fly-by of the second floor, she heard Sasha Hernandez's scream. Katie froze. Was it a joke? Someone dreaming? Or was there an actual assault occurring in one of these rooms?

Katie's mind flashed to the story of Kitty Genovese, the famous case of the New York woman who screamed for help for approximately thirty minutes as she was stabbed and raped. Although dozens of people heard the screams, according to legend, not one of them came to her aid or called the police.

The story still stuck with Katie.

If something bad was happening in one of these rooms, Katie intended to help. She wouldn't be a passive bystander. *Evil can only triumph when good men do nothing*, she thought.

She hid in the stairwell and peered out at the second-floor hallway.

One of the doors opened.

A man stepped out into the light.

Katie saw *him*.

His dead, blood-red eyes.

His gray, blood-splattered cardigan.

That dull, blood-dipped hammer in his hands.

He stood alone in the hall for a moment. He seemed huge.

The man didn't notice Katie hunkering in the stairwell. Instead, he stepped toward another room and tried the handle. Locked.

Then he moved to the next door. Locked

He worked his way down the hall, gently trying each door, checking for fresh opportunities and fresh meat.

In the stairwell, Katie wanted to scream. She wanted to wake the world and warn her friends to lock their doors. But she couldn't. She knew that to break the silence meant death. He would find her before help could. He would find her, and he would kill her.

The rational part of her mind clicked off then. She was in the stairwell. One floor from the ground... from the exit... from freedom. She was also one floor from her room... her phone... a solid door she could lock.

She chose the latter. For whatever reason, getting access to her phone suddenly seemed more important than getting access to the outside world.

She tiptoed up the stairs to her room. She went inside and quickly locked the door. She woke her roommate, Trish, and urgently explained the situation. Katie called 911 while Trish sent a message to the dorm email list advising everyone to lock their doors—there was an intruder on the premises.

Katie stayed on the line with 911 while Trish searched the room for something to use as a weapon. A desk lamp? A vodka bottle?

They briefly tried to move a dresser in front of the door as a barricade, but the noise caused by the process seemed too loud. Silence felt more secure. The 911 operator assured them that police were en route and the best thing they could do was to lock the door, turn off the lights, and stay calm and quiet. That's exactly what they did.

Until they heard the knock.

And the weak, gasping voice.

"Please... help... Katie..."

Katie knew immediately that it was Maddie. She was in trouble. The door's peephole revealed nothing, just a narrow fish-eye of empty hallway.

"Help... help..."

Katie had to do something. The 911 Operator ordered her to not open the door. The best course of action was to keep the door locked and stay hidden until the police arrived.

But Maddie continued weakly clawing at the door. She was right there. Two inches away. And she needed help. It would take only seconds to open the door, drag Maddie inside and close and lock the door behind her. Katie knew she could do it. She was strong. An athlete. Katie made up her mind.

Trish was terrified but found comfort in deferring to Katie.

They came up with a plan—Trish would open the door, Katie would drag in Maddie, then Trish would close and lock the door. Seconds. That's all it would take. There wasn't a moment to lose.

Katie crouched by the door, ready to grab Maddie.

In one motion, Trish unlocked the door and flung it open.

He barged in immediately.

With Katie crouching down, he had an elevated position. His single hammer swing had so much force that it went right through the crown of Katie's skull. The hammer got stuck. He had to dislodge it from Katie's bone.

That distraction is probably why he never noticed Trish hiding behind the door.

He pulled the hammer from Katie's skull and left.

***

Officer Cornett arrived in the third-floor hallway.

When Officer Cornett saw him step out of Katie and Trish's room, he didn't fire. He had been expecting to find a student attacking fellow classmates. Maybe a crazy homeless person. Perhaps a gang of Satanists. What he saw didn't fit his expectations. And so, he didn't fire. He didn't shoot to kill. He didn't end it there and then.

He saw a man that looked like his own grandpa. That gray cardigan over grease-stained overalls. That pure white ring of hair on an otherwise bald scalp. Those reading glasses. That full beard, trimmed daily with pride.

This wasn't a killer. It couldn't be a killer.

This must be a Good Samaritan neighbor. Or a maintenance worker. Or the residential faculty advertiser. An old man with a kind heart who had heard the distressed cries of the kids under his care and grabbed the only weapon he had access to—a hammer—and rushed to their defense.

Yes. That must be it.

As Officer Cornett watched the old man turn and face him, saw the blood splattered on the cardigan, saw his red, lifeless eyes, it just didn't make any sense.

The old man saw the officer aiming the gun at him. His muscles seemed to relax. It was as if he had been expecting this moment. He dropped his hammer. He put his hands on his head and lowered himself to his knees.

It *still* didn't make any sense to Officer Cornett. Not even as he pinned the man down and slapped handcuffs on his wrists.

This guy can't be the killer.

***

As police teams flooded the building, freeing residents and cataloguing the extensive crime scene, a reporter managed to grab Officer Cornett and pull him aside for a sound bite.

"What were your first thoughts when you laid eyes on him?" the reporter asked.

Officer Cornett hadn't yet been briefed by the department's PR officers. He was still too young and too shaken to give a "no comment." He felt the role of a police officer was to preserve the honesty and integrity of society, and so, he gave an honest answer.

"I thought he was the handyman," he said. "But he was actually The Devil."

That single clip played around the country.

A legend was born.

The fascination began.

The Handyman became America's most famous killer.

CHAPTER 1

Isaac Luce sat in his car.

He was determined to not give Best Buy a single extra *second* of his life. It was 5:50 a.m. and Isaac knew he only required eight minutes to exit his car, blissfully amble across the parking lot in the cool, damp Oregon air, walk through the front door, cross the sales floor and swipe his fob on the pad in the stock room to punch-in for the day.

Eight minutes from car to clock. And he had ten.

Two extra minutes for him to try to shock his system awake with the gangsta rap blaring from his too-cheap-to-handle-the-bass speakers.

Two extra minutes where he wasn't wearing that damn back brace, moving flat-screen TV boxes around a windowless stock room.

Two extra minutes of solitude in his car.

Not that his car was any great joyful place to kill some time. The early-90s Honda only had two things going for it—it *generally* started when Isaac wanted it to, and it *generally* stopped when Isaac needed it to. Other than that, it was thread-bare upholstery that flaked small bits of foam, and a smell that could only be described as "old car"—some mixture of burning oil, exhaust that leaked up through the heater vents, and the remnants of spilt beef-and-broccoli sauce that had soaked into the seat back when Isaac was in high school.

He was sure the car was slowly killing him. But... it *generally* started and stopped when he wanted it to. And this made it the most valuable thing that Isaac had ever owned in all his twenty-two years. What more could he want?

He glanced again at the clock. He still had time.

As Isaac sat in his car, he heard an engine. He looked over and watched as a Jeep pulled into the spot next to him. Not just any Jeep. It was a green Jeep.

The green Jeep.

Kim Rivera's Green Jeep.

Isaac immediately turned off his music. He didn't know what music Kim listened to, but it probably wasn't rap. It was probably some indie rock from some obscure Portland band that was only known to the cool people of the world.

Despite the coolness of the morning, Isaac felt traces of nervous sweat forming on his palms. It was his chance to talk to Kim.

Ever since he started this job six months ago, Isaac had tried to finagle a conversation with Kim. She worked the sales floor and he worked the stock room. Their paths only crossed when an obnoxious customer demanded that Kim check the back to see if something was in stock. Those micro-interactions convinced Isaac that Kim was, in fact, cool. He couldn't define what exactly made her cool. Maybe it was just that she was actually nice and friendly toward him.

Isaac had wanted to invite himself along on Kim's lunch breaks, but she almost always took her breaks with her friends. Isaac never had the nerve to try to crack into those groups. He knew his weaknesses—the more people in a group, the more he withdrew into himself and slinked around the periphery. The real world was like high school all over again.

But here was an opportunity.

His mind spun up with all the different ways this scenario might play out. If he timed this right, he would have the full walk across the parking lot alone with Kim. There was no telling what kind of witty conversation might develop. Maybe they'd talk about movies, or basketball, or music. There might be that slimmest of openings for Isaac to prove to Kim that he was worthy of her attention.

For the briefest of moments, he could feel his muscles involuntarily cringing at the realization that his heart was pounding and his palms were sweating at the *possibility* of a three-minute walk with an attractive girl. It seemed that every other bro wandered in and out of such interactions with confidence and ease.

But, at long last, it was Isaac's moment to shine.

He rustled around his car for a few seconds, waiting for the timing to be just right.

He glanced in his rear-view mirror and eyed her stepping out of her Jeep. *Plotting intercept course in five... four... three... two...*

He put his hand on the door handle, and then...

His phone rang.

At 5:52 a.m.?

He looked at the caller I.D. The number wasn't in his contacts. Isaac sent the call to voicemail and stepped out of his car.

He was too late. Kim was already ten steps ahead, walking toward the entrance. Isaac could jog and catch up, but that would look like he was *trying* to jog and catch up. Lame. Pathetic. Intrusive. He could call out to her, but she had her ear buds in. He would have to yell. Lame. Pathetic. Intrusive.

The timing hadn't worked. The opportunity was gone. His well-laid plans were totally and royally screwed.

His phone rang.

Again?

He checked the caller I.D. He wasn't sure if this was the same number that called earlier, but he could swear the area code of the first caller started with a 3-something, and this was a 2-something. Weird.

He sent the call to voicemail.

As he walked behind Kim, the thought occurred to Isaac that Kim might not even know his name. Had she ever said it out loud?

Riiiing!

What. The. Actual. Fuck.

Isaac answered his phone with a curt "Hello."

He expected to hear some accented voice trying to sell him the latest and greatest scam of his life, but instead he heard, "Hey! My name is Ben Stewart. I'm doing some background. This Isaac Luce?"

The guy's voice had the pacing of a go-getter who was juggling five tasks at once. Isaac stopped walking.

"Um, yeah. This is Isaac Luce."

"I'm an editor at DOPER Magazine..."

Isaac's mind raced. *DOPER Mag? Defenders Of Public Enlightenment and Recreation Magazine.* Isaac knew it well. They were at the checkout stand of every grocery store. They had spun off into one of those gossip sites that published anything from celebrity nip-slips to celebrity suicide photos.

Ben talked fast. "I know the crews will probably be setting up outside your place soon—"

"My place?"

"Your apartment at 113 Brookfield Road? Unit 201?"

Isaac didn't respond. Yes, that was definitely his apartment, but he wanted to figure out the hook of the scam before he relinquished any personal details.

But Ben didn't care. He was already on to the next piece of business. "Look, they're gonna be shoving cameras in your face, shouting out questions, trying to get you to say something on record. I'd like to bring you in for an actual interview. Something professional, good lighting, makeup."

Isaac stood silently. He tried to piece together the information.

Ben continued, "I know what you probably think of us, but I gotta say, as someone who's been working here for a long time, we're very respectful to the families in these stories. Do you read our stuff or go on our site?"

"Uh, no."

"The families aren't the story. They're our lens into the story. They're sympathetic. They're the normal people caught up in this shitstorm. That's how we like to portray them. We'll let you get your side out. But the vultures who show up at your door with a camera are going to pick over your carcass. They don't want a story. They don't want a human. They want sound bites. Give us the exclusive and we'll be fair."

Ben rolled seamlessly into a list of questions. "Let me just get a few background things on record. When was the last time you were in your father's house?"

Isaac was so confused that he found himself blurting out responses. "A few years ago. I guess. I think it was... I don't really remember." His *father*? What the hell was this about?

Ben continued, "When was the last time you spoke with him?"

"I dunno. Christmas?"

"Did you go *in* his house on Christmas?"

"No. We met up for lunch."

"Is that how you traditionally celebrated holidays with him?"

Isaac didn't know why, but his heartrate increased. His hands again began to sweat, just as they had when he thought he might get a moment of conversation with Kim. He had been terrified of that simple interaction, afraid he might make a fool of himself in front of a pretty girl. Somehow, talking to Ben with his no-nonsense fact-finding questions felt far more dangerous and consequential.

He chose his words carefully. "We started doing that a couple years ago. What's going on?"

"I see your mother died seventeen years ago. Is that correct?"

"Uh, yeah. I guess."

Isaac felt like one of those soldiers who dumbly put his foot down and heard a click. Any second now, a Bouncing Betty mine was going to jump out of the ground and fill him with shrapnel.

"What can you tell me about her death? Was it suspicious at all? Did you ever see her body?"

Isaac blinked in astonishment for a moment. His hand clenched on the phone and his jaw drew tight. His confusion gave way to a defiant rage that boiled up through his system.

"I'm hanging up."

Ben's voice on the other end immediately dropped its cocky demeanor. An urgency overtook it. "Wait, wait, wait," Ben said. "How 'bout pictures?"

"Pictures?"

"Your social media's fair game, and I'm sure it's been picked clean by everyone else. But honestly, there's not much there. Anything else that paints a fuller picture and helps us tell a story would be great. Him as a kid, him at work. If you have any of him holding a tool, that would be best."

Isaac didn't respond.

"We'll throw you a little something for any and all images of just him, depending on how good the shot is. It can be in front of a Christmas tree for all I care. But I can budget a hellava lot more for any images of him holding a tool."

Isaac couldn't hold his confusion any more. "What is going on?"

Ben went silent for a moment. "You really don't know?"

"I'm hanging up."

"I'm sorry, man. Offer stands on those photos. You got my number on your phone. And..." Isaac heard Ben gulp. A moment of sincerity overtook the conversation. "It's gonna suck, man. From my experience, it's best if you just roll with it. Others will call. Don't give away anything for free. Charge for it all. Get what you can, while you can. My rate will always be fair, and I'll always respect whatever privacy limits you want to put on the material you send me. Make the best of it. Good luck."

Isaac finally hung up. He wished he had done it sooner. Maybe this was all a prank?

His phone rang again. This time, the call came from a blocked number. Isaac sent the call to voicemail, only for — *RIIIIING!* — another call to come in from a different number.

He sent that one to voicemail. Not a moment later—*RIIIIING!* The calls came in fast. Isaac realized they must be stacked up; dozens if not hundreds of people dialing, and redialing, and redialing, all waiting to break through to speak to Isaac. He powered off his phone and shoved it into his pocket.

For a moment, Isaac stood alone in the Best Buy parking lot. It was silent. It was still. Kim had already entered the store. His earlier excitement at having the chance of talking with her felt like an entirely different day. All he could register was how quiet and alone the parking lot felt.

Isaac liked the quiet. Isaac liked being alone.

It was a typical overcast Oregon morning. A damp crispness hung in the air. Last night's rain lingered on the world, making everything feel clean. Isaac walked the final few yards across the parking lot and into his work.

CHAPTER 2

Everything in the store felt weird. Different.

No one manned the register. No one stocked shelves. No one gathered to listen to the manager, Owen, discuss the day's schedule.

Isaac looked around, wondering where everyone had gone. The answer soon became clear. They were grouped together at the wall of mounted flat-screen TVs.

Isaac approached them, a weight forming in his stomach. He knew they weren't watching the demo displays. Someone had hooked one of the screens to a digital antenna and every employee's eyes were glued to the morning news.

On the screen, the news showed shots of what looked like a dorm. The camera never went wide, never provided context. It stayed focused on the building's door. That door swarmed with police officers, SWAT members, and paramedics, all hustling in and out. Everyone had a job to do.

And then, all the police parted, stepping out of the way of the door as paramedics wheeled a body bag out on a gurney. And then another body bag. And another.

Someone in the store gasped at the sight.

The news anchor announced, "Police now report eight dead. All classes have been cancelled for the day, and students are being urged to stay in their rooms. Police stress that they have a suspect in custody. They say they do not believe that he had an accomplice."

Isaac walked over and stood beside Connor Brooks. He was a young guy, about Isaac's age.

"What's going on?" Isaac asked.

Connor kept his eyes on the TV. "Some guy went into a dorm last night and killed like eight kids."

A fear rose in Isaac. "Here?"

Connor nodded. "UCO."

UCO. University of Central Oregon. Undergraduate student body of eighteen-thousand. Only an hour's drive south down I-5.

Isaac didn't go to college, but he knew the campus well. A dozen of his high school classmates went to UCO. It was the school of choice for kids who were expected to attend college but didn't want to put thought or effort into actively pursuing a college education.

The phone call with Ben replayed itself, and suddenly Isaac began to put the pieces together.

"Do they know who?" he asked.

"They got him in custody."

"What's his name?"

"Dunno. He did it all with a hammer so everyone's just calling him The Handyman."

The Handyman.

The news had already created a label.

Isaac's mouth and mind locked up. He fixated on the TV screen as the anchor made an announcement. "And we now go to a large police presence that has gathered near the town of Woodburn." A gasp rose among Isaac's coworkers when they heard the name of their city.

The news cut to a video feed from a helicopter hovering over green fields and woodlands. This was rural country. A land of family-owned farms. From the air, all houses in the area looked the same. The helicopter's camera focused on one particular house, a house isolated from its neighbors by an acre on each side. Police cars surrounded the house. Their lights flashed. Officers roamed the ground.

The video of a reporter appeared in the corner of the screen. He stood on the gravel road, talking to the camera as police lights flashed behind him.

"SWAT teams entered this Woodburn area home early this morning. We're not allowed to go closer because this is an active crime scene. However, the SWAT teams have stood down and are allowing police investigators to enter the house. They do not seem to think that anything in this house presents a threat to their officers or the community."

"Jim, has anyone said if this raid is related to the tragedy unfolding at UCO?" the anchor asked.

"No one with the police is confirming or denying that. But the speed and force with which they descended on this home in the immediate aftermath of identifying the suspect at UCO does make it appear the two are related."

"Jim, we're watching helicopter views of the area. We see a lot of K-9 units searching the grounds around the house..."

It was true. On the screen, officers combed the expansive property, slowly walking it with dogs.

"... are those bomb dogs or cadaver dogs?"

"I haven't been told, but judging by the fact that the police don't consider our position to be dangerous, I can only assume that those dogs aren't looking for bombs, but for bodies."

At that moment, one of the dogs went rigid. Its handler frantically motioned for others to come help him. Several police and investigators descended on the patch of ground.

The anchor said, "They seem to have discovered something. We don't know what it is. We'd like to warn our viewers that it may be something disturbing. As a precaution, we're going to zoom wide right now. Again, it appears that local police, state police, and I believe I see an FBI jacket, have converged on this house in the Woodburn area. We do not know what for, and we do not know if it is related to the attack at the University of Central Oregon early this morning."

The camera zoomed wide.

Isaac looked at the area. He looked at the aerial view of the house. He looked at the gravel road connecting to the highway at that clump of trees. He had never seen it from this perspective, but he knew. At that moment, he knew.

The screen returned to the reporter. "We're receiving unconfirmed reports that human remains have, in fact, been discovered in the basement."

"Do you know how many human remains?"

"The police aren't releasing an exact number. But it does seem to be substantial."

"Thanks, Jim. Keep us informed," the anchor said.

The image then cut back to the studio and the anchor at her desk. She looked sternly into the camera, speaking slowly to build some suspense, "We have just received word that, according to county records, this house is owned by a sixty-two-year-old retired contractor."

Isaac held his breath.

The anchor's dramatic pause became unbearable.

He knew what she would say. It was inevitable. But he hoped, and hoped, and hoped that she would say some other name. Some other person. Some other guy's father.

"His name is Walter Luce," the anchor said.

The words slammed into Isaac, their pure force seeming to knock the breath out of him and send his stomach churning. His legs wobbled. He tasted bile in his mouth. His eyes narrowed into a myopic focus, shutting out the astonished looks from his coworkers who recognized the last name.

It was true. His fears were true.

The anchor announced that they had a photo of Walter Luce taken from his son's Facebook page.

An image faded onto the sixty-inch, mounted, flat-screen TV. It was the face of a white-haired, bearded man. He looked like a grandfather. Like someone who might be cast in a caramel candy commercial. Innocent and friendly.

In the picture he was even smiling as he knelt to pet a black lab. Kneeling beside this old man and this dog was another person. The news had tactfully blurred this person's face, but Isaac knew exactly who it was.

Isaac stumbled from the TVs to the aisle of laptops. He felt himself floating, as if his limbs weren't quite connected to his mind anymore. Some impulse had taken over through the fog that his mind had become. He soon found himself logging into his Facebook account.

Messages piled up on his page. Every second that passed, new ones appeared, the counter always climbing higher.

18 unread messages...

43 unread messages...

He clicked around through his photos until he found a picture. *The* picture. The picture of the man, the dog, and the blurred face. But on Isaac's Facebook page, the face wasn't blurred. It was a picture of Walter Luce, his dog... and Isaac.

82 unread messages...

107 unread messages...

In his fevered haze, Isaac clicked on his settings. He searched around the tabs.

115 unread messages...

131 unread messages...

He deleted his account. *"Are you sure you want to proceed?"*

Yes, damnit!

He clicked on the verifications.

Then he stumbled away from the computers.

"Oh god... oh fuck..." he muttered to himself.

His gaze drifted up. All his coworkers watched him. Some stared. Some looked away. Some let their faces warp in confusion. But they knew.

They all knew. They knew that last name. They knew the man in the photo looked like an older Isaac. They knew.

Kim stepped forward. "Isaac? Are you okay?"

She walked toward him, but Isaac turned and stumbled away.

To the front door. To the outside. But he didn't make it.

As he approached the door, he leaned over, dry-heaved once, and vomited onto the floor.

CHAPTER 3

Nine months after his arrest, the State of Oregon tried Walter "The Handyman" Luce for sixteen counts of murder. After four weeks of trial, the jury found him sane and guilty on all counts.

The judge sentenced Walter Luce to death by lethal injection.

He was assigned to Death Row at Willamette Valley Correctional Facility, one of two facilities in the State of Oregon equipped to handle executions.

The prosecution warned the victims' families that although justice had been served, the execution might not happen for years, or even decades. From California to Florida, the glaring spotlight and publicity that serial killers generated meant a lengthy appeals process.

Ted Bundy. The Campus Killer.
Sentenced to death in 1979. Florida. Executed in 1989.

John Wayne Gacy. The Killer Clown.
Sentenced to death in 1980. Illinois. Executed in 1994.

Richard Ramirez. The Night Stalker.
Sentenced to death in 1989. California. Died in 2013. Of lymphoma.

Everyone accepted that Walter Luce might not face the lethal injection chamber in his own lifetime. Regardless, everyone in America knew his face. Everyone knew what happened in his basement.

Walter Luce was famous.

But no one understood why he did what he did.

He refused to talk about his crimes to the police. Or the FBI. Or his lawyers. Or in trial. Or to any of the hundreds of reporters, authors, and journalists who requested interviews. He wouldn't even speak to the *thousands* of people who wrote to him in prison. He didn't speak to his fans, or to preachers, or to the women who wanted to have his baby.

He wouldn't speak to anyone.

It made the hunger for what he had to say grow.

It made his legend expand.

What made a recently-retired contractor snap?

What created The Handyman?

CHAPTER 4

"Why didn't he try an insanity defense?"

The moment Isaac sat down for this interview, he knew the conversation would go in that direction. The interest in The Handyman had tapered during the two years since the arrest, but every now and then the questions popped back up. And always in the least convenient of places.

What really annoyed Isaac about being asked this today was that this wasn't even a news interview. It was a job interview.

He was interviewing for a janitorial position at a movie theater. Just sweeping popcorn and sterilizing doorknobs. Something to help pay the bills. But soon after he shook hands with the manager in that dim office, the interview veered off into questions about Isaac's famous father.

"His public defender *tried* an insanity plea," Isaac said, attempting to sound detached and matter-of-fact about the whole thing. "But all the evidence in the basement indicated a level of planning and higher thought. It showed that he had a realization that his crimes were wrong and punishable if he were caught. It was pretty easy for the DA to swat down insanity."

"Do *you* think he should have gotten insanity?"

Isaac paused and considered his response. "I think the death penalty was a fair sentencing for what he did."

"When's the execution?"

Isaac shrugged. "Honestly, it probably won't happen in his lifetime. He's old. The appeals process in high profile cases like this can drag on for ten to twenty years."

"What was he like?" the manager asked.

Isaac tried to think of a way to answer the question while also shutting down follow-up questions. "I never really noticed anything odd about him. He seemed like a normal dad. He kept his emotions to himself.

But that's that generation, you know. I don't know what happened. I don't know why he snapped. It's just a really tragic thing. I wish I knew more."

"It's so interesting," the manager said. "Man, I would have loved to have been a fly on the wall in that house."

"Yeah. Crazy, ain't it?"

Despite his best efforts, Isaac could sense that he wouldn't be able to transition this conversation. He had always heard of serial killer groupies—the strange women who wrote love letters to incarcerated men who were convicted of horrific murder. Even Ted Bundy—a man who struggled to maintain genuine relationships as an attractive law student— found a wife and fathered a child only *after* he was convicted, and his crimes were made public.

Bundy confessed not only to murdering women and burying them in the woods, but to going back to the graves, digging them up and having sex with their dead bodies. *What kind of woman is attracted to a confessed and convicted necrophile?* Isaac wondered.

But the groupies who really surprised Isaac weren't the women.

It was the men.

It wasn't long after the crime that Isaac started receiving fan mail. Some people simply wanted interviews or a pen pal. But as the months went by, the requests got weirder.

A husband and wife once sent Isaac a letter, complete with return postage, asking for a set of his father's clothes. The husband wanted to dress up as The Handyman so that he could chase his wife around the house and tie her up in the basement as part of a "game." According to the letter, the wife was not only on board with it, but it was her idea.

Another time, Isaac received a box in the mail filled with framed portraits of each of his father's female victims. The instructions offered Isaac five-hundred dollars if he would ejaculate onto the photos and mail them back. The sender had even put his real name and address on the return label.

Isaac looked the man up. He was married with three boys, owned a small real estate company in Louisville, and coordinated his church's canned food drive.

And he apparently had a fetish for serial killers.

After those experiences, Isaac recognized that the manager interviewing him wasn't a concerned citizen, amateur psychologist, or everyday news-consuming American. This man was part of a large population of people whose interest in serial killers went deeper than mere fascination. Isaac couldn't find a good word to describe it but "envy" was probably the closest. These were normal, law-abiding people who identified with, and were sometimes aroused by, the darkest slivers of society.

Isaac understood these men well.

"Did you ever do any, um, you know, father-son stuff?" the manager asked, his face starting to glisten with excitement as he forced the conversation deeper.

"Like what?"

"Oh, I don't know. Camping. Hunting. You know, father-son stuff. Were you ever out in the woods with him?"

In truth they *had* done "father-son" stuff throughout Isaac's childhood, but it always felt forced. Isaac's dad seemed to view fatherhood as an inconvenient chore; something that had to be done with certain regularity, like cleaning the gutters or replacing fence posts. And so, on schedule, Walter would build him a tree house or take him camping or buy him a dog.

These experiences never bridged the distance between them.

"Nah. We didn't do much together."

"Did you guys have pets?"

"A black lab named Buddy."

"Did he ever *do* anything to Buddy?"

"Buddy ran away during my senior year of high school," Isaac said, this time more forceful in his attempts to move the conversation along. "There was never any animal torture in our house. No arson. No bedwetting. Nothing. The warning signs weren't there. I wish I knew what triggered him. But I guess I'm lucky I was mostly raised by my mom."

The manager got quiet.

Isaac took the opportunity to slide his resume across the man's desk. "Anyway, this whole incident is what caused that gap in my work history. But I assure you—"

The manager scanned Isaac's resume, but it was clear his mind was elsewhere. "Have you visited him?"

Isaac's smile became forced. "I don't really care to. We have nothing to say to each other."

"You should. I mean, he *is* your father."

"In name." Isaac motioned back to his resume. "I've mostly worked in retail. I have a high school diploma, and I'm a few credits away from—"

"If you want to discuss your father's motives or anything, I just want you to know I'm a bit of an expert on serial killers."

Isaac sighed. "Cool."

"I watch all the shows, and I've read a few books. They fascinate me, man. I love figurin' them out. The shit that humans can do to other humans—and this is real life I'm talking about, not that Hollywood stuff—it's unreal."

"They're something else."

"Your dad was pretty cool with the whole 'Handyman' angle. That's what you need to do if you want to be a famous killer. You need an angle. A hook. John Wayne Gacy was a clown. That's real nice and creepy. Ed Gein made lamps out of human skin. Awesome. That's why these guys are famous, just like your dad."

"Good to know."

"Yeah, I'm real into this stuff. There's this one guy from Alaska I read about. You'll like him."

Isaac leaned back in his seat. "Robert Hansen."

"I don't think that's his name."

"Alaskan serial killer? Trust me, you're thinking of Robert Hansen."

"No. The guy I'm thinking of would—"

"—abduct women, fly them up to the Alaska tundra in his small bush plane, set them loose and then hunt them," Isaac said.

"Yeah! You've heard of him."

"Robert Hansen."

"That's so raw, man. I mean, that's other level badass."

"The guy had bad acne."

The manager stared at Isaac. "Huh?"

"Robert Hansen had bad acne as a teenager. This made him self-conscious and probably not very attractive. The girls rejected him. And so, he grew up hating women. After hiring some hookers, he realized that wasn't enough. He wanted to hurt them. That's why he was abducting prostitutes, raping them, and hunting them."

"Wow. I guess you know your killers."

"Most of these guys are sexually frustrated losers. Women rejected them. And now they want to punish those women. They want to feel powerful. They're not particularly deep. And they're not very interesting."

The manager straightened in his chair. His face flushed in annoyance. "Well. Your dad had female *and* male victims. Sounds like he was an equal opportunity torturer. Was he just a sexually frustrated loser?"

Isaac looked down as he thought for a moment. "I don't know," he said. And he truly didn't.

The manager gave a reassuring nod, like a professor counseling a student. "I've read a lot about The Handyman. I think there's more to him than meets the eye. He had some sort of mission or goal down there. That's why he won't talk about it. But I don't think it was just simple sex or anger. There's something bigger to him. I can feel it. Dads are weird like that, you know. They all got their secrets. God, I'd love to hear what he has to say for himself."

He cupped his hands behind his head and leaned back in his chair, staring off, deep in thought as he contemplated the nature of murder.

Isaac let the silence sit for a moment. When it became clear that the manager wasn't going to break it, Isaac nudged his resume further across the desk. "So, about the position..."

The manager forced an awkward *Yeah... about that* smile. "I'm just not sure you're a good fit here," he said.

"We haven't even discussed my experience. Or the position."

"Corporate's protective of their brand. You may be a bit too... you know."

"I'll be in the supply room. I won't be interacting with the customers. And my hours are flexible. I can come in after you close."

The manager shook his head, "Sorry. My team needs to feel safe here. When they look at you, they'll see your dad."

And there it was.

Throughout his life, people always commented how much Isaac looked like his father. Photos of Walter in his youth could easily pass for Isaac. Even by father-son standards, the resemblance was uncanny. It was true, and Isaac knew it; anyone who saw his face, even if just passing on the street, felt a chill. Isaac had the face of the most famous Oregon resident in history. A face that had run on the local news, on and off, for two years. A face that caused national media outlets to descend on Woodburn during every trial update and anniversary of the massacre.

"You seem like a nice guy," the manager continued. "And if it were up to me, I'd hire you in a second. But there are a lot of people who think that bad things run in families. I'm not saying that psychopathy and anger and violence are inherited, but, well, you know..." he trailed off without completing the thought.

In that instant, an image flashed into Isaac's head. He could practically see his hand reaching for the scissors on the desk and plunging them into the man's neck. It would be so quick that the man could only gurgle, not scream, as his blood drained onto the floor.

Isaac pushed the thought out of his mind. He took a deep breath, keeping himself calm. "If you weren't going to hire me, why bring me in to interview?"

The manager shrugged. "I'm a big fan of The Handyman. I mean, not a 'fan' per se, but... you know. Anyone can use an AR-15. But your dad? A sledgehammer? No matter what you think of the guy, that's pretty raw."

"He didn't use a sledge."

"No, not in the dorm. But in the basement."

"He didn't use a sledge," Isaac repeated.

"No, no, no. The news said..."

"I know what the news said. I saw the field reporter demonstrate it on a watermelon. Ten-pound sledge with a thirty-four-inch fiberglass handle. Wasn't my father."

The manager leaned in, finally getting the juicy insider details.

"What do you mean that wasn't your father?"

Isaac rose from his seat and walked toward the door of the office.

"Wait, wait, wait!" the man called after him.

Isaac paused, his hand on the doorknob, and turned.

The manager licked his lips, eager for more details. "Just between us... What do you know that wasn't reported?"

"Nuthin."

And with that, Isaac walked out.

CHAPTER 5

Isaac stepped out of the theater and into a dreary day.

His eyes glanced at the "Now Hiring! Inquire Within!" sign posted on the window. He flipped it off and trudged to his car.

A thin mist of Oregon drizzle floated in the air—enough moisture to be clammy and annoying, but not enough to warrant a hood or an umbrella. Not that Oregonians used umbrellas. It wasn't their style. And Isaac didn't even feel the cold.

He drove down Woodburn's main drag, Highway 214. The movie theater was on the same strip as the grocery store, a Big Five, and the dollar store. With two sports bars and two Mexican food joints on this stretch of road, it was the most happening place in town.

To the immediate west, across Interstate 5, were the factory outlets. People from Portland would make the thirty-minute drive there to do their Christmas shopping. As far as any of them knew, that marginally discounted mall with the excessively big Christmas tree was "Woodburn."

But the real town was a few miles east, composed of a stretch of auto-part stores, farm machinery retailers, and tractor repair shops.

When a farmer in Elliot Prairie said he was "going into town," he meant that he was going into Woodburn to pick up some forty-weight oil at O'Reilly's and a cherry pie at Shari's.

Isaac drove alongside the railroad tracks for a mile and then turned down a quiet, tree-lined road. He pulled into the parking lot of a colonial house in bad need of paint and repairs. A sign above the house's door read "Thrift Shop."

He walked in, avoiding eye contact with the old man in the plain clothes at the register. The store was owned and operated by the local Mennonite Church. Ol' Jacob at the register never watched TV, never read the papers, and never laid eyes on the internet. As such, he was one of the few people in town who had never heard the last name "Luce."

Ol' Jacob regarded Isaac with the same detached apathy that he regarded all the other Hell-bound creatures of Earth, an anonymity that Isaac relished. As far as Isaac could tell, the man spent his days reading scripture, tidying the store, and glaring at the kids who took selfies with him thinking he was Amish. Isaac wasn't quite sure of the difference himself.

Having been here multiple times and knowing exactly what he wanted, Isaac strolled past the racks of unsorted used clothing, all donated from some estate sale of some recently deceased grandmother. He figured the inventory must change, but it always looked the same. Flowery old lady dresses on the women's racks, and extra-large tweed suits on the men's.

The whole place had a musty smell. Lifetimes' worth of body oils soaking into clothes and fermenting. It was a smell that, while not foul, lingered and clung to everything, like cigarette smoke.

He went past the vacuums, the racks of boxy tube televisions (the Mennonites might not watch the damned things, but they had no problem with selling them), and walked directly to a staircase that led to the house's basement.

There, in the dimly lit cellar, spread before him in unorganized rows of crates, were three folding tables of donated hand-tools.

Isaac moseyed through the collection. At this point, he was a fine connoisseur of the used hand-tool trade, and he knew that most of these bins had only one organizing principle—they were lumped together according to whichever dead man had unknowingly donated them.

Each tool told a story. Isaac could spot the drywall dust on a saw blade, and he could tell this tool's owner knew his way around manual labor. A blunted screwdriver head might indicate that the owner, through lack of knowledge or just plain laziness, had inappropriately used the tool as a prybar or chisel.

New, shiny, unused tools, with their unfaded wood and unworn metal, were of no use to Isaac. Isaac needed dull and dirty. Tools that held history within their imperfections.

At last, he came upon a pile that held promise. A cluttered heap from an era when wood was cheaper than fiberglass or plastic. No bright colors. No name brands. He didn't want a tool that could be bought at a Home Depot or Lowe's, and definitely not something that could be found in Target or Walmart. It had to be nameless and timeless.

Old, classic, last-for-your-life-and-your-grandson's-life tools.

A smile formed on his lips as he found his prize—a bevel-headed chisel of solid forged metal. The blade was scraped and chipped, probably from being pounded into concrete. The handle, which might have been shiny twenty years ago, was now tarnished and dark. The striking head had the pock marks of hundreds of blows with a hammer. It was perfect.

Into Isaac's basket it went.

He followed it up with a set of channel-lock pliers. The rubber grips had long since worn off the handles, leaving only bare metal, but the teeth were still sharp.

Then, for good measure, he tossed in a wooden hand-screw clamp. The clamp looked relatively new, but it was only two dollars and Isaac felt he could leave it out in the rain and sun for a few weeks. It might darken and swell the wood just enough to give it the well-used look that Isaac required.

He paid in all cash. He went back to his car and drove home.

Isaac changed apartments every six months or so, usually to downgrade to something cheaper. At this point it meant that he lived in a second-floor studio so close to Interstate 5 that the constant hum of traffic almost formed its own white noise, akin to living next to the ocean, Isaac liked to tell himself. Unfortunately, that white noise was constantly punctuated by the wail of an Oregon State Police siren or a double-trailer trucker laying on the horn.

Isaac's studio apartment was nothing special. A desk, a bed, a kitchenette. He couldn't afford furniture. Well... except for *one* thing.

Against a corner of the apartment sat a small, circular table. A blood-red velvet cloth was draped over it. Surrounding it were floodlights on tripods. At some point, Isaac intended to buy actual photography lights, but eventually he came to believe that the intensity of the halogen work lights gave his products the crude, intimidating look he wanted.

He flipped the lights on. He laid the chisel on the velvet cloth. The bright lights revealed its blemishes to the world, exactly as Isaac intended.

He took his phone and snapped photos of the chisel. An overhead angle first. Then a front angle, looking straight at the edge of the blade. He finished with a few wide shots showing the full body of the chisel.

The bright lights threw Isaac's shadow onto the white wall, and Isaac made sure that the hint of the shadow was caught in the photo. A professional photographer would ensure that his or her own shadow never entered frame, but Isaac didn't want the pictures to look professional. He wanted it to look exactly as it was—a loner in his apartment taking photos of tools. Besides, he liked the shadow. It felt menacing, like an evil force loomed over the otherwise innocent chisel.

Isaac always fancied himself a creative person, but he never took an art class. He never took a photography class. He just instinctively knew how this chisel needed to look for his purposes.

With the photos done, Isaac powered off his lights and sat down at his computer. He uploaded the photo and super-imposed a caption on it:

> *"Bevel-Edged Chisel. Owned by Walter 'The Handyman' Luce.*
> *Guaranteed genuine authentic by his son, Isaac Luce.*
> *Only $199!!!"*

It was hard for Isaac to believe the prices people would pay. He had found out only from desperation.

When his old landlord had served him an eviction, he dealt with the matter by getting drunk. Really drunk. While he was wasted, he opted for one final monetary Hail Mary; he pulled out the box from his dad's admirer—the box with the framed photos of Walter's female victims, and the request that someone with the Luce bloodline ejaculate on them.

It took him a few hours, but Isaac did what was requested. He attached the self-addressed return postage and sent it back.

Only later did he realize that it was probably illegal to send semen through the mail. He became paranoid that this was a set-up, and soon it would be blasted all over the news that The Handyman's son was a pervert. He couldn't even deny it; his DNA was smeared over everything.

But then... a check for five hundred dollars arrived. The perv in Kentucky got his semen smeared photos and paid up. In full. Isaac couldn't believe that he just made the easiest five hundred bucks of his life.

And so, he tried again. He remembered the husband and wife who wanted to do some Handyman cosplay. Isaac had a flannel shirt he had stolen from his father for a camping trip. That shirt also happened to be the same shirt that Walter wore in the picture of the two of them with Buddy, the dog. Isaac boxed it up and mailed it with a request for three hundred dollars.

Two weeks later, a three-hundred-dollar check arrived.

Isaac had stumbled into a strange, but lucrative, underground market for serial killer memorabilia.

The normal online marketplaces, like eBay and Amazon, banned such products, but Isaac found other sites, other nooks of the internet where morbid fanatics gathered and traded their goods: Love letters from Ted Bundy, clown paintings by John Wayne Gacy, nonsensical scribbles from Son of Sam.

And now, the hand-tools of Walter Luce.

Isaac decided to be strategic about it. He, and he alone, could claim authenticity on the product. Sure, the police confiscated all of Walter's possessions, including his tools, but a murderabilia buyer wasn't going to walk into Woodburn PD and ask if the chisel he just paid top dollar for was the one that was used to chop off so-and-so's middle toe.

And so, Isaac began buying tools and marking them up.

He made sure to not flood the market. Each tool needed to have its place to shine. And hammers were of particular value. Those were Isaac's rainy-day fund.

By this point, Isaac had two crates full of old, rusty, wood-and-steel tools stacked in a corner. Some were already on market. Others would be soon.

He hit "Publish" on the chisel ad and leaned back, wondering when he should start drinking for the night.

His phone rang.

He didn't want to answer. Isaac changed phone number periodically, often when a new stalker tried to go through Isaac to get a love message to his dad. But he had changed his number only a few months ago, and there was always a bit of a lag before the creepers caught on. Any call on a night like this would probably be business-related.

With a sigh, he picked up his phone. "Hello?"

The man's voice on the other end was deep, gravelly, but pitched slightly higher than natural out of an eagerness to please. "Hey, Isaac. It's Teddy."

Ah, Teddy.

Isaac didn't know much about Teddy, other than that he was a Death Row prison guard and that he had some sort of *amazing!* get rich quick scheme. Isaac figured it was probably stupid, like selling Walter's autograph or something.

In any case, Isaac didn't much care. Despite his business relying solely on his father's infamy, Isaac had no interest in involving his father as a partner. He would hear Teddy out, and probably blow him off.

Teddy continued, "I know we said we'd meet at Shari's at seven, and I'm really sorry, but I forgot I had a prior commitment. Would it be cool with you if we met at the high school? My daughter has a lacrosse game tonight. I can't miss it. We can discuss the proposal in the stands."

"Is it a big game or something?"

"No, no, no. But when she was born I promised I would always be there for her, and these are the kind of things that fathers should always be there for."

Isaac sighed. He didn't want to go to the high school. "It's fine. Let's just meet some night you don't have a game."

"Sure, whatever's best for you. But..." Teddy trailed off, letting that "but" linger.

"But?"

"But I think you'll want what I have to offer. I got a buyer arranged and everything. She's really interested."

"Well, she can wait another day."

"She's offering sixty grand."

Isaac sat up. "Wait. What?"

He could almost feel Teddy's excited grin over the phone. "Sixty thousand bucks."

"Legit? On the table?"

"If you knew who my buyer was, and if you knew what we're gonna sell, you'd know it was guaranteed."

Isaac sat silently.

Teddy took the silence as an opportunity to continue, "I'll be at the high school lacrosse field. 7 p.m. I'm six-two, about 270 pounds, wearing a blue coat and a green cap that says 'Philmont.' Just listen to what I got to say. What do you got to lose?"

The truthful answer to that question, Isaac knew, was "nothing."

CHAPTER 6

Isaac walked through the gate of the high school athletic field.

Under the bright field lights, a women's lacrosse game was in full swing. It was intense. Violent. Brutal. The pads, helmets and facemasks gave the players the freedom to unleash a week's worth of high school aggression on each other. Their elbows and sticks swung wildly.

In the bleachers, a smattering of parents cheered, shouted encouragement, or zoned out and chatted among themselves.

Isaac eyed the field and momentarily watched the high school girls shoving each other and racing for the ball. Then he glanced around the bleachers at the assembled parents. He knew that as a male in his twenties— obviously *not* a student and *not* a parent—he stood out. Were the parents watching him? Were they suspicious? Would they recognize him?

He wanted to walk away right then. Screw Teddy and whatever he was selling.

But as Isaac pivoted to leave, he heard, "Hey! Hey, Isaac! Over here!"

Isaac looked.

At the top of the bleachers, waving down at him, sat a large man, a complete bear of a human who would have been terrifying if not for that meek smile on his face. The man's entire body had a bit of a slouch, as if he was trying to hide his massive size so as not to intimidate the people around him. But that slouch also contained a weariness from the weight of the world pushing down on the man's spine for a decade too long.

This was Teddy, a gentle giant in the truest sense.

With a sigh, Isaac trudged his way up the steps to the top of the bleachers.

Despite there being plenty of empty seats, Teddy scooted over to offer up his seat to Isaac. And then, realizing that that wasn't enough of a greeting, rose to shake Isaac's hand.

"Hey, buddy! I'm Teddy."

It was an enthusiastic shake that hurt Isaac's hand.

"I gathered." Isaac pointed to Teddy's coat and hat. "Blue jacket and green Philmont hat, just like you said."

"You ever been to Philmont?"

"I, uh, don't even know where or what that is?"

"It's a Boy Scout ranch in New Mexico. It's, like, thousands of square miles of hiking trails. Gorgeous, just gorgeous."

"Is your son a Boy Scout?"

"No, no, no. I wish. I mean, I wish I had a son." Teddy's face flushed as he realized how that sounded. "No, no, no, what I mean is I wish I *also* had a son." He was getting flustered. "I have one daughter. She's great. She's my world, and I don't wish she was a boy at all. The hat is from when I was a Boy Scout. You ever do Scouting?"

"No. Cub Scouts for a bit, but—"

"Cub Scouts is nothing. Boy Scouts is where the real fun is. Best time of my life. I mean, other than being a father which is its own daily, rewarding—"

"I get it."

Isaac looked down at the seat. They were still standing, talking about Boy Scouts for some reason. Teddy seemed to realize this and quickly motioned toward a seat.

"Sit, sit. Watch with me. We're rooting for White. They're the good guys. Number 69 is Lauren, my daughter."

Isaac stifled a giggle. "Number 69?"

"Yep."

Teddy seemed oblivious that "69" might have any humor or significance beyond being a randomly assigned jersey number. Isaac couldn't help but grin as he sat. He looked down at the field with renewed interest; he wanted to see what kind of girl would wear 69 on her lacrosse team.

On the sideline stood #69, Lauren.

She was the only player who cheered on her teammates, and, boy, was she getting into it. She held her helmet in her hands so that her shouts could project even more. With her dark hair and pale skin, she was only a few piercings from being at home in a punk band. She seemed almost too cool and popular to be emo, and too emo to be cool. She seemed like a girl who transcended labels and just did whatever she wanted.

Lauren shouted at her teammates, "Come on, ladies! What makes the grass grow? —BLOOD! BLOOD! What makes the grass grow? —BLOOD! BLOOD!"

Isaac couldn't decide if she was being seriously intense or hilariously ironic. Was she really into this game, or was she making a statement that to be really into sports is akin to warfare? Or maybe she had just recently seen *Full Metal Jacket* and liked the quote. Isaac figured that it didn't matter *why* she chose that chant, but he fucking loved that she did.

Teddy caught Isaac grinning as he watched Lauren shout.

"That's my Lauren."

"She's... intense."

Teddy beamed. "Smart too. She got into Columbia." In the off-chance that his fatherly brag was confusing for any reason, he quickly added, "Columbia the Ivy-League university. Not Colombia the coffee exporting country."

Isaac nodded, "Ah, got it. And I thought you were gonna dismember her and dump her corpse in the *Columbia* River."

Isaac glanced over at Teddy. But the face looking back at him had none of the warmth and cheer he had come to expect from Teddy.

"That's my daughter," Teddy said, his lips tight and his fists impulsively clenching.

The smile vanished from Isaac's face. "Sorry. Bad joke. Totally inappropriate."

Teddy's eyes sized Isaac up.

Isaac felt like a Terminator was scanning him, ready to strike. "I've gotten used to a certain macabre, serial killer humor. People kind of expect it of me. I don't mean anything by it."

For an extra moment, Teddy held that glare. And then, almost by strength of will, seemingly remembering that he had business to attend to and still had to woo Isaac to participate, his smile returned.

"It's fine, it's fine. Single dads. We get a little crazy, you know. Heck, you know more than anyone."

"Um, so, what's she studying?"

"Journalism. Always wanted to be a writer. Loves reading the news and doing research too. She probably knows more about your dad than I do. Her mind, it's just, it's incredible how she can absorb and process information. Not like this old guy." Teddy whacked his head with the palm of his hand as if to demonstrate that there was nothing in there.

"If she's doing journalism, New York is the place to be."

"Oh, uh, yeah. So, I said she *got into* Columbia. She's probably gonna go to UCO."

"I see. Cool."

"UCO's a good school too. Totally underrated in the grand scheme of things. And, well, it's just cheaper, is all."

Isaac nodded. "I had a lot of friends go there. My dad went there too. Not as a student, of course. But as a mass murderer."

Teddy's face went cold again. He obviously didn't approve of the joke. But he forced a smile. He gave Isaac a friendly punch on the shoulder that was so hard it made Isaac wince. "That's a good one."

"So, what Handyman paraphernalia are you selling?"

A grin formed on Teddy's face as he looked around, making sure no one was listening. "Access."

Isaac looked at him. "You're his prison guard?"

"Corrections Officer. And I'm also the facility coordinator for all visitations to the Special Housing Unit."

"Which includes Death Row?"

"Yep."

"So... you schedule my dad's visits?"

"You got it. But only for one week. You see, Hank is the one who approves all Special Housing Visitations, but he's on vacation in Maui. Now, Rick usually subs for him, but he's caring for his mom who was in a hit-and-run."

"Jesus."

"Which means, for three days and three days only, *I* approve the visitations. I control access to The Handyman."

"But he doesn't do visitations," Isaac said, "Or interviews. He didn't even testify. No one's heard his voice."

"He'll speak to you."

"I doubt it."

"Inmates submit a list of potential visitors. You only get to see an inmate if he invites you and the facility approves you. Otherwise, groupies and priests and reporters would just be showing up in the visitation rooms. So, once the inmate submits their list, we check the people, trying to weed out gang affiliations and prostitutes and stuff. Most guests are wives, girlfriends, mothers, family and friends, so forth.

"Walter's been with us for about 24 months now. His list only has one name. That's all it's ever had. That name isn't a lawyer. Not a priest. Not a brother. Not some stripper that he fell in love with. The one and only name that Walter Luce put on his list is...Isaac Luce."

For the briefest of moments, Isaac thought of his father, sitting alone in an isolated cell in the prison, wanting only for his son to walk in the door and say hi.

But Isaac shook off the image. "Nah, I don't think he—"

"I'll get you a private room," Teddy said.

"I'm not—"

"—and record your conversation without his permission. Or the prison's."

Isaac suddenly realized that Teddy wasn't offering some father-son cathartic resolution. And he wasn't offering Walter's signature on some fan mail. This was something else.

As Isaac's mind spun up, trying to put the pieces together, his gaze drifted out over the field.

***

Lauren was now in the game, struggling to box out her opponent. She found herself matched up against the other team's biggest and best, a beast of a player whom Lauren, her teammates, and even her coach referred to as "She-Hulk."

She-Hulk wasn't only big, she was dirty. As Lauren tried to back her down, She-Hulk sent a sharp elbow into Lauren's spine.

"Watch it, bitch!" Lauren snapped.

She-Hulk responded by sending another low elbow into Lauren's back. At that moment, the ball sailed through the air on a pass to Lauren. Lauren and She-Hulk went up for it together, but in the process, She-Hulk's stick smacked Lauren hard in the face. Lauren leaned over and rubbed her cheek as She-Hulk ran off with the ball, leading the teams the other direction.

Lauren jogged alongside the ref, shouting at him, "Jesus, dude, you gonna regulate?"

The ref simply shrugged. "Incidental contact."

"Incidental my ass!"

The ref gave her a stern look. "Watch it, sixty-nine."

Lauren huffed and ran off in pursuit of the ball.

***

Teddy's gaze drilled into Isaac, waiting for his answer.

Isaac shook his head. "Even if he confesses, it won't be admissible at his appeals."

"Appeals? What? This doesn't have anything to do with appeals or trials or guilty verdicts or what not. I mean, CSI needs a single drop of blood to pull enough DNA for a conviction. Your dad practically handed the DA sixteen *bodies*. He's guilty. He's not even arguing that. He ain't never going free."

"So, this isn't about his execution?"

"There ain't much of anything you can do about that one way or the other. I've been doing this job a long time and I can tell you that diabetes is the real executioner in there. We pump those guys full of salty, fatty, carb-heavy food. Keeps 'em drowsy and easier to handle. The inmates, they make this one thing called The Spread. Just ramen noodles crushed up, mixed with mayo, chunks of pepperoni sticks, cheese spread and eaten with Doritos. Every prison has their own Spread recipe. And let me tell you, that stuff kills more of these guys than potassium chloride ever does."

"So, you want to sell his story?"

Teddy winked. "Already sold it. Folks love serial killers. I dunno why."

"Wish fulfillment. It arouses them."

"What? Nah. That's... nah. I hear these guys talk all the time, and there ain't nothing arousing about it."

Isaac didn't say anything.

"Not your dad, though. He don't talk about it at all. But the other guys? Just sick stuff. They're not normal. They're wired differently than you and me, you know? I think serial killers are just so different that they get people curious. I used to drive Lauren to the Oregon Zoo every month when she was young. Her favorite animals were the elephants and giraffes. And when you think about it, they're just weird-looking animals. The neck... those ears... that trunk. Kids just can't get enough of 'em. I think that's what it's like with killers. They're just so different. Most people would never do that kind of thing, so when you see someone who does, it just..." Teddy shook his head, seeming saddened by the thought.

"I guess," Isaac said with a shrug.

"I may not know much about why your dad did what he did, but I do know one thing about people. They'll pay to hear him talk about it. Now we just gotta get him to speak. He won't talk to me, but he'll talk to you. I got a buyer for the recordings all lined up."

"Who?"

"Her name's Joan. She's a film producer. She's really into the story."

"Do I know her work?"

Teddy looked off to the side, evidently trying to answer the question without answering it. "Well..." he said. "Joan's just starting out in this whole media business thing. But she wants to see this through, and she's got money on the table. Sixty grand." Teddy gave a little wink.

Isaac's eyes narrowed. "What kind of split?"

"Hey, I'm not greedy. Just a workin' man who's gotta pay for college."

"The split."

"Fifty-fifty. But remember, with me, you get access, the room, a recording—"

"—and the joy of seeing him again," Isaac said.

"Come on, buddy. Everyone in America wants this. He might actually tell you something. What if you found out why he did it? Think of all those families that are waiting to hear that. Maybe he'll be sorry. Maybe he'll ask for forgiveness."

"You really think so?"

"I dunno. He's *your* father."

"I'll think about it."

Isaac rose from his seat.

Teddy stood with him and grabbed his hand in an overly-vigorous handshake.

"You only got this week. After that, I can't set it up for you, and I can't record it no more," Teddy said.

"I got your number."

"You gotta do it, buddy. You could buy yourself a new life. And you sure look like you could use it."

Despite his best efforts to remain stoic, Isaac found himself nodding in agreement. It was true. A new life sure couldn't hurt.

***

Down on the field, a player lobbed the ball high. It arced up and sailed down toward Lauren.

She-Hulk and Lauren both reached up with their sticks to catch it, but She-Hulk jumped a bit higher, swung her elbow, and nailed Lauren in the side of the head.

She-Hulk caught the ball and made a turn to take it on offense.

Lauren seethed, "Fuck it. Mercy does not exist in this dojo."

She reached up, and with She-Hulk building a head of steam in the other direction, Lauren grabbed her by the ponytail with a vise-firm grip. Lauren yanked hard, pulling She-Hulk off her feet and to the ground.

The crowd gasped. That gasp turned to boos.

The ref blew his whistle. "You're outta here, sixty-nine!"

Lauren pulled off her helmet and plodded toward the bench. She glanced down at She-Hulk, being helped to her feet by her teammates.

Lauren batted her eyes in She-Hulk's direction and made little kissy sounds, the kind a mother would make to a poor baby who got a widdle boo-boo.

She giggled as She-Hulk's teammates suddenly had to push She-Hulk *down* onto the grass to keep her from charging.

As Lauren strolled off the field, she looked up at the bleachers, searching for her father whom she knew must have watched the entire scene. She expected to see that disapproving, sad look on his face. The look that let her know that a lecture was forthcoming. But for once, her father wasn't looking at her. No, he was shaking hands with some guy. Some *young* guy.

She watched as the guy turned away from her father and walked down the bleacher stairs toward the exit.

There was something about that guy. Something familiar. Something that nibbled at Lauren's mind.

CHAPTER 7

The parking lot was quiet enough for Isaac to make his call.

He usually liked complete silence and privacy for his business calls, but he was too excited and too curious to wait. Besides, if it was 7:30 in Oregon, then it was 10:30 in New York. He needed to get in touch before it was too late.

The first number he dialed was Ben, the editor at DOPER Magazine.

The day of the college attack, Ben had been the one who blew apart Isaac's world. At the time, Isaac thought that Ben was just another in a wide sea of douchey, brotastic parasites who sucked blood from his father's fame. But quite soon after, Isaac himself became a similar parasite, using his father's fame to pay his own bills. Once he relinquished the moral high ground, he actually found Ben to be a remarkably honest asshole.

Ben always gave him the best rates on photos and interviews. Even Ben admitted that he was purposefully setting a high price-point, and that the more traditional news outlets would hesitate to match it out of some idealized adherence to "journalistic integrity."

Those early paychecks from Ben kept Isaac alive.

Isaac felt that Ben had always been real with him. When Isaac uncovered a home movie of his dad taking a young Isaac on a trip to Crater Lake, he spent weeks shopping it around to various outlets, getting bids and counterbids, trying to drive up the price. After all that effort, after all the lies and half-truths he had to tell to various producers, all the credibility he wasted, he only managed to pull the field up to Ben's initial offer. It was as Ben said when he made the offer, "*This* is the market price." He was right. Ben was always right.

And unlike the other outlets, Ben's interest in the subject never waned. He had been committed to the story from Day One.

He foresaw the grand narrative structure and the unwavering interest of the public in this most peculiar serial killer. Other news rags and cable channels came circling only during the predictable bumps in public intrigue—the massacre, the discovery of the bodies, the beginning of the trial, the sentencing.

Isaac resigned himself to the fact that they wouldn't come calling again until the story reached its inevitable climax—Walter's execution. Whenever *that* might be.

Ben saw something different.

When Ben looked at Walter, he saw his own father, *anyone's* father. To Ben, Walter *looked* like a stunt double for Alec Guinness's Obi Wan Kenobi. That gray stubble, that twinkle in his eye, that kindly smile.

On top of it, Walter was blue-collar, a self-made man who owned and operated a business that required a lifetime's accumulation of every-man skills. This man represented every Millennial's father—the distant Baby-Boomer who had diligently worked hard to build this country and now had lost his place in it. The American Dream had failed Walter.

At one point, Ben had said those exact words to Isaac. "Your dad's story is our generation's *Death of a Fucking Salesman*. The American Dream is fucking toast. You work hard, you develop a trade, it's supposed to get you somewhere. But the system just chews you up, dumps you in stomach acid, and shits you out. There's this deep fucking anger out there, man.

"Your dad shows how if society ignores that fucking kettle, it will hiss and screech until, finally, it either fucking explodes or melts down on the fucking stove. But unlike *Death of a Salesman*, your dad doesn't just drive his car off a bridge, or whatever. He starts fucking killing people. Young, strong, attractive, high-socio-economic-status, predominantly white people. I get that. The public gets that. This isn't a fifteen minutes of fame story. The market for this story has a tail here, and I'm betting it's a long one. He's your dad, he's my dad, he's everyone's dad."

When he made that pitch, Isaac thought it was just that, a pitch. But Ben, if nothing else, proved that he knew his stuff.

Certainly, the story disappeared from the six o'clock news within the week. But there was a definite floor to the public intrigue. Walter Luce's name continued to hover at a certain level on the search engine histories. The messages boards dedicated to him kept an audience engaged and discussing.

While Isaac dithered on whether or not Ben was a charlatan, three different books on The Handyman were published, one in the first year, two the next year. Isaac tracked their sales rankings. Those authors, who simply compiled news reports into a tidy timeline, were probably making a few thousand a month in royalties for their efforts.

Ben was right. The market was there. If that audience could be fed, they would continue to open their wallets.

Isaac stood in the school's parking lot, hearing the drifting applause from the nearby lacrosse game while he listened to Ben's phone ring. He assumed he would have to leave a message at this late hour. But then—

"Yo, wazzup, I.L.?" Ben answered.

"Hey, man. You still at work?"

"Yeah, just knocking out a mock-up for next week's front page. I got the dick pics of an Oscar winning actor."

"Who is it?"

"Subscribe and see, bro. Although, I will say, give him the right make-up artist and this guy could play your dad. Might be a good way to rehabilitate his acting career after we crush him. He's Royal Shakespeare, so everyone thinks he's all refined and shit. Always plays the wise, older voice of reason. He's gonna need to rebrand himself now. Anyway, what's up?"

"What would you guys bid for audio recordings of The Handyman?"

"Content determines pricing point, mi amigo. If it's just his voicemail away message, well, we ripped that Day One. If he's talking sports, meh. We can give you a little something. But if he's talking tools or construction, then we'll be able to allocate a lot more."

Isaac smiled. "What if he's talking about his basement?"

The other end of the phone went silent. The shuffling of papers, the clicking of the keyboard, the multi-tasking that was a constant when dealing with Ben, a guy who always did four things at once, all ceased.

"Clear audio?" Ben asked.

"Sure."

"Like, 100% his voice, talking about fucked-up torture, murder, sledgehammer shit?"

"What pricing point does that bring us to?"

Ben paused as he considered the question. Isaac knew that any other producer would try to low-ball him at this point. He wondered if Ben was about to get greedy.

Finally, Ben replied, "One that I'll need to kick upstairs for authorization."

At that moment, Isaac knew he was set. Ben could habitually authorize payments of thousands of dollars and then ask for permission, or forgiveness, from his bosses later.

Isaac wanted to nail him down. "You got an estimate?"

"How long are the tapes?"

"Hours. Full conversations. I'm not talking about sound bites here. I'm talking something you can stretch into a long-running series on your site. You could turn them into a tie-in podcast and pull in that *Serial* audience."

Ben took a breath. "I'll have to hear them first, of course. But if you got hours of him talking about his life, his pain, his breaking point, the fucked-up shit he did and why... We're talking a floor of six figures. I could probably push to $150,000."

$150,000?

Isaac couldn't breathe. He wasn't sure he heard the number correctly. His mind raced. It was enough money to get out of town, to find a life out from under the shadow of his father. As Isaac started to mentally scroll through the options of where he might live, Ben asked, "So when can I hear your demo?"

"I, uh, I don't have them yet."

He didn't *quite* hear Ben let out an annoyed sigh, but he did hear the clicking of Ben's mouse resume. Then some tapping on the keyboard. Then a scratching of a pen on paper.

"Send 'em my way when you got 'em. I'll give a listen and then we'll talk. Coolio, bro?"

"Yeah, yeah. Totes cool, bro." Isaac immediately regretted trying to meet Ben on his vernacular level.

"Later, man."

Before Isaac could even say goodbye, Ben had—*click*—hung up the phone.

Isaac stood in the school's parking lot for a long moment, staring off. He looked at all the parked cars—mostly pickups and mid-90s Hondas. Each one, Isaac figured, was owned by someone who would be trapped in Woodburn for life. All these kids would grow to be farmers, mechanics or, at best, the manager of one of the outlet stores. Until this very moment, such a future was also Isaac's best-case scenario. But for the first time in his life, Isaac felt that Woodburn wasn't his coffin.

He looked down at his hand and found that it was trembling in excitement. Now seemed like as good a time as any for a celebratory cigarette. He had been rationing them for the past year, partly out of health concerns, but mostly because they were so damn expensive. This felt like the time to treat himself.

He pulled the pack from his coat pocket, popped a smoke into his mouth, and lit up. He took a deep drag and exhaled a puff out over the parking lot. He glanced at a "No Smoking" sign—this was a *high school* after all—and grinned to himself. Smoking in the parking lot; what a rule breaker he was!

"Can I bum one?"

The voice startled Isaac. He pivoted around. Approaching him, lacrosse stick and gym bag in hand, was Lauren.

She strolled up to him with the confidence that only the cool girls in high school possess. She leaned against his car. Her eyes locked onto his, making it abundantly clear that there was no mistake, no misunderstanding. *She*, Lauren Anderton, the kind of girl who actively campaigns to *not* be on the Homecoming Court ballot, was actually talking to *him*, the loser son of a serial killer.

Isaac hesitated.

Lauren sighed, "I'm eighteen, if that puts your arbitrary societal morals of decency at ease."

Isaac held out the pack and Lauren pulled one out. She held it and looked at him expectedly. "Umm... and can I get a light?"

"Oh, yeah. Sorry."

Isaac fumbled into his pocket to get his lighter. Despite seeing suave leading men light an attractive girl's cigarette all the time in the movies, it was the kind of simple thing he had never done in his life.

The flame sprouted on his lighter. Lauren leaned in and inhaled. The paper smoldered. She took a puff, her eyes wandering over Isaac, trying to figure him out.

"So, you know my pops?" she finally asked.

"We're friends."

"Yeah. That makes sense. Dad is *sooo* sociable and has *sooo* many friends that I just can't fucking keep track." She smirked at him. Her tone wasn't necessarily sarcastic, but an honest, *Why bullshit me, man?*

"We're business associates."

She nodded, "Ah! Money. His social lubricant." She took another drag on the cigarette. "So what *business* do you have with a corrections officer?"

There was a bluntness to her that unsteadied Isaac. He didn't have a lie, he didn't have a pivot. And so, he simply said, "My dad is one of his... *clients*."

For a moment, Lauren quietly smoked, thoroughly unimpressed with the answer. Isaac watched as her mind ran through the possible scenarios. Did she think that Isaac worked at the prison? Some young guard whom Teddy had taken under his wing? Maybe a vendor for a laundry detergent company or something?

Then, as she looked at Isaac, her eyes went wide. A realization hit her. That face. That nose. That cheek structure. She knew it. She knew it intimately. She stared at Isaac, and for the first time in a while, she had nothing to say.

Finally, she croaked out, "Oh shit. Handyman?"

Isaac nodded. He usually hated this recognition, but usually it came from lecherous, middle-aged, over-weight men. When an eighteen-year-old was staring at him in awe, though, he felt... well... like a badass.

Without consciously doing it, his posture had straightened, a slight grin had formed on his face, and his pose—cigarette in his cupped hand being coolly brought to his lips—was like James fucking Dean. He felt no need to reply, no need to justify or deflect. His curt nod, and a puff on his cigarette, was enough. *Jesus Christ, don't cough man. Please don't fucking cough.*

Lauren's eyes stayed wide. She was gazing at a celebrity. Well, as much of a celebrity as Woodburn could produce.

"Whoa. Fuuuuuuuck," she finally said.

Whoa, fuuuuuuck, indeed.

Her gym bag suddenly vibrated, yanking her from her star-struck state. She reached into the bag and pulled out her phone. She checked the caller ID.

"Fuck. My prison guard's waiting. I gotta run, but..." she had no way to complete that thought. So, she finished with a, "Holy fuck, dude."

She crushed out her cigarette, her eyes never leaving Isaac's face. "You got your dad's nose."

"I found it in a box he kept under his bed," Isaac said. He didn't know why he made that stupid joke, but he liked the confidence with which he delivered it.

Lauren laughed. It was a genuine guffaw.

"Glad I didn't say 'You got his dick' then," she said.

Then she pulled some gum from her bag and popped it into her mouth. She jogged off across the parking lot, calling out over her shoulder, "Later, Junior Handyman!"

Isaac watched her go. He smiled to himself.

CHAPTER 8

Isaac stepped into his apartment. His mind still hummed from everything that had just occurred.

The excitement of his potential windfall was quickly replaced by an overwhelming dread. This entire plan, and thus Isaac's payment for successfully executing it, relied on one variable—his father openly discussing his crimes, preferably with excessive amounts of gory detail and maybe an ounce of armchair psychological self-analysis.

Isaac wondered if he could actually get the man to talk, let alone say something interesting and marketable.

He decided he needed a drink to help his mind relax.

A vodka orange juice.

He started drinking it as a bad joke. *The Handyman's son drinks screwdrivers!* But at a certain point, he discovered that it was the only drink he could both afford and stomach.

He went to his sink. The plastic jug of vodka that waited there was down to its last few gulps. Not enough to get the job done. He opened his pantry, which was essentially a single shelf of ramen noodles, instant oatmeal, and three more plastic jugs of vodka. He cracked open one of the jugs and then emptied its contents into a nearby Brita pitcher. It was a trick he learned from his college buddies, back when he had college buddies.

During the past two years, though, what was once a fun alcohol hack became a necessary component of his survival. The cheap vodka used to burn out his throat and upset what he was sure was a growing ulcer. Running it through a water filter didn't turn it into *good* vodka, but it turned it into nicely bland vodka. A little orange juice and it went down smooth.

As the filter slowly dripped the vodka through the charcoal filter and filled the pitcher, Isaac sat on his bed and waited.

He thought about the best strategies for getting his dad to talk about his crimes. His father had always tried to engage Isaac with talk of construction, but Isaac habitually closed off any meaningful dialogue with his father by acting like a typical teenage boy—unwilling to mutter more than one-word answers in response to any and all topics.

They lived together for thirteen years. Did they have any conversations that contained depth or nuance or insight? Isaac couldn't remember any.

He didn't feel that he grew up with any friction or anger toward his father. They never fought and never yelled. But when he thought of his childhood and his father, the main visual that came to mind was of coming home from taking the dog for a walk and seeing his father seated in his recliner, watching the Portland Trailblazers on TV. The old man would have a beer in his hand, an empty microwaveable dinner tray on the coffee table, and would be zoned out. He neither cheered nor napped during the games. Just watched.

Sometimes, if the game seemed close, Isaac would sit down and watch too. Other times he'd go to his room, plug in his headset, and either listen to music or watch porn on his phone. That was it. That was what it was like to live under the same roof as The Handyman.

Isaac figured that he *could* try to open up his father by talking about the Blazers. The old man hadn't missed a game since they won the championship in 1977, and he would definitely be curious as to how they were doing. Isaac wasn't sure how they were doing himself. He had concluded recently that all professional sports were simply a product being sold. The players were shuffled via trades and free agency every year so that the product was always recognizable, but still slightly new and exciting— much like how a new iPhone or Taco Bell menu item was unveiled every year. But while other goods produced a tangible product to be purchased, with sports, you were buying... hope? Hope that this year is the year? That things are better now that we have *this* rookie and *this* power forward? And if things aren't better, well, there's always next year.

If sports were the business of selling hope, at some point Isaac had realized that it was a product he had no interest in buying or possessing.

That realization bothered Isaac. He used to be so invested in basketball. As a kid, he would wear good luck charms during the games and actually pray during free throws in the fourth quarter. But then he realized that when the season ended, the world kept spinning, and spun directly toward the *next* season, and the one after, and the one after...

No, Isaac didn't want to talk Blazers with his dad. He didn't know if he could do it without criticizing the very fabric of something his dad loved. The old man had invested three hours a game, eighty-two games a year, into his fandom. It seemed cruel to rant to the man about how it was all some bullshit marketing strategy to sell TV commercial time.

The vodka finished filtering. Isaac stood and fixed himself a screwdriver.

Maybe there were other memories.

He tried to think of one. A happy one.

There was, of course, Christmas Land.

When Isaac was a kid, Walter seeded three acres of their property with Christmas trees. It took about ten years for the trees to grow to a usable size. Isaac spent much of his youth wandering the lot, waiting for the trees to get bigger. By the time Isaac reached middle school, the trees had grown, and Isaac excitedly helped his father open a U-cut tree lot. It was his first job, and, really, his first passion project.

Walter built a gravel parking lot in the middle of his tree farm, and it was there that he and Isaac set up a little Christmas village, complete with plywood cut-outs of Santa, elves, reindeer, and even an abominable snowman hiding behind some of the trees.

Over the course of five years of preparation, Walter stockpiled lights from every after-Christmas sale from every store in a twenty miles radius. They spent all of Thanksgiving weekend stringing the lights and hanging decorations.

When they finally flipped the switch, and the lights and characters came to life, Isaac felt a rush that no drug or booze ever came close to reaching since. It was the most joyous experience of his life. It was his little project. He dreamed of a never-ending string of cars arriving from Portland, all to experience and partake in the Christmas that Isaac had built.

He manned that tree lot every day after school, deep into the night, huddling under a canopy as he listened to Bing Crosby and the Mormon Tabernacle Choir on repeat.

But few cars came.

They sold maybe a dozen trees that year, not even enough to cover the plywood and the discounted lights. As had often been the case, his father had failed to advertise or promote. The only people who drove past Christmas Land were farmers driving to the city for supplies. Families didn't know. All that effort yielded nothing.

That was the only year of Christmas Land. The next year, Walter abandoned the project. His lack of interest crushed Isaac.

For a time, Isaac debated whether he should try to run the tree lot himself, but he chickened out, partly from laziness and partly from Walter's assurances that it was a losing business. The decision made Isaac resent Christmas and its commercialization.

No, Christmas Land wasn't a good conversation starter either.

There was nothing to talk about.

Now three drinks deep, Isaac still didn't have a clue of how he was going to break the ice with his father. Maybe the whole plan would fall apart. Maybe Teddy wouldn't be able to schedule the meeting. Maybe he wouldn't have to go through with it. Maybe this was just another Christmas Land—a fun idea, but too difficult to actually implement and destined for a quiet, ignominious death.

Isaac poured himself another drink. Instead of wasting his time thinking of conversation starters, he decided to look up how many drinks per week is considered a drinking problem.

He got halfway through typing the question on his phone before opening a new browser tab to see if his chisel had gotten any hits.

***

Isaac's phone woke him.

He still wore his clothes from the previous day. His night had been spent huddled and shivering on top of the blankets because he had been too drunk to figure out how to get beneath them. His head hurt, and his mouth was dry. All his saliva felt thick and creamy.

He picked up his phone and saw Teddy's name on the caller ID.

"Hello?" he said, trying to sound alert, awake, and professional. He didn't want Teddy to think that he was just waking up on a Wednesday at 10 a.m. with a hangover.

But Teddy didn't seem to notice or care. "Hey, buddy. Today's the day. I got a private room booked for you and your dad at 1 p.m. Your name's on the list. You just need to walk in the visitor entrance."

"Oh. Cool."

There was a long pause on the phone. Teddy finally cleared his throat. "I, uh, I just gotta be sure, man. Are you coming? Because he's such a high-profile inmate that if I take him outta his cell for nothing, he might get mad and not agree to future visitations. And then it'll create a whole stink where the superintendent might find out, and I might get reassigned and not be able to..."

"Yeah, yeah, yeah. I'll be there. One o'clock."

"Super! Don't bring any bags or metal objects, obviously. You'll have to rent a bin to lock up your phone and keys and whatnot. Or just leave them in your car. Don't wear blue denim, including jeans, because that's what *they* wear. I guess they don't want no one to pull a switcheroo or something. Also, if you want snacks, you gotta bring your own quarters. We can't break bills."

"I got it, I got it."

"Cool, man. Well... see you this afternoon at Wavecliff!"

Isaac hung up. He took a deep breath.

He was going to Willamette Valley Correctional Facility.

He was going to Death Row.

He was going to see his dad.

CHAPTER 9

It surprised Isaac how close the prison actually was to Woodburn. Only a thirty-minute drive. A quick shot down I-5 to Salem.

When Isaac's phone directed him to exit the freeway, he was sure that he had entered the wrong address. The road was lined with trees and grassy walks. He passed a high school, a park, several banks. This was the suburbs.

Immediately, Isaac worried that his phone was directing him toward the prison's *mailing* address or administrative offices. Was he going to be late? Was he going to miss his appointment?

The thought actually calmed Isaac. *I fucking tried*, he thought. It wasn't his fault that his navigation app fucked up.

His phone told him that he would arrive at his destination in four hundred feet on his right. No way this was the right place. Prisons, especially supermax prisons, should be isolated, right? They're way out in the middle of nowhere, like Alcatraz. And Oregon certainly didn't lack for middle of nowheres.

There was zero chance they would build this facility in the middle of the city, right off the same road that one would drive to get to the state's capitol building.

All Isaac could see were high trees growing along a mill creek.

When signaled, Isaac took his right turn. He thought he was driving into a state park. Pink rose bushes dotted the well-manicured grassy fields. The perfect place to pull some friends together for a game of Ultimate Frisbee. Isaac could see walking paths and even a low stone wall that rose only a foot off the ground. *Well, that ain't fucking secure*, Isaac thought.

He followed the road past some unmarked white houses. It curved to the right.

Suddenly, the beautiful nature park vanished.

Spread before him were twenty-five-foot concrete walls connected to a labyrinth of chain-link fencing, all topped with razor wire. Guard towers dotted the area. Peeking out from beyond the walls were the cell blocks.

Willamette Valley Correctional Facility.

Its acronym—WVCF—was pronounced "WAVECLIFF" among the prison population. More than one elderly mother, having received word that her inmate child had just been transferred to WAVECLIFF, had searched for the facility along the Oregon Coast and been frustrated at not finding it there.

There were no waves and no cliffs here. Just a supermax prison in the middle of the capitol city, disguised from its suburban neighbors only by rows of greenery.

But now, as Isaac approached, it had pulled off its mask.

WAVECLIFF was an old prison that had grown and expanded over time. In truth, it *had* been built in the middle of nowhere, but, over the century, the city had grown and swallowed it up. More wings and cell blocks had been added over the years to create a hodgepodge of the old and the new, all somewhat tied together by the creamy-yellow paint job and encircled by multiple rows of chain-link.

Isaac pulled up to a gate.

There was no guard booth. Instead, looming over Isaac's car, was a cream-colored concrete tower that looked very much like a lighthouse. A sign at the gate read, "STOP! Wait for directions from tower."

Isaac rolled down his window and leaned toward the callbox that extended from a post in the ground. There was a brief crackle of static, and then a voice called out.

"Name."

"Um, Isaac Luce."

"Spell it, please."

"Isaac. I-S-A-A-C. Luce. L-U-C-E."

Isaac heard the clicking of a keyboard.

The voice came back. "Purpose."

"Visitation."

"Inmate ID number."

Isaac had no idea. "Uh, I don't know his number. But last name Luce. L-U-C-E. First name, Walter. I should be on the list," Isaac said, and then added, "I'm his son."

Another pause. Finally, the voice said, "Drive around the tower to the left. You will see a checkpoint that says, 'Visitor Parking.'"

With the sound of a buzzer, the gate slid open. Isaac drove through.

He did as told and followed the road to the left, around the tower. His tires clunked over a spike-strip meant to rip out the rubber of any vehicle trying to go the wrong way. Then he wove through a tight pathway of concrete median dividers.

As he emerged from the maze, he came upon a guard booth.

The guard stepped out and jotted down Isaac's plate number.

"Pop your trunk, sir."

Isaac pulled the trunk release lever. He immediately cursed himself. He had meant to clean out the trunk and now realized that a prison guard was going to sift through his crates of rusty hand tools. He may as well have baked a cake and put a file in it.

But the guard just poked around a bit then shut the trunk and came back to Isaac's window.

"I, uh, sell tools," Isaac explained.

The guard didn't seem to care either which way. "Just be sure to leave them in your car. Park in any numbered spot. Bring your ID to the front door of that yellow building."

And with that, he waved Isaac through.

Isaac parked his car and put everything except his keys and wallet under the driver's seat. He stepped out and walked across the small parking lot toward the tall yellow building marked "Visitors."

Upon entering, he placed his keys in a tray and walked through a metal detector. He was told to raise his hands above his head. A guard patted him down under his arms and along his inner thigh. They had him open his mouth and they inspected his throat and under his tongue.

A guard waved him through and motioned him toward the clerk's booth.

He walked up and passed his ID through the Plexiglas partition. She entered his information, asked him for a contact phone and address, and then handed him a red visitor badge to hang from his neck.

He looked at it: "Visitor—DEATH ROW."

Then he was directed to enter an adjoining waiting room.

He took a seat in a hard-plastic chair.

He glanced around and immediately felt out of place. He was the only adult male in the room. There were some children playing with one of those "move the wooden blocks along the wire track" toys. It was the kind of diversion that entertained a child for all of 30 seconds. Some of the kids were growing fussy, and the adults in charge of them—apparently wives, girlfriends, and mothers of the inmates—didn't know how to handle a fussy child without the use of a phone or tablet.

The nervous hum of the women, combined with the near-breakdown of their children, made Isaac uncomfortable. The women fidgeted. Some played with wedding rings, others continually ran their fingers over their hair, trying to smooth out any strays. They wanted to look good for whomever they were visiting.

It occurred to Isaac that this was a school day. All of these kids had been taken out of the classroom. This must be a big event in their week. A face-to-face conversation with a loved one. They all probably looked forward to this day all month.

Watching these families made Isaac wonder how far they traveled for the occasion. The prison system shuffled inmates around due to space and need, but with no concern for a family's schedule or ability to visit. Isaac glanced at the women and tried to guess—Who drove from out of town? Who had to rent a hotel? Who had to borrow money from a friend or family member to make this experience happen? And were these women doing it for themselves or for their children to grow up knowing their father's face and voice?

All of these thoughts made Isaac shift in his seat. Everyone else here *wanted* to have this visit. They looked forward to this visit. They altered their lives for this visit. All for one hour of face-to-face conversation.

Isaac, meanwhile, felt put out by having to wake up before noon on a Wednesday.

With a buzz, a door opened. Isaac looked up.

Teddy stepped into the room. He was dressed in his beige and brown uniform. He had a baseball hat and a tactical belt of cuffs, mace, and a club. He glanced over the room. His eyes lingered on Isaac for half a second and an excited smile spread on his face, but it quickly vanished. He read aloud from a clipboard.

"Isaac Luce visiting Walter Luce?"

The room went silent. Everyone recognized the name.

Teddy looked around the room again, pretending not to recognize Isaac. He repeated, "Isaac Luce visiting Walter Luce?"

Isaac glanced to his left and right. He was the *only* guy in the room. The only person who could possibly be named "Isaac." Sure, Teddy wanted to play dumb and pretend that they had never met before, but this was *too* dumb.

He raised his hand.

Teddy looked around again before finally noticing Isaac.

"Come with me, sir."

Isaac stood and walked over.

"ID."

Isaac handed over his license.

Teddy looked at it, then looked at Isaac's face, then back at the picture, then back at Isaac. Finally satisfied that this person before him was in fact Isaac Luce, he jotted down some notes and handed back the license.

"I will escort you to your visitation room. Please follow me."

The door buzzed. Teddy pulled it open, holding it for Isaac to follow.

They walked down a narrow corridor. They reached another door that buzzed as Teddy approached. He pulled it open.

Isaac glanced up at the security cameras mounted to the ceiling. Some guard in a security booth must be following their every move, unlocking the doors as they approached.

Teddy held the next door. They stepped outside.

It was a thin, outdoor alley, surrounded on both sides by tall concrete buildings topped by razor wire. Isaac briefly thought that this would be a horrible place to be trapped during a prison riot. Or zombie attack.

Teddy spoke quietly out the side of his mouth, "We don't get a lot of male visitors. Mostly wives and girlfriends. During this part of the walk, I'm usually telling people to not expose their breasts to their inmate, no matter how intimate they are."

"I don't think that'll be a problem for me."

"I'm always surprised by how horny people get on these visits. Sex, man. It's all people think about. It's a sad, sad world we live in." Teddy sighed.

"How are you handling the recordings?"

Teddy smiled. He looked around. Then he motioned to his shirt. Peeking through a button hole was the microphone of a standard phone headset. It was well-disguised, to be sure, but Isaac was dubious.

"Will it sound okay?" Isaac asked.

"Sure. Yeah. I mean, I guess. Why wouldn't it?"

"We should've done a test run."

They reached the end of the outdoor walkway. The door of one of the cellblocks buzzed and Teddy led Isaac inside.

They entered a white, concrete hallway. The fluorescent lights were all held in cages. Every door was metal and remotely sealed. They passed through more doors, more checkpoints, more hallways. Isaac never saw another prisoner. He occasionally heard their voices—their arguments and their laughter—reverberate around the metal and concrete, but mostly he felt that he was being guided through a side-universe, one that ran parallel to the universe of prison life. An unending, twisted castle of well-lit hallways that only the loudest echoes of the other world were allowed to penetrate.

"It's usually not this far a walk. But he insisted on a private room," Teddy explained. "He's a little paranoid of the general population. Had some death threats and got beat up a bit during his first month here. Some guys just wanna punch him because he's famous. Other guys got kids of their own and don't like what he did."

Isaac couldn't help but feel bad at the thought of his dad, huddled naked in the middle of the shower room as prison gangs beat him.

"We don't usually accommodate things like private rooms for inmates, but he's kinda like a VIP around here."

Teddy held open a door and for once there wasn't a hallway on the other side, but a room. A windowless, concrete room.

In the center was a white metal table. Isaac almost chuckled at the sight. The table looked like one that fast food restaurants used for their outdoor seating—a picnic bench too heavy to steal. It was a big, white square with arms extending from its base that attached to chairs on either side, facing each other. Isaac figured the design made sense. An inmate couldn't lift the whole table to bludgeon someone, and he couldn't rip off a piece to make a shiv.

"Have a seat, sir," Teddy said, motioning to one of the chairs.

Isaac sat in the chair that faced the door.

As he looked around the room, he noticed the metal rings embedded in the concrete floor. A place to fasten the inmate's restraints, Isaac figured. It crossed his mind that his dad had devised a similar system in his basement.

Teddy stood behind Isaac and spoke into his walkie-talkie. "Visitor is seated."

There was a long silence. Isaac stared at the table. He thought that he would have been feeling something, *anything* by now, but there was nothing. Maybe this was all going to be easier than he expected.

He told himself that he wasn't feeling anything because he didn't actually *know* the man. In some ways, he was as removed from this old man as he was from those crates of tools in the Mennonite basement. This was a job. This man was a product. And Isaac was going to pick through him until he had extracted all potential resale value. He was going to repackage and sell this man.

If Walter had walked in at that moment, then Isaac would have been in a good place to start the conversation. But five minutes passed.

Then ten.

His father was surely being escorted down a similarly labyrinthian pathway.

In those moments, Isaac's mind wandered further.

Perhaps, he thought, he felt an emptiness toward his father not because of anything his father had done, but because of an emptiness in Isaac. The primary sign of a psychopath is lack of empathy. Isaac had read theories that psychopathy was a brain and chemical imbalance that might be hereditary.

Did Isaac feel nothing toward his father because he was exactly like the old man?

The thought ate at him.

Before he could purge it, rationalize it, or at least analyze and explore its depths, there was a loud buzz.

The door clanged open.

Two guards escorted a man into the room.

Isaac looked down at the table, unable to raise his head, unable to cast his gaze on the man.

The guards brought the man to the chair across from Isaac and the man wearily plopped into it. Then the guards stepped back.

After a full minute of silence, Isaac looked up.

He looked into the face of Walter Luce.

The Handyman.

His father.

CHAPTER 10

Isaac's first thought was that the old man had aged a few decades since the two last saw each other. But Isaac couldn't tell *why* he thought that.

His father had always had those crows' feet that merged into a face of wrinkles. His cheekbones were always high (Walter liked to say he was part Cherokee, but Isaac could never prove it and never put the effort into looking hard). The flesh on his face always hung loosely from those cheekbones, like the melting watch in Dali's painting. And as long as Isaac could remember, the old man had always had that scalp that was picked clean of every single hair follicle on top but had a full bushy donut around the side.

So, what was different? Why did he look so much older?

Then Isaac realized—the beard.

A full bush of hair that had always maintained its natural color. So thick and stiff that Walter joked he could sweep asphalt with it.

Isaac remembered that the old man began every morning, no matter how early he had to rise, with a ritualized landscaping of his face. Not a hair was allowed to rise above the rest. Walter may have allowed his business to slack off, but he never allowed his beard to. Isaac never realized how much maintenance his father had put into that beard over the years.

But for the first time in Isaac's life, he saw wayward hairs on the old man's face. There had apparently been attempts to rein it in, but the mustache was looking unruly with some stragglers extending below the upper lip. The hairs on his chin were getting long and starting to naturally twist into that goat look that Walter always criticized on hipsters.

It appeared that Walter either didn't care to sculpt his beard, or he didn't have the means to. The thought made Isaac wonder how inmates shave. Surely the prison didn't issue razors that could be turned into weapons. How did they do it then?

In that fleeting moment, Isaac felt sad for his father. All his freedoms had been taken away to the point that his simple daily shaving ritual had vanished.

"Hey, kiddo," Walter said.

Once he heard the old man's voice, Isaac's sympathy evaporated.

"Hey, Dad," Isaac said. He tried to make the words sound genuine, or at least ambivalent. Despite his efforts, there was some spit and bile woven into his tone. "Um, how are you?"

"Alive. You?"

"I'm, uh, fine."

They looked at each other for a long moment.

Isaac expected for Walter's gaze to be hardened, or at least empty and uncaring like he always remembered. But instead, Walter's eyes were soft and wide. He was leaning forward in his seat. This meeting actually seemed to mean something to him.

"You working?" Walter asked.

"No. I mean, yeah. Kinda."

"You either work or you don't."

"A little side gig."

"Mmm-hmmm." Walter seemed none-too-impressed.

They sat in silence.

Isaac cleared his throat. "How are they treating you in here?"

"Fine."

"Just fine?"

Walter shrugged. "Food's too salty. Showers are too hot."

"Do you get to work in the shop or anything?"

"Nope."

"You read any good books?"

"Nah."

"Watch any good shows?"

"Not really."

The two men looked at each other. Isaac had rattled off every conversation starter he had brainstormed. "So, um, you wanna talk about it?"

"About what?"

"*It.*"

"And what is *it*?"

Isaac sighed. "You know what *it* is, Dad. Don't play stupid."

Walter raised an eyebrow. "*Stupid*? Did you just call me stupid, boy?"

"Sorry."

They looked away from each other.

Isaac glanced up at the clock. They had been face-to-face for less than two minutes and they'd not only run out of things to say, but they were on each other's nerves.

He looked over at Teddy whose eyes urged Isaac to get on with it and say something. Anything. Break the ice and get the man talking.

"Blazers almost made the semis this year," Isaac said.

The old man's head perked up. "Really?"

"Yeah. First round was a real tight series. It went all seven games."

"What happened?"

"Oh, you know how it is these days in basketball. Everyone's shooting threes and sometimes the shots don't fall. When they don't, teams today can't win."

Walter wrinkled his face and nodded in an annoyed agreement. "They need to get down low and bang some more."

"No one likes doing that," Isaac said. "It's all spread offenses and switching on defense. You know what the Blazers need?"

"What?"

Isaac knew exactly what his father wanted to hear—a callback to the "good old days" of basketball. "They need someone like Big Mo down on the block. Get that toughness back," Isaac said. It was the kind of statement he had heard his father mutter during games all the time. Isaac had never engaged in the discussion, but he was now glad that part of his brain processed his father saying such things.

Walter rewarded Isaac by grinning wide in agreement. He wagged his finger, not at Isaac, but at the general state of basketball. "Mmm-hmmm. Exactly. Exactly."

"Every championship team has that brawler," Isaac said. "That tough guy. The guy who's just a little dirty. Throws his elbows a little hard. The one you want on your side in a fight."

Walter was positively beaming by now. "Like in the '77 Finales when Dawkins was pushing around Gross, and Lucas just comes up behind him and..."

Isaac completed the thought by miming a massive roundhouse punch. "That shit'll get you kicked outta the league now."

"Bunch of pussies."

The two men smiled at each other.

"Now *that* was team ball," Walter stared off, wistful.

Isaac realized that he had never seen his father wistful until now. He stayed quiet, letting the silence settle the room for a moment.

"1977," Walter said, shaking his head in wonder. "Greatest Blazer team of all time."

Isaac nodded, not wanting to admit that he hadn't been born yet and had never actually seen that team play.

"I really wanted to head up to Portland for the championship parade that year," Walter said. "Sure, it was all a bunch a hippies hanging from lamp-posts and stuff, but gee, it woulda been a riot."

Isaac sat quietly, waiting for him to continue.

Walter sighed. "Unfortunately, it was a work day and I had a business to run. Didn't get no calls or jobs that day. I remember that plainly. All that beautiful June day, I sat in the garage, waiting by the phone, listening to the parade on the radio. I guess anyone who woulda hired me for work took that day off anyway. I swore that I would head up for the next parade, the next time they won the championship." He chuckled to himself as he looked around at his concrete surroundings. "Guess I gotta keep waiting."

"You never told me that."

"I ain't one to bitch an' moan."

"You worked hard, though. And you sacrificed a lot for your business."

Walter leaned back in his seat and looked at his son. A sly smirk formed on the old man's lips. "Oh, it wasn't nothing much. You seen one parade, you seen 'em all. And those Clyde Drexler teams in the 90s, that was some pretty good basketball too. That was about the time of the Dream Team, you know. The sport was never bigger. If that Blazer team had gotten past Jordan and won a title...woo-weee... in terms of Oregon history, I think it woulda been bigger than Lewis and Clark."

Isaac pounced on his opportunity. "Well, something bigger *has* happened in Oregon since then."

"Them Jail Blazers? Nah. I mean, they got close, if not for Game 7 in the 2000 Western Conference Finals."

"No. Not basketball."

"Then whatcha talking about?"

"You're famous. Hell, more kids in Portland probably recognize your face at this point than they would Clyde-the-Glide Drexler. You wanna talk about it?"

Walter dismissively waved his hand. "I'm sure it's in the papers."

"I don't want the media's story. I want yours," Isaac said. "I want to understand."

"Why on Earth?"

"Because..." Isaac took a deep breath. "Because you're my dad."

The words sat there for a moment, neither man was sure how much they actually believed in the earnestness. But, nonetheless, Walter leaned back and didn't say a word. It was a tacit permission to continue.

"What changed?" Isaac asked. "You weren't always like this."

"Maybe I was. Maybe that's why your mom left me."

"Let's not talk about Mom," Isaac said with an ounce more curtness than he intended.

For the briefest moment, a devilish smile appeared on Walter's lips. But the smile quickly vanished and Walter merely nodded, agreeing to the rule to not speak of Isaac's mother.

They sat quietly for a moment before Isaac continued. "The media has a theory about you."

"Do I care?"

"They think you snapped when Luce Contracting went under."

Walter released an angry sigh. "Christ."

"They got all sorts of experts in psychology and psychopathy saying that a major life disruption like losing a business, especially one that bears your own name, is a major stressor. Aside from the stress of money problems, losing a business that you've invested so much of yourself in... well... it fucks with a man's ego. And when a man's ego feels threatened, he tends to lash out."

"Does *he*?" Walter sneered. "Psycho-mumbo bullshit."

"You don't see a little truth in it?"

Walter leaned forward, his eyes piercing Isaac. "That there is ancient history. I folded Luce Contracting five years before this whole mess happened."

"But it was personal. It was a family business."

"What family? You never lifted a goddamn finger to help. Other than that Christmas tree thing."

"The company had your name on it."

"What else was I supposed to fucking call it?"

"You started it with grandpa's inheritance."

Walter's hand suddenly shot up so quick that Teddy, standing nearby, flinched and almost tackled the old man. But Walter had no intention of striking Isaac; his hand had shot up so that he could stretch out his finger and wag it in Isaac's face. A lecture.

"Don't you dare call that man 'grandpa.' You didn't know him. You never met him. He didn't do nothing to earn that sort of honorific title from you."

"Sure, but—"

"And he didn't leave me some fortune, either. He was a cheapskate, never spent a dime on anything that wasn't McDonalds or Jim Beam. He had a union pension, was all. Ever hear of those things? Yeah, they're like unicorns now, but back in the day a pension could take care of a man. Let him go into old age with some dignity. So yeah, he left me some money. $120,000. I bought a house, a bunch of tools, and leased a back-hoe and a trailer. That's it. I didn't get gifted nothing. I built Luce Contracting with my own two hands, one callous at a time."

"$120,000 ain't nothing."

"Doesn't go as far as you'd think."

"Then why have we never talked about him before?"

Walter took a deep breath and calmed himself down. "I didn't really know him. He was a stranger. We shared a last name and a house, but never a beer nor a kind word. He was an angry sonabitch."

"Why was that?"

"Never gave it much thought. Just the way some people are." Walter looked off and considered the question. "There're a lotta men, they get beaten up out there, day after day. They go into work, they go to the bank, they go to the store, they go to the car dealership, and they're just getting punched in the face. Over and over. So, these men, they go home. Waiting there is a child. Crying, wanting food and whatnot. These men finally see something in their life that *they* can punch. Something that can't punch back."

"Wait, wait... did he *beat* you?"

Walter stopped and looked at him. "What? No. Don't be dumb, boy. You think I'd put up with that?"

"But you just said—"

"Maybe by today's bubble-gum standards he was a rough man. But that's the thing. He was a *man*. He wasn't doing anything that all the other kids' dads weren't doing."

"That still doesn't sound like a healthy relationship."

"Look," Walter said, "I didn't love my dad. But I understood him. And I'm grateful for all he did to provide for me. You and your generation don't know the meaning of the word gratitude."

"High praise."

"He didn't have time for a kid. He was a man with a job."

"When *you* lost *your* job, how did it feel?

Walter leaned back in his seat and crossed his arms. "Same as ever."

"I moved out about the same time. Were you lonely?"

"Boy, it ain't like you were the cure to loneliness. Always hanging out with your buddies. Coming home late. Sleeping past noon. It was like living with a zombie."

Isaac leaned in, not giving up on the question. "Were you lonely?"

"Do those TV experts say I was lonely? That I needed company?"

"Kyla Perkins was a prostitute."

Isaac intended for the words to land hard, but Walter merely raised an eyebrow, seemingly not recognizing the name. Isaac let the silence thicken, hoping the awkwardness would stir Walter to speak. But Walter made no motion to pick up the conversation.

The only sound was Teddy shuffling his feet, checking his watch, and gulping nervously.

Finally, bored with the game, Walter simply said, "Who?"

"The dead prostitute in your basement," Isaac said.

"Is this really what you want to talk about?"

"Yes."

"I'd rather talk about the Blazers, if it's all the same to you," Walter said, sighing as if he was bored by it all.

"Jesus fucking Christ, Dad! You're the only serial killer who *doesn't* like to talk about what he did. Most of them won't shut the fuck up bragging about it. Especially when they've already been found guilty."

Walter's gaze wandered around the room, searching for something more interesting.

But Isaac persisted. "Her name was Kyla Perkins. She was the first one who went missing. Meaning she was probably your first victim. Do you have anything to say about that?"

"I'm afraid I just don't know anyone named Kyla."

Isaac sighed.

"Unless you mean Trixie," Walter said.

Isaac looked at his father. The old man's mustache was ruffled into a mischievous grin.

"Trixie?" Isaac said.

"She was a friend of mine. I met her after you moved out."

"She was a prostitute."

"Oh, yes. A relatively cheap one. I'm not too familiar with the prices in that particular market. But for a hundred bucks for the entire night? You can't beat that deal with a stick."

"How long have you been seeing prostitutes, Dad?"

"Trixie was my first." He thought for a moment. "And only."

"What made you go out and get a prostitute?"

The smile on Walter's lips widened. "The day I bought Trixie was the day I met Elizabeth."

"*The* Elizabeth?"

"Yes, boy. *The* Elizabeth."

"Tell me about her. And Trixie. And everything."

Walter looked off. His lower lip sucked on the hairs of his mustache. It was a habit he had for whenever he was about to tell a story...

CHAPTER 11

I was knee deep in shit when I saw her.

Some moron had planted Chinese sumac by the entrance of the West Creek Apartment Complex in Salem. Big trees. Grows fast. Gives a lotta shade. Looks nice, but they smell like sour peanut butter when the leaves die. Damned things are a downright invasive species. Their roots grow crazy in the spring, and they rip into any water source they can ball themselves into.

Well, the sewer line ran right underneath them. As the trees grew, their roots ripped into the old pipe. Tore right through it and took a big ol' drink.

Now, if these were actual adults living there, they woulda called a plumber the moment their drain started making that "glug-glug-glug" sound. But these apartments mostly had college kids. College kids don't know how to stand on their own two feet and actually deal with a problem.

So, the roots got worse and worse and worse, and well, by spring, you flush a toilet on the second floor and shit bubbles up the kitchen drain on the first floor.

It was a mess.

Now, the owner of West Creek, well, he's a real tight-ass. Always has been, always will be. Didn't like hiring the union guys to work on his properties, and so, he'd call around to the desperate old-timers like myself.

What can I say, I needed the money.

I couldn't snake out the roots; the pipe was too far gone, and my auger would just punch a hole through that brittle old cast iron, tear it to shreds. The whole line needed to be replaced. So, I had to dig a trench from the front door to the street.

I'd turned the water off to the building, but of course the college kids would turn it back on if they wanted to take a shower, or run their dishwasher, or flush their toilet. These fucking kids are lazy as slugs when it comes to actual adult work, but try inconvenience them with two days of limited water and they'll figure out a way to get that water back on.

Which meant my trench would fill, all day, with their shit.

To boot, it was April, so of course it was pouring rain. The runoff from that mixed right in there, made it harder to find the leaks.

Well, I was crouching down, my back aching, measuring PVC fittings as a fucking fraternity turd would float by. This was my life. No, no. This *wasn't* my life. This was what I had to do to prevent my life from getting worse. From becoming truly disgusting.

And then, I heard her voice.

"Hey. How's it going?" she said.

When I looked up, I saw her. She was in her twenties. She had on a jogging suit. I suppose it was a tight and attractive suit, and the rain probably made it hug her figure even closer, but I didn't pay any of that no mind.

Instead, the only thing I saw was that her blonde hair was pulled back underneath a Blazer hat. *That's* what made me smile.

I realized I had been staring for what felt a day and hadn't answered her question. "Tree roots in the septic system," I managed to say.

"Looks awful," she said.

The smell must've wafted up to her as she covered her nose with her hand right then. To be honest, the stench wasn't too bad. It was open air and all. Although the rain had spread it all out into a larger soup, it had also beaten back the fumes.

Still, for a pretty city girl like her, I imagine it don't take more than a teaspoon of shit to ruin the barbeque. She wrinkled up her face in disgust at the situation, and sympathy for the poor devil who was knee deep in it.

I tried to downplay it all. I shrugged and said, "I'm used to it."

I immediately regretted those words as they most definitely implied that, yes, I spend my days digging through shit. I am beneath you.

But she kept smiling back down on me, as friendly as ever.

"I've seen you working all week," she said, "And, anyway, I run past a donut shop and thought..."

At that moment, she held out a small paper bag, its sides splashed with rain, and its bottom wet from the grease of some delicious fried dough.

"Here ya go," she said as she held it out.

"Maybe after I wash up," I said.

"Yeah. Good call."

She set the bag on the grass. It was then that I pointed at her hat.

"Blazer fan?" I asked.

"Rip City, baby."

"Catch many games?"

"Taking the bus into P-town this weekend. My mom's got courtside seats for the Jazz game."

"I'll keep an eye out for you on TV. I'm Walter, by the way."

"Elizabeth. Stay clean, Walter."

She gave me a wave and turned to jog back into the apartment. But then she paused and turned around to face me.

"Is there water for showers?" she asked.

I smiled up at her. "Of course."

She gave me another little wave and jogged up into the building. I pulled myself out of my trench and walked over to the main line.

I picked up my water valve key, which I welded myself, by the way. Most keys they sell are rebar, but I twisted mine up once, so I welded a couple steel pipes into a five-foot T-bar. You fit the notch right on the valve. Now, these valves are old, often rusty. You just need to move it a quarter turn, but you gotta do it real slow with steady, even torque. Don't just use your arms. That's what them frat boys like to do. They would just try to crack it with brute strength. You'll snap a valve that way. You should be using your whole body, like you're rowing a boat. Those frat boys can surely best me at any bench press competition, but I can out-muscle them at any real-life skill. That's where it really counts.

Where was I?

Oh, yeah. I turned on the water.

Immediately, it looked as though twenty toilets flushed directly into my trench. It filled to the brim with mud and shit.

And you know what? I didn't mind.

The only thing that I saw was that paper bag with that donut.

And for the first time in a long while, I smiled.

CHAPTER 12

Isaac looked across the table at his dad. "That's it?"

The old man was still staring off, wistfully imagining that paper bag sitting on the grass. "That's it," he said.

"A fucking *donut* started all this?"

Walter shook his head, annoyed. "No. A genuine human interaction started all this. Simple decency. Compassion. The things that I had been missing."

"So, some nice college girl gives you a donut. You realize how lonely you are, how much the world sucks, and so forth. So to not be lonely anymore, you go out and bring a prostitute home, then chain her in your basement. I get it."

"No, you don't. You don't get anything. You never did."

"What was it you called her? Trixie? Was that her street name or was that the pet name you came up with for her? Either way, it's not very original."

"It's not like you think."

Isaac leaned forward. "Then help me understand."

Walter shrugged. He took a deep breath and continued. "It was innocent, really..."

CHAPTER 13

I must've driven around town for hours.

I went through every mobile home park, behind every motel, every dark corner of town. I knew I could probably find someone on the internet, but somehow, I didn't like the idea. Call me old-fashioned, but I feel a hooker is something that should be picked up in person, not ordered online.

I saw her step out of one of those motels off Highway 214. Her and her John walked out together. She didn't look much like a hooker, though. I mean, she was dressed up pretty, in a skirt too short for the cool temperature, but her face wasn't covered in clown makeup like you see in the movies.

She just looked normal. Pretty. Nice.

I figured I had a narrow window from between when her John left and her pimp returned, so I quickly pulled up and made my offer.

Fifty bucks to have a home-cooked meal with me.

I probably fumbled out the words as I didn't quite know how to phrase that proposition, but she didn't seem at all confused by it. I guess plenty of guys met with her out of companionship with no intents on sleaze. She bartered me up to an even hundred, and then climbed in the car.

We didn't talk about anything during the drive.

But when I reached out my hand, she grasped it. That was nice. Just sitting there, driving down the highway, holding hands and listening to the radio.

When we reached the house, I heated up an old pot roast in the microwave. A couple rolls. Some instant potatoes. Set two places and we sat down to a lovely dinner.

I told her about my day at work. She asked questions. Seemed genuinely interested. I didn't ask about her day, and she didn't volunteer anything as I'm sure she felt it would break the moment.

It was probably one of the best meals I'd had in ages. It felt natural and good.

I had actually forgotten that we weren't an item when I said, "There's a Blazer game starting in a few minutes. Wanna go to the living room?"

She looked at me. Her face was completely emotionless. All business. "That'll be another couple hours."

She said it with that detached voice that a bartender might use to remind you the price when you order a second beer. I had forgotten that this was merely a transaction to her. It was a perfectly natural response from her, but it caught me a bit off guard.

In my rush to be polite, I hurriedly pulled out my wallet.

And that there was a big fucking mistake.

You see, when Luce Contracting went under, the creditors had swooped in and hovered over all my bank accounts, waiting to descend and pluck out any loose entrails that might present themselves. Because of that, I had gone to an all-cash lifestyle.

I had actually gotten paid for the plumbing work that very afternoon, and I had immediately cashed the check. My wallet held north of three-thousand dollars.

When I opened it to pull out a hundred, Trixie saw it all.

Our eyes met right then. I remember time stopping and us just staring at each other. We both knew that I had made a fool's move to flash so much cash, truly all the money I had in the world.

When that moment of stopped time ended, the world suddenly sped up to a pace that was practically incomprehensible to me. Somehow Trixie had grabbed the carving knife out of the knife block. She held it ready, in front of my throat.

"Give it to me," she said. "All of it."

I was confused. Betrayed. But what could I do? I closed my wallet and set it on the table.

"Now give me the keys to your truck," she hissed.

"I need that truck."

"Give me the fucking keys."

I just looked at her. I didn't say a word.

"I will cut you, old man."

I pulled out my keys and dropped them on the table.

That truck was my livelihood. It may not look like much, but I couldn't replace it. Especially not without the money from this plumbing gig. And I didn't know if she was going to start looking around the rest of the house for more hidden cash. Maybe my TV or computer.

If I let her leave, then this would be a financial blow from which I could never recover. The thin sandbar on which I stood, keeping my head above water, was crumbling beneath the weight of some greedy, filthy whore.

I didn't make a conscious decision to fight back. Survival instincts travel much too fast for that. But I wasn't letting her get my truck and money.

When she reached down to pick up the wallet and keys, I grabbed the lamp right off the counter. That old accountant's lamp. You know the one I mean? I always kept it on when you were in high school, out having fun with your friends, so you'd never come home to a dark house. I liked that lamp. Got it from that old Mennonite secondhand store. Why the Amish are selling lamps, I'll never know. Damn hypocrites.

Anyways, I took that lamp and slammed it into her fucking face.

She recoiled and stumbled to the ground, but, oh, did that old skank have some fight in her yet. She swung that knife around, even as the blood poured from her nose.

She was jabbing it, slicing it. Anything she could to hurt me.

I managed to grab her knife hand. We wrestled for it. She was scrappy, and she was strong.

But here's a trick one of the old boys taught me when I worked at the mill. If you're ever in a fight for a weapon, grab the other guy's pinkie. It's the weakest muscle in the hand. Yank it hard to the side. Ain't nothing they can do to stop it. Once that thing breaks off, they'll be screaming to high Hell.

And that's exactly what I did. Wrapped my thumb and index around her pinkie and I tore the tendons on that thing on down to her wrist.

We both heard it snap and then all I could hear was Trixie hollering and howling in pain. The rest of her fingers completely forgot that they were holding a knife. She dropped it right to the floor.

She was stunned.

I had my chance. I grabbed that lamp cord and wrapped it full around her neck. Pulled on both sides and I cinched it so tight she couldn't slide a dollar bill in there.

Even then she didn't stop fighting. She tried to kick me, head butt me. Her arms flailed about. She made the most awful gurgling, hissing sound that whole time. But I held on.

After a while, her legs gave out and she slumped down.

It happened so suddenly that I thought her fall might have enough force to snap her neck or rip her head clean off. But no. She just kinda dangled there a moment.

When I finally let go, it truly was like a sack of potatoes hitting the floor. I bent down and checked her. She was still breathing. She was still alive. Any moment she might spring back to life and try to attack me again.

I wrapped the lamp cord around her wrists.

But I needed a place to put her. I dragged her across the kitchen to the broom closet. I threw the brooms, the mops, the buckets, everything, out. And then I threw her in.

She was coming to by this time, but the only words she could come out with were, "No... no... no..."

I slammed the closet door and wedged a chair under the knob to keep it closed.

I knew that was a short-term solution, so I hurried to the garage, grabbed my drill, a couple of two-by-fours, and some good three-inch wood screws. I drilled those boards across the door, straight into the studs of the door frame. She wasn't going to be able to force that open.

But the door, of course, was hollow-core, so it was only a matter of time 'fore she might be able to bust through it.

The world finally stopped spinning long enough for me to think. I had an angry whore locked up in my broom closet. Fuck me.

She must have a pimp. They always do. If I let her go, she'd run off to him and they'd hunt me down. She knew where I lived, what kinda truck I drive. I didn't have the finances to change any of those realities. She could find me again. And she could cause trouble.

But could I kill her? No. I didn't have it in me for that.

What could I do? The broom closet wasn't gonna hold forever. It was a temporary solution. I needed to put her somewhere more functional while I figured out my plan. Somewhere more permanent.

If there's one thing I've always strived for as a builder and as a man, it's permanence.

CHAPTER 14

I opened the basement door and walked down those long, steep steps. When I stepped into the basement, I knew this was the spot. Sure, it was cluttered with all that crap from that damn Christmas tree lot, but that was an easy clean job.

It was a solid half-basement. Mostly subterranean. Good concrete walls that were strong enough to hold the foundation of the house. A lot of homes in this state don't have actual basements. Just crawl spaces. Too much rain and flooding. And, yeah, moisture build-up has been a battle I been fighting down there for decades, but I wasn't about to complain about that now.

So, I grabbed a box of Christmas lights, heaved it up the stairs, and went to work. Took me two hours of trudging up and down them steps to move all that junk to the garage.

But I admit, it was fun to have a task.

A job.

Something to be accomplished.

First step, of course, was to get accurate measurements. I measured that room—measure *twice*— and made a plan.

I knew she was gonna have to relieve herself, and I didn't want to mess with carting around chamber pots and buckets. I wish I coulda hooked something up to the septic tank, but I didn't have the time.

So, I brought out the jackhammer and hacked a little trench along the back wall. Right down to the dirt underneath. I installed a grate in it and ran a hose line down from the kitchen. That way, she could rinse her piss and shit down into the dirt. Not good for the house's foundation, mind you, but I figured I wasn't gonna be around for that old house to appreciate much more, so I dug down into that concrete.

Next, that basement, as you know, has got that small window. Well, I couldn't have that. That'd be her first place to look to call for help or get away. I mixed up some mortar and laid brick over that whole window. Fastened it into the wood frame with brackets. I had a leftover box of security screws from another project; you know those screws that you can only tighten, but not loosen because the Phillips groove is angled? I used those to fasten it down.

It still occurred to me that the way sound waves travel, her screams were just gonna bounce around in there. So, I nailed some old rolls of carpet to the ceiling. I had some rolls of foam, too, that was leftover underlayment from a laminate flooring project. Ghastly looking stuff, those laminate floors. Just cheap. Tacky. Anyone who can't tell the difference between laminate and hardwood floors, or doesn't care, is a fool who ain't got no taste and ain't got no business owning property to begin with. Anyway, I glued that foam underlayment to the walls in spots. Seemed to help.

Oh wait, I should take a step back. As I was doing all this other stuff, I was waiting for my concrete to dry. See, what I did was I drove an anchor bolt right into the floor. On top of that, I built a wood frame, about a foot wide, and filled it with concrete. I embedded a thick chain in the concrete. I needed something to hold her to, you see.

Finally, I reinforced the basement door. Swapped out that old hollow core with a solid wood door that I'd gotten from a job site and had been holding onto out in the shed. That's why you should never throw things away, boy. You never know when you'll need a door for your whore. Ha! Now, *that's* a rhyme worthy of Seuss. Anyway, I put on a new deadbolt and latch. At that point, if she ever got outta those chains, there was no way she was breaking through that door.

There it was. Took a day and a half and I was done.

And not a moment too soon.

This whole time, I could tell that Trixie was up to her tricks. Whenever my tools were making noise, I would stop suddenly and could hear a couple bangs on that broom closet door. She was using my noise as cover to break free.

When I went up to the kitchen, I could see she was getting close. The hinge screws were about to pull right outta the door.

By this time, she had gotten her hands free, I imagined. I was gonna have a hell of a time getting her out of there and into the basement. She wasn't going down without a fight.

So, here's what I did.

I took my drill and I bored a half-inch hole right into that door. She knew right then something was up. She started looking through that hole and she started hollering, "Please! Let me out! I won't tell anyone. Please!"

Total lies. She was all bullshit. But what do you expect from a whore?

I shoved a rubber hose into that hole in the door. Sealed it in with a rag and some duct tape. I shoved a wet towel down at the base of the door to seal that off too.

"Please! Please!" she cried, "I promise you won't get in trouble!"

You think I was born yesterday?

I walked the other end of that hose to the stove. Had to pull the oven out away from the wall, but there was the gas line. I unhooked the stove and clamped my rubber hose onto the line. I turned on the valve. The whole thing started hissing. Her little closet was filling with gas.

Woo-wee, she knew what was up immediately.

She pounded on that door. Hard as she could. She kicked at it. Punched at it. Threw her back into it. And to be honest, I was glad that she did. She used up more of her oxygen that way, and believe me, at that exact moment in her life, there was no resource more valuable, and she was frittering it away.

Pretty soon she wised up. She knew she had to stop that gas from filling her tiny room before it knocked her out cold.

First, she tried to shove the hose back out the hole. But I held on tight. Then she tried to yank the hose all the way through, maybe she was thinking she could rip it off the clamp. Again, I held her off.

She was scrappy. In a straight up fight, I think she might've had a chance against me. But in a tug-a-war over this rubber hose, just a battle of arm-strength, she wasn't gonna win or even come close.

Eventually she tried to plug the end of the hose. I couldn't see her through the door, but I knew I had won. I had punched holes up and down the first foot or two of that hose. She wasn't gonna be able to plug them all.

Even her begging was getting weak at this point.

"Please, please," she gasped.

In a little while, she was out. I heard her body slide down to the floor. I waited a few more minutes just to be sure. What did I care if she got a little brain damage? It was her fault for fighting it so much.

I unscrewed the door and there she was. Limp as a daisy. Kicked her a few times. Nothing.

I put her on that old red toboggan of yours and I dragged her down the stairs.

By the time she woke up, her leg was chained to a block of concrete that was anchored to the floor.

And she was mine.

All mine.

CHAPTER 15

BZZZZZZZZZZZZ!

Isaac looked around, angry that whatever alarm was making that sound had just interrupted his father and ruined the flow of his story. His glare finally fell on Teddy who could only respond with an apologetic shrug.

"That's, um, that's it for today," Teddy said.

"But we were just getting started," Isaac snapped back.

"I know. I'm real sorry. But visitations can only last so long. There's nothing I can do about that. We gotta clear the room and we gotta get him back for count. You're allowed a brief hug before you go."

Isaac stared at him. "*Seriously?*"

"I'm sorry. If both of you are willing to meet again, I can set up another visitation for tomorrow. There are restrictions on frequency, but I have the authority to pull some strings for you," Teddy said as he glanced from one man to the other, "You two want to meet again?"

Walter and Isaac looked at each other. Finally, Walter chuckled. "I admit that I wasn't looking too forward to this. Since you showed no interest in seeing me all these years, even when I wasn't in here, I didn't see any real point to us meeting. When Teddy said you wanted to visit me, I nearly said, 'Thanks but no thanks.'"

"Really?" Isaac asked.

"I had to be dragged out here."

"Me too. I didn't know what I'd actually have to say to you."

Walter smiled. Isaac couldn't help but return the smile, bonding with his father over the realization that they at least had one thing in common—neither of them wanted nor asked for this meeting.

"I thought we might end up sitting and staring at each other for an hour, and that wouldn't be no fun for no one," Walter said. "Or worse, maybe you had found Jesus or something and was gonna pour out that bullshit onto me." He leaned back. A thoughtful quiet overtook him. "We've never talked like this boy. It feels good."

"You'd like to meet again?"

"I don't have nothing on the books for tomorrow."

They stood from the table and faced each other. Walter held his arms wide for a hug. Isaac stepped toward him. And then Isaac held out his hand. Walter's face fell as he closed his arms and instead grasped his son in a firm handshake.

"See you tomorrow," Isaac said.

The doors opened, and two guards stepped into the room with Walter's shackles in hand.

CHAPTER 16

Isaac waited outside Teddy's house.

The sun had long ago sunk behind the mountains of the Coast Range, and now the Oregon evening air hung chilly. It wasn't raining or even misting, but there was a such a dampness that Isaac could practically smell the moss growing.

Isaac had found Teddy's address online. Digging it up was surprisingly easy. He didn't even have to pay for one of those stalker websites. He simply searched around and about three screens deep, there it was: "THEODORE ANDERTON: WOODBURN, OREGON." Listed beside it was a home address. The document was some kind of public record lawsuit over the property. It seemed to be related to a messy divorce, but Isaac's eyes glazed over the legalese. He didn't really care about Teddy's life or marriage.

He only cared about the recordings.

After hearing his father speak in such vivid detail—something that Isaac had not expected—it took him a while to process just exactly what had happened. But as his car pulled out of the WAVECLIFF parking lot, it struck him just how valuable these recordings could be.

He expected his dad to mumble his way through the hour. But instead, it was as if sixty years of built-up non-expression finally ruptured something in the old man. The words came spilling forth, flooding Isaac. Such introspection. Such insight. And such cold detail. *Hearing* The Handyman describe his construction of his torture basement was more than Isaac would have prayed for. Ben could put a paywall on the site and still get a million hits.

Isaac wanted his hands on those recordings. He wanted to hear them. He needed to know their sound quality. He needed to be confident in their very existence.

And so, he waited on Teddy's front step.

The house was small. It was only a step removed from "mobile home park," and even those, despite the stigma in the name, tended to be brightened up with a certain pride in ownership.

Teddy's house, on the other hand, was purely functional. In some ways, it reminded Isaac of his own childhood home. Although his father was a contractor and overall handyman, projects tended to linger. White primer patches on the siding would last for years. Gutter joints that just needed to be snapped and sealed back into place would hang open, forgotten until the next heavy rain when the water would shoot down and bore a hole in the dirt of a flower bed that hadn't held plant life in a decade.

Isaac noticed similar imperfections in Teddy's house, but he made it a point not to judge them. A poor, single-father in a blue-collar job didn't have the hours in the day to deal with "curb appeal."

Unlike Isaac's childhood home out in the farming country, Teddy's home was in the Woodburn suburbs. Isaac couldn't help but think, *If Teddy locked up a prostitute, someone would surely hear*. It both amused and worried him that he now looked at the world through this serial murder lens. *"Is this person... or this location... or this blunt object conducive to killing someone and getting away with it?"*

It reminded him of that period in his late teens when he was obsessed with zombie fiction. It seeped into his brain to the point where he couldn't walk into a room or a building without mentally cataloguing the area's strengths and weaknesses for surviving the zombie apocalypse. At the time, he considered it a funny little brain-worm. That worm had passed on through, and a new one had taken its place.

The loud, grinding motor of an ancient garage door interrupted his thoughts. The gravel crunched beneath the tires of an approaching car.

Teddy was finally coming home.

Isaac rose as Teddy's old stick-shift Ford Escort—its engine alternating between glugging and whirling, a decade's worth of delayed maintenance and duct-tape repairs disrupting the timing on all its belts and pistons—coasted up to the house and came to a stop.

Teddy climbed out of his car and stepped into the driveway. He cast a confused look at Isaac.

"Oh, hey, partner," Teddy said as he gathered his belongings from the backseat. "You don't need to come to my house."

"I want to hear it."

"Oh, it's good. Don't worry about it. I got it covered."

Isaac stepped toward him, "I need to hear it. Send it to me."

Teddy shifted. "I, uh, don't even know how to send it. I mean, I'm sure there's a way, but it'll take me some time to figure out. But you can trust me. It sounds great."

"You recorded it on your phone, right?"

"Uh. Yeah."

Isaac let out an annoyed sigh. "So, you tap the file and it will give you options. One of those options is going to say 'Email.' So then, get this, you *email* it to me."

"Oooooh. Yeah, yeah. I can do that." Teddy made no move to take out his phone.

"Is there a problem?"

"No, no, no. It's just... I mean, you can listen to it right here with me. Why do you need a copy for yourself?"

"I'm soliciting bids and I need a proof-of-concept."

Teddy's face turned sour. "*You're* soliciting bids? But... but I got a buyer. Joan. She's all lined up, ready to go. Money on the table."

"Who is she?"

"You'll love her. She's a TV producer. Wants to do a whole documentary series on The Handyman. She's way into this project. She's been researching this for years. She said things like 'syndication' and maybe a 'theatrical' release. You know, this is big stuff. This is big Hollywood kind of stuff. It could go viral."

"What's her name?"

"Joan. Like I said."

"I assume there's more than one 'Joan' who works in movies. What's her *last* name?"

"Full disclosure, she's just starting out her production company. You're not going to find out a whole lot on her, but she wants this to be the project that launches her."

"Her *name*."

"Joan Larkins. Now, I know you think you might be able to get more elsewhere, but you can't buy her passion for this project. Anywhere else, they might pay a lot, but then they just throw it on the web and it's gone. But with Joan pushing it, we're talking about a lifetime of residuals. Like, this can set us up forever."

Isaac just shook his head in disbelief. "This is *her* saying that?"

"I mean... no-no-no. Not *just* her. I mean, she's local. She's from Portland, so she knows the story. And she's got money. She was a big-time lawyer, so you know we're going to be well-protected."

"Why does she care?"

"She wants to branch out. She's made her money and now she wants to become an independent producer."

"You lost me at 'independent.' Give me the file. I'll make the deal."

Teddy made no move to pull out his phone. "She's got money."

"Not mainstream major media corporation money."

Teddy stood firm. "I... I can't give it to you."

"Why not?"

Teddy looked away. His hands went into his pockets and his right foot dug a little hole in the dirt. He was an enormous man who could easily rip Isaac's arm off, but in that short moment, Isaac saw a little boy. A kid who felt terrified that the world only existed to take advantage of him.

"You're afraid I'm gonna sell the recordings without you," Isaac finally said. "And since you're breaking prison rules to set up these interviews and make these tapes, a signed contract between us probably isn't too enforceable. Or smart."

"No, no... I trust you."

"Then how do *I* know that you're not going to run off and sell them without *me*?"

"We're a team, you know. I got the buyer. She's all set to go. This is a good thing. You just gotta trust me."

Isaac thought about that for a moment. Then he shook his head. "I'm not going back in that room with him unless I get some guarantees. You're going to send me the recordings and I'm going to shop them around to my contacts."

Teddy shoveled a few more grains of dirt out of the hole with the toe of his shoe. His eyes stayed on his feet. His whole body shifted uncomfortably.

Isaac's annoyance grew. "Look, I'm not going to cut you out. I wouldn't screw over little Lauren's state-school college fund like that."

And suddenly, Teddy's eyes shot up. His body stopped shifting. His foot planted itself firmly on the ground. His hands even came out of his pockets and balled into fists at his side. None of this was for show. It was a completely subconscious reaction.

"What's that supposed to mean?" he asked, his voice steady and threatening.

For the briefest moment, Isaac wondered if he was going to have to fight Teddy. He thought about how his father would fight off a big man like Teddy. Isaac's mind flashed to an image of kicking Teddy hard in the kneecap. If he did it with enough force, he could send the big man straight to the ground. Then Isaac would get in his car, and while Teddy was immobilized, he would swerve around and run over the man's head. He wondered if he would be able to feel it pop under the weight of his tires.

But Isaac quickly buried these thoughts. He put his hands up for peace. "Sorry. I didn't mean anything by it," Isaac said.

Teddy calmed down. He took a few deep breaths and his body relaxed again.

"But if you want me back in that prison, I need the files," Isaac said.

After considering for a moment, Teddy pulled out his phone. "Okay, okay. Sending."

DING! — Isaac looked at his phone. The message went through. "Thank you for your trust," he said.

"Yeah, yeah. Sorry. I really wanted to... you know what, never mind. Have a good night, Isaac." With that, Teddy pushed past Isaac and without a second glance, walked into his garage

"You too, Teddy. See you tomorrow..."

But Teddy was already inside. The garage motor spun up and loudly lowered the door on Isaac's words.

Isaac muttered under his breath, "... you fucking dickwad."

As he walked back to his car, he opened the file on his phone. He immediately heard his father's voice. First came the awkwardness of them greeting each other.

Isaac scrolled forward.

He stopped and listened just as they were wrapping up their basketball conversation. Isaac scrolled forward again.

Finally, he heard the voice of his father, speaking in that trance-like state as he regaled Isaac with the story of bashing in Trixie's face with the table-side accountant's lamp.

It was just as surreal as Isaac remembered it.

That detached voice.

So matter of fact.

So removed from what he was actually saying about his crimes.

That voice made Isaac shiver, and yet he found himself unable to fast-forward. He couldn't skip ahead, he couldn't press stop. He *had* to listen. He was hypnotized. Until…

A car—an old hand-me-down of a hand-me-down—suddenly sped around the corner and screeched to a gravelly stop at the edge of the driveway. Isaac could hear the bass of an indie rock band reverberate around the neighborhood. The passenger door of the car opened, and a plume of smoke drifted out.

Isaac watched as Lauren stumbled out of the car. In her stoned delirium, she nearly tripped and face-planted. She was high in the way that only teenagers got high—half from the drugs, and half from acting in the way you *think* you should be acting because of the drugs.

She staggered out and tried to slam the car door, but whiffed badly, not touching it at all. This made her explode in a hysterical cackle. The girl who was behind the wheel also laughed.

Lauren finally steadied herself and managed to place her hand on the door.

Her friend called out to her, "Later, masturbator!"

"After while, chunky bile!" Lauren responded before slamming the door.

The car peeled out and drove off down the street. Lauren, a grin on her face, ambled up her driveway.

Despite Isaac standing in clear view, watching her, the first thing she noticed was his car. She stood and analyzed it for a moment, not sure what to make of this strange car in her driveway. She shrugged and continued on until her eyes finally realized that there was a man standing beside the car in the shadows, watching her. Isaac.

She jerked to a stop, unsure if she was hallucinating or not. Finally, she realized that she did in fact recognize the man, but it still took an extra second for her to place him.

"Luce???" she finally asked. Then her eyes darted to the garage. Her grin vanished. "Shit. Is he home?"

Isaac could only nod.

Lauren immediately pulled her shirt toward her nose and started smelling it. Her face creased up in worry and fear. Then she undid her ponytail and pulled her long, dark hair toward her nose. She frantically inhaled, over and over, trying to convince herself that the scent was just trapped in her nostrils, or maybe her mind.

Isaac knew exactly what she was worried about. He glumly shook his head. "Yeah. It's pretty obvious."

"Is it really?"

"Smells like good weed, at least," Isaac said.

Lauren couldn't help but grin at the comment, even as she covered her face with her hand.

"You should get a vaporizer. Or at least a dedicated smoking hoodie," Isaac said. "It would keep it out of your hair. You can also take a paper towel tube and shove it with fabric softener sheets. Exhale into that. Your mileage may vary."

"Thanks for the tip."

"None of this solves your red-eye, though."

Lauren hurried over to Isaac's car and examined her eyes in his side-view mirror. Sure enough, they were glazed and pink.

"Fuck my life, fuck my life, fuck my life," she said as she closed her eyes and leaned against Isaac's car.

"He probably won't even notice."

She responded with a look of *Are you fucking kidding me?* "He may not have passed the police exams, but I'm pretty sure he'll notice if I'm high.

He can walk by a guy getting his fucking head hacked off with a machete in the street, and my dad wouldn't notice a fucking thing. But when it comes to me, he's got this weird delinquency sonar. It's like I ping out my disobedience to him or some shit. So, yeah, he'll know I'm high."

Isaac smiled. "I guess you'll have to wait for him to go to bed then."

She nodded, resigned to the realization that it was her only solution. "What the fuck do I do 'til then?" Then her eyes fell on Isaac. Her gaze roamed up and down him, finally settling on his face. She cocked her head to the side in a slightly flirtatious move.

"Wanna hang?" she asked.

"Me?"

She looked to her left and right and behind her, as if to say, *I don't see anyone else.*

"Don't you have homework?" Isaac said as he took a step back.

"Yeah. But I've been recently diagnosed with this crippling case of senioritis."

"Your corrections officer father would not approve."

"Ah, but your serial killer father totally would." She crossed her arms and gave him a smirk.

"I'm sorry. I've got plans."

"Which are?"

"Um, drinking alone?"

She gave an exaggerated look toward the heavens, as if pleading with God for Isaac not to be so lame. Then, with a weary sigh, she turned her grinning face back to him. "Look, I gotta kill a couple hours as I sober up and the air clears. Before my dad goes to bed, he's gonna use his phone-stalky-app thingy to find my GPS location. Which means–" She pulled out her phone and held it up for Isaac to see her power it off. "–I have to play the 'my battery died' card. I only get to play that card once or twice per year before my dad gets pissed and suspicious and really starts cracking down. So, the question is, are you going to make me fucking waste my 'dead battery card' or are you going to show me a good time?"

"You should hang out with a friend or something. I don't even know what kids do for fun in this town anymore."

She smiled. It was such a welcoming smile. The smile of someone who genuinely wanted to spend time with Isaac. It was so infectious that, in spite of his efforts, Isaac found himself smiling back at her.

"I got an idea," she said.

CHAPTER 17

Isaac drove down the highway, leaving the borders of the town.

There were no street lights out here. Isaac's headlights illuminated the road as they traversed it. The forests, hills, and farms all merged into an indistinguishable blackened mass of shadows a few feet from the windows.

The car took a right on Grand Valley Road, a paved two-lane street. A little bit later, he slowed and turned left on a one-lane gravel road. They were driving through a forest now with tall darkened pines lining their path. Nothing but trees for miles.

"Jesus, you lived in the ass-end of nowhere," Lauren said.

"Your phone's off, right?"

"Yeah. Why?"

"Nothing. Just making sure the cell towers can't ping your last known location."

"Be warned, I'm a biter."

Another left turn on an even narrower gravel road. Isaac knew the roads by heart. He had learned to drive a stick-shift on these roads when he was thirteen. By the time he was eighteen, he could navigate the area with his eyes closed, which he nearly did a handful of times when coming home wasted from a party.

With one final turn, his car pulled to a stop in a driveway.

Lauren stepped out of the car first. She stood there, her eyes wide and her mouth open. Goosebumps formed on her arms and neck, partially from the cold but mostly from the thrill.

"Fucking badass," she managed to say.

Isaac climbed out of the car and walked over to stand beside her.

"Always glad to meet a fan," he said.

For a quiet moment, they both looked out.

They were parked in front of the house.

It was a gray ranch-style house, tucked away among the trees. It had been unoccupied for years, neglected for decades, and was showing all the signs of dilapidation. The peeling paint, busted gutters, boarded-up windows, and missing shingles could have made it look like a stock image for abandoned property. But then there was the yellow crime scene tape, shredded from age, but still fluttering from where it was wrapped around the boards.

A sectional chain-link fence had been erected by the county to completely encase the house. This too was accented by the tattered yellow police tape. But the fence did little to keep people out. The house had been heavily graffitied. Most of the plywood covering the windows had been tagged with "666" or "The Handyman Can!" The garage door proclaimed in large block letters "ABANDON ALL HOPE, YE WHO ENTER!" Two giant cartoon eyes had been drawn above the front door to make the front of the house look like a screaming face.

Isaac and Lauren stared at the house, taking it all in.

"My phone is off. Take my picture," Lauren said as she turned and struck a pose—a big smile with an exaggerated two-thumbs up.

Isaac pulled out his phone and snapped a photo. She looked good. Cute and goofy. Then a thought hit him.

"I have a better idea," he said.

He went back to the car and popped the trunk. He rummaged around, digging through his crate of tools. When he emerged, he had a hammer in his hand.

Lauren's eyes went wide. "Whoa."

"A prop for your photo, milady?" Isaac said as he held out the hammer.

Lauren reached out, but as her hand neared it, she hesitated. It was as if the hammer had an aura that she didn't want to, or couldn't, penetrate.

Finally, her hand found the courage to grasp its handle. She lifted it from Isaac's grip and held it aloft, eyeing it in wonder and feeling its power.

"Is... is this real? Like, legit?" she asked.

"Nah. The police kept all the actual murder hammers. I kinda thought that maybe I'd get his tool collection in an inheritance or something, but the cops cleaned out the place and nothing came my way. I didn't really want to ask either."

"Then what is this?" Lauren rotated the hammer to examine it.

Isaac looked at his feet and gave a little shrug. "I buy used tools and sell them online. I sign my name to it and say they were owned and used by The Handyman."

"And people buy them?"

"Yeah. There's a whole murder economy. The major online resellers don't let you do it, but there are a bunch of dark web boards where these trades go on."

"But these aren't real. They're not genuine."

"No. But remember, my target demo is also buying old Nazi medals and used Zyklon-B canisters. My buyer-beware sympathy level is fairly low on this." He finally glanced up to check her expression. She nodded in agreement, the impressed smile still on her lips.

"Badass," she said.

Isaac readied his camera.

"Ooooh! What about a sledgehammer?" she said. "Can I use one of those for my picture?"

"The claw hammer is more universal. It's what he used at the dorms."

"But we're at his house. And in his basement, he used a—"

"He didn't use a sledge in the basement."

"Are you sure about that?"

Isaac sighed. "Yeah, I'm sure."

"I thought I read..."

"I don't got a sledge. Do you want the picture or not?" The words came out a hint terser than he intended, but Lauren didn't seem to mind. She raised the hammer above her head and stretched her mouth into a fierce, maniacal screaming face. Isaac pointed his phone and took a picture. He showed her the screen so she could admire their work.

"New profile pic," she said with an approving grin. She leaned back against his car and took in the view of the house.

"So, what now?" Isaac asked.

A sly grin appeared on Lauren's face. "Shit's about to get real."

With that, she jogged off toward the house. She tucked the hammer into her belt and leapt onto the chain-link fence. She scampered up it with ease, throwing her leg over the top and hopping down to the other side.

She went up to the house and wedged the claw of the hammer beneath one of the sheets of plywood that covered the front living room window. She began prying. She loosened one nail. Then she wiggled the claw along the seam of the wood and loosened more.

Isaac waited by the car. He held his breath. Despite there not being a soul within a mile radius, he couldn't help but glance up the road, half expecting a police cruiser to race around the corner and arrest them.

"You're fucking insane," he finally called out.

"No. I'm a teenager, and therefore indestructible."

She moved the claw of the hammer toward another nail and pried it loose. The entire sheet of plywood suddenly swung free. It dangled by one remaining nail in the top corner and rocked like a pendulum twice before the weight broke it off. Lauren jumped back as the entire sheet crashed to the ground.

The loud whump of the wood slamming into the concrete reverberated and echoed around the forest. Even though he was fifty feet removed from the action, even Isaac jumped.

As the sound died away, Lauren let out a laugh. She was having fun.

She went up to the window. Shards of glass from the long-gone pane still protruded from the window frame like jagged teeth. She used the hammer to break them off.

"What the fuck are you doing?" Isaac called, trying to keep his voice bemused instead of worried.

"Investigating the haunted house. I'm going all Nancy-fucking-Drew, bitch." She turned, put her hands on her hips, and called back to Isaac, "You coming?"

Isaac wanted to decline, or maybe pretend to be too cool and mature to engage in such teenage shenanigans. But he couldn't.

"Yeah. Yeah. I'm coming," he said as he jogged forward. He leapt onto the chain-link fence. As soon as his weight slammed into the section, he realized that his feet didn't have a good grip, and his hands weren't strong enough to hold his weight. His legs kicked at the fence. His foot finally got a toe-hold just as his grip gave out. He plummeted backwards, his foot still stuck in the chain-link, and landed hard on his back.

Lauren doubled up in laughter.

The fall knocked the air out of Isaac, but he forced himself to put up his middle finger and shout, "Fuck you, Fence!"

Lauren laughed even harder.

He bounded to his feet. He consciously tried not to walk with a limp or rub his stinging hands, fingers, and wrists.

On his second attempt, he took his time, getting his hand and foot placements ready. He slowly climbed up the fence, gripped the top bar, and cautiously swung himself over. He jumped down to the other side, and immediately felt that he might have turned his ankle. He tried not to show it as he calmly strutted up to the window.

"Gravity is the real serial killer," he said.

Lauren let out another joyous laugh. "True dat."

She brushed off the final glass shards from the windowsill, pulled her long sleeves up over her hands for protection, then grabbed hold of the sill and hoisted herself in.

Isaac rubbed his aching hands, taking that extra moment to shake off the sting—both physical and emotional—from his fall. He looked at the window.

He knew this window led to the living room. It was where they always set up their Christmas tree so that Isaac could see it when he walked home from the school bus. Once, when he was ten, school was canceled because of snow. His father went to a job site anyway, and so Isaac spent the day home alone. He opened this exact window and sat at this exact windowsill, beside his Christmas tree, watching the white flakes drift down onto the driveway for hours. He played a Bing Crosby Christmas CD on loop; it was his mom's favorite.

He struggled to think of a happier memory than that day at this window.

"Need a hand, old man?" Lauren called from inside. "Hurry up! I need a light."

Isaac gripped the sill and hoisted himself inside.

CHAPTER 18

Isaac turned on his phone's flashlight and looked around. There was no furniture and no fixtures. Someone, at some point, had come through and pounded out holes along the sheetrock which they had then reached through to rip the copper wiring out of the walls. They even made off with the outlets and switches. This resulted in long gash marks on every wall, looking like veins running throughout the house.

A layer of dust and cobwebs had settled in. Water damage from an untended roof leak left large brown stains on the ceiling. The smell of must and rot, mixed with a whiff of rat shit, hung in the air.

They stood silently, the floorboards creaking under their shifting weight.

"How long did you live here?" Lauren finally asked.

"My dad owned this house pretty much his whole life. I lived here from... let's see... age five to eighteen. Before that, I lived with my mom in Salem."

"Where's she at?"

"Dead. Aneurysm."

Lauren stopped walking and looked at Isaac with genuine sympathy. "Oh shit. Sorry. That sucks."

"No worries."

"Was she cool?"

"Yeah. She was pretty cool."

"What exactly is an aneurysm?"

"It's when a blood vessel in the brain bulges out and ruptures. A lot of people don't even feel it happening. They just suddenly keel over dead. That's what happened. Woke up one morning and there was Mom, still in her bed. She seemed peaceful, though. At least that's how I remember it."

Isaac wandered off to inspect the room. There was something about talking about his mom that made his muscles feel the urge to move. To be active. Standing made him uncomfortable.

He walked over to a heater vent in the floor and shone his light down it. The grill was gone. As far as Isaac could tell, so was the ductwork. All stripped away. Isaac wondered if whoever made off with the ducts found the green Army men he had shoved down there when he was kid.

"So, what happened after your mom died?"

"The state found me, packed me up and sent me off to live with my dad."

"What about grandparents?"

"Never knew 'em. Grandma left when Dad was a kid. Then a few years before I was born, Grandpa wandered into the backyard, put a rifle in his mouth and blew off the back of his head. Dad came home from work and found him lying across the woodpile." Isaac let out a nervous chuckle. "My family has a bad history of stumbling on our parents after they've died."

"Shitballs," she said, "Your dad's cray and all, but that really sucks."

"Yeah. My dad never had much luck keeping people around. At least not without a padlock."

Isaac flashed Lauren a grin and then he walked toward the hallway. She followed after him.

The hall spliced off into two bedrooms and a bathroom. Isaac walked into one of the rooms. He looked around at the empty ten-by-ten-foot space. His eyes settled onto the wall by the closet door. There were markings: *1st Grade... 2nd Grade... 3 Grade...* Isaac's childhood height. He gazed at those markings, remembering his dad commanding him to stand up straight, back to the wall, as he pressed a carpenter square against the top of Isaac's head and drew a line.

As a kid, Isaac had a growth spurt in 7th grade and fully expected to surpass his father's height. But Isaac's growth leveled out in the following years, and his old man always seemed so much taller and stronger than him. That is, until this recent reunion at the prison, when Walter, for the first time, seemed so small and frail.

Isaac's gaze was interrupted by Lauren joining him in the room.

"Whatcha looking at?" she asked.

"*That* charming little display of fuckedupedness," he said, pointing toward his feet. It was a small pile of used condoms.

"Apparently, people are breaking in so they can have sex in my childhood bedroom. Because... just because, I guess."

"Hot."

Isaac looked down at the base of his height wall. There was another condom there, encroaching upon his childhood. He tried to kick it away, but it merely flopped along the floor. He tried again, but this time the condom stuck to his shoe.

"Goddamnit," he grumbled.

With it clinging to the top of his shoe, he jerked his leg a few times. Finally, the condom broke free, floated through the air a foot, and then plopped down back on the floor. Isaac rubbed his shoe along the wall, trying to wipe away any remaining residue.

He walked off. Lauren followed behind.

They went back down the hall and entered the kitchen. The appliances had long since been stripped away, but their outlines were still visible on the faded linoleum. Isaac walked to the window where the breakfast nook used to be. He shone his light around. Something caught his attention. He bent down and examined the wall, inspecting the baseboards.

"What's up?"

He stood. "Just checking out something my dad told me."

"Care to illuminate me?"

"It's nothing. Just one of his stories."

Lauren didn't press it further. Her attention was distracted by a door next to the kitchen pantry. She ran her hand over the holes in the door where a column of locks, latches, and deadbolts once existed. "Is this...?"

"Yep."

"Can I see it?"

Isaac nodded.

He stepped over and grasped the knob. A lump formed in his throat. He swallowed it down and pulled open the door. A long, wooden staircase descended into a thick, black abyss. Isaac and Lauren walked down.

Their weight made the old steps creak loudly. It was a sound Isaac remembered. The floorboards had expanded and contracted with age so that several of the nails had worn loose. The boards had warped and now rubbed together. But with no furniture in the house to absorb the sound, the creaking echoed loudly. It was amplified and uncomfortable, as if the house was screaming.

Even Lauren seemed unnerved by it.

She began softly singing a children's playground rhyme:

"*Handyman, he played one.*

He used pliers to break my thumb.

With a dick slap, hammer whack, break all of your bones,

The Handyman is in your home."

Isaac stopped and turned to face her. "Wait, what?"

She continued:

"*Handyman, he played two.*

He gave a bucket for me to poo.

With a dick slap, hammer whack, break all of your bones,

The Handyman is in your home."

"Does everyone know this fucking song?" Isaac asked.

Lauren flashed him a grin. "*Handyman. He played three...*"

She left the final note hanging. Isaac just looked at her dumbly. She repeated the verse, slowing it down and accenting it with jazz hands. "*Handyman. He played three...*"

She motioned for him to finish it off.

Isaac thought. Then he finally sang, "*He pounded a chisel below my knee!*"

Together they finished the song as they walked down the final couple steps, "*With a dick slap, hammer whack, break all of your bones. Han-dy-man is in your h—*"

The last line faded from their lips as they entered the basement.

The light from Isaac's phone was only powerful enough to illuminate small sections at a time, leaving most of their surroundings in milky blackness. But what they were able to distinguish was enough to make the world fall silent. Song no longer existed. Neither did laughter nor fun. The weight of the darkness struck them and crushed their joy.

They were standing inside a concrete prison.

Everything was as Walter had described it. The carpet nailed to the ceiling. The latrine trench hacked into the concrete floor. And the concrete block with an embedded metal ring.

But there wasn't just one block.

There was another.

And another.

And another.

Human hitching posts formed a horseshoe around the basement floor. *Seven* blocks in total.

Seven spots for seven humans.

Isaac and Lauren stood silently and stared at the blocks.

CHAPTER 19

"Park right here. At the corner. I don't want him to see you."

Isaac rolled his car to a stop. They were a block west of Teddy's driveway.

He smiled at the memory of performing such a maneuver himself back in high school. Having briefly dated a girl—Tanya Cheng—whose parents disapproved of all their daughter's potential teenage distractions, such as boyfriends. Isaac learned to park a block away and walk to her house in the darkness of night before sneaking in through her window. That way, a parent sitting up in the living room wouldn't hear a car engine or door.

In hindsight, Isaac realized that he could have invited Tanya over to *his* house and up to *his* room. His father might not have approved, but certainly wouldn't have interfered. In any case, it didn't matter. He never *wanted* to bring Tanya, or any girl (or any*one,* for that matter) back to his house. He wondered if he knew something about his dad back then, some inkling of what was to come.

"Thanks for the tour. That shit was intense," Lauren said. "What do you think is the value of the Handyman Experience you just gave me?"

Isaac thought. "Honestly, if I owned the house and charged ninety-nine bucks just for the walk through, I'd get maybe ten customers a month. There are a few out there who'd pay a couple hundred bucks. We'd get all kinds. More during Halloween."

"Oooh, you could set up mazes through the house and hire actors to jump out at people with hacksaws and sledgehammers and shit. And then the rest of the year, you could set up one of those escape rooms in the basement. They'd have to solve a bunch of puzzles to find a key. And they'd have to do it before the Handyman comes to murder them." She thought for a moment. "I can name about fifty kids who would pay for that. And then, you add all the kids in all the high schools in Portland, and you got a fucking legit revenue stream there."

"I like the way your mind works."

"I'm serious."

"So am I. These are genuinely good ideas. The market is there. The interest is there. Just need to capitalize."

"When you set up Handyman Inc., give me a ten percent commission." She smiled at him and opened the car door.

"Will your dad be asleep?" Isaac asked.

"Nope. Because he couldn't find me on GPS, he's sitting in the living room right now. He's too shy to call my friends to track me down, so instead he'll sit there and stew about it. I'll tell him I was studying and lost track of time and didn't know my phone had died. I'll apologize profusely. He'll tell me to be more responsible. We'll both go to bed."

"Life is much simpler when your dad's a sociopath who doesn't give a shit about you."

"We can't all be so lucky." She climbed out of the car, then poked her head back inside. "Lemme see your phone."

He handed it to her.

She entered some information and then passed it back. "I just put my number in. Send me those pics of me with the hammer."

"Sure thing."

"Let's hang out again," she said. She closed the door.

Isaac watched as she jogged off and disappeared into the darkness.

He looked down at his phone and saw her name and number in his contacts. He opened his photos and scrolled through the pictures of her posing with the hammer.

This brought a smile to his face.

CHAPTER 20

The door clanged open.

Two guards led in Walter.

"Inmate and guest may share a brief hug," Teddy announced from his position behind Isaac's seat.

Walter waited a moment, his arms slightly raised in anticipation of the hug, but Isaac made no motion to rise.

"Have a seat," Teddy said.

Walter shuffled over and plopped into the chair. His restraints rattled against the metal chair and concrete floor. The two escort guards stepped away and left the room, clanging the door shut behind them. The echo died, leaving just Walter, Isaac, and Teddy looking at each other.

"I'm glad you came back," the old man finally said.

"There's no outlet by the dining table," Isaac replied.

Walter looked at him. "Excuse me?"

"When I was in middle school, you installed recessed lighting throughout the kitchen and dining area. The wires and boxes are all gone, but the hole is still there. There's no outlet along those walls."

"You went in the house?"

"No outlet means that there was no place to plug in that green accountant's lamp you liked so much."

"I don't understand."

"You said that when Trixie pulled the knife on you, you used the lamp for self-defense. You hit her in the head with it. And then you tied her up with the cord. And yet, there's no fucking *place* for that lamp where you say it was. Unless you happened to keep your favorite lamp unplugged on the floor in the event you needed to fight off your rowdy prostitute dinner guests."

"What are you getting at, boy?"

"You didn't keep a lamp there. But I remember where you used to keep it," Isaac said as he leaned in. "On your nightstand."

Walter's face remained motionless.

"I can see it all right now," Isaac continued. "You hiring a prostitute. Taking her up to your room. Grinding away at her. Why else would you hire a prostitute if you weren't going to fuck her? And if that lamp is by your bed... Did she try to rob you there? Or, while she was faking her orgasm, did you just grab the lamp and slam it into her face for no reason?"

"I don't know what you're drivin' at, but—"

"Here's what I'm *drivin'* at—I don't want the sad story of the lonely old man who invites the hooker to dinner. I want the one where you bash her head in while fucking her."

"It wasn't like that."

"Fine. Then you can tell me about the other six."

"Other six what?"

"*People*, dad! The other six people! The ones in your basement. There are seven blocks of concrete down there. You had seven people, all at the same time. Men and women. And no one can piece together what the fuck was going through your mind."

"I told you. It was an accident."

"That's bullshit. The whole story about Trixie pulling a knife on you is total fucking bullshit. I'm not going to sit here and let you fucking lie to me like that. Seven concrete blocks in a reinforced basement. That's seven premeditated abductions. Why?"

Walter's eyes searched for answers.

Isaac continued, "Most serial killers who abduct and imprison their victims do it out of some desire to create a sex slave. Charles Ng, Gary Heidnik, hell, even Jeffrey Dahmer."

"Jeffrey Dahmer? Who do you think I am? I didn't eat anybody. I didn't keep peckers in jars."

"If we can just set aside Dahmer's necrophilia, cannibalism, and dicks in jars—"

"That's a *lot* to set aside, boy."

"—Dahmer was insecure. He was gay at a time when it was really bad to be gay. He didn't like that about himself, and he didn't like the rejection that came from dating in the underground gay world of the 80s. So, he would find guys, bring them home, drug them, and then drill holes in their heads and inject acid into their brains. He was trying to lobotomize them. He wanted to turn them into zombies. He wanted to make it so they wouldn't leave him like everyone else in his life did. And when they died from having acid injected into their brains, Dahmer would consume their flesh as a way for them to always be a part of him."

"You're making me all weepy for Jeffrey Dahmer. You know that guy would take out their hearts and beat himself off with them. Is that what you think of me?"

"His motivations made perfect sense. I'm just trying to figure out yours."

Walter cocked an eyebrow as he looked at Isaac. "You been doing a whole lotta reading up on killers, ain't ya?"

"It's a recent interest."

"Who's your favorite?"

"Let's talk about you, Dad."

"You don't got a favorite?"

"No."

"But you gotta have one. Someone that interests you. Or that you admire." Walter paused and leaned in. "Or that scares you."

"Ted Bundy, alright," Isaac said.

"Everyone says Bundy. That ain't no answer."

"What do you *want* me to say?" Isaac said, getting annoyed. *"The Handyman?"* As much as Isaac had attempted to say the name flippantly, the words sounded weird as he spoke them to his father. His voice had cracked in way that sounded almost like reverence.

The old man's face softened. Not from remorse or embarrassment, but from what seemed like a sense of genuine pride. By saying the name out loud, Isaac had elevated The Handyman to the highest levels of serial killer fame.

Ted Bundy. Jeffrey Dahmer. And now, Walter "The Handyman" Luce.

They sat for a quiet moment. Then, Isaac's gaze met his father's. "Help me understand, Dad. There must've been a reason."

Walter took a deep, long breath. His body relaxed. His lips curled into a nervous smile. "It all just kinda happened."

"How did chaining and torturing seven people in your basement 'just happen'?" Isaac paused, then added, "You weren't always like this."

"No. No, I wasn't." Nobody spoke. Nobody moved. Walter's eyes silently cast down onto the table, but they didn't focus on the table. They appeared to veer inward with their gaze, turning back around and searching through himself. "You know what a GFCI is?" Walter finally asked.

Isaac nodded. "It's that little switch on the bathroom outlets. Keeps you from electrocuting yourself."

"Good boy. Stands for Ground Fault Circuit Interrupter. You drop a hairdryer in a sink filled with water, and that little switch says, 'There's a whole lotta current passing through here. I better shut this down or someone might die.' And so, it just goes 'click.' Kills the outlet. No more power until you hit that little button that says 'reset.' Now, I'm not one to really buy into the whole concept of evolution, but I think there's a GFCI in all of us. Too much current passes through, and at some point, the body, mind, and soul, well, they just—"

"—go click."

"Precisely. Shuts it down. Couldn't tell you when exactly it happened. Or why. It's not like a hairdryer fell in my sink. The current just built and built, until finally, all my circuits were fried."

"What does it feel like?"

Another silence passed. Walter sat thinking. He finally said, "Have you ever stood at the edge of a cliff? Staring down into the nothingness?"

"And had the urge to jump?"

"No. And had the urge to grab the nearest person and throw them off."

Isaac couldn't help but chuckle. "Of course. Everyone jokes about that."

"And why do they joke about it?"

"Because it's true. They really want to see how it feels to throw someone off."

"Exactly. Or has a pedestrian, a total stranger, ever walked in front of your car and every impulse in your body wanted to step on the gas? There's no reason. They did nothing wrong to you. You don't even know them. You would achieve no monetary gain from running them down. No sexual pleasure. No political statement or religious victory. There is no reason for you to kill that person except to know how it feels to kill that person. To watch their face as they crumple beneath your bumper. To feel the shocks on your wheels bounce as if you're going over a speedbump, but knowing that it's a human head or torso. Has *that* urge ever struck you? The urge to just hurt someone for no reason other than because you can?"

A rigidness overtook Isaac's body. Every impulse told him not to gulp, not to fidget, not to betray his true feelings. But when he saw his father's eyes probing him, desperate to find that connection, a strange sensation overwhelmed Isaac.

He couldn't lie to this man. Not to his father.

And so, Isaac simply replied, "All the time."

Walter smiled wide. "There are so many liars out there who swear that such thoughts would never cross their minds. They're too 'pure.' They're too 'good.' But in my experience, only one thing on this Earth separates good from evil."

"And what's that?"

"Restraint."

Isaac's smile matched his father's. A strange bridge, imperceptible to Teddy or anyone else watching, had formed between man and child at that precise moment. "So why did you start hurting people?" Isaac asked. "Why did you lose your restraint?"

Walter leaned back in his seat, his eyes gazing off in memory...

CHAPTER 21

Prison's an interesting thing. My whole life, I ain't been bored for more than ten minutes. Always something to do. Work to be done. Some project I been putting off.

But in prison?

There's nothing.

You sit. You eat. You think.

Now, most of the guys in here with half a brain spend their free days—and for the first time in their lives, they got plenty of free days—thinking about one of two things: Their court appeals, or how the fuck they got here in the first place.

Now, I don't give two shits about my appeals. They got me. They know it, and I know it. I'm not gonna start smearing feces on my face, pretending I think it's mascara, to get some bullshit insanity plea. And I sure ain't gonna get all weepy-eyed in front of some judge—pleading my sins and my heartfelt remorse—so I can get some more favorable death sentence.

I'm here 'til I die. Ain't my fault that Oregon don't have the balls to kill me fast.

So, if I'm not spending all this time thinking about my appeals, then I must be thinking about my life. How did I end up here? When exactly did that GFCI click off for me?

I've always had those thoughts of running down the pedestrians who passed in front of my car, especially those fat ones waddling all slow across the intersection. I used to smile at myself at how easy it would be. On a busy day, like when you'd get a whole family crossing the street on their way to after-church brunch, I'd give myself points for how many I think I could kill on one swerve.

That game ran through my mind for as long as I remember. But I never acted on it. There was power in the dream, though. Every day that my foot stayed firm on that brake pedal, I was sparing lives. I was judging those strangers as being worthy of life.

You may think I'm pulling your leg when I say that Elizabeth giving me a donut made me go "click," but I've had much time to think about it. There was something about that simple, kind moment. It made me ask a question that never occurred to me to ponder—Why *was* I sparing lives?

That's when the game began.

I distinctly remember it. I saw a guy in Safeway, some rich, preppy, polo-shirt wearing mother-fucker. The kind of guy who always laughed at me as I fixed his leaky shit-sucking pipes.

Well, he was standing at the snack shelf, reading the back of some bag of chips, probably making sure it didn't contain no whatever nonsense they're avoiding these days. Anyway, he was distracted. So, I stepped right up behind him. I stood there. Coulda grabbed him by the hair if I felt like it. Coulda stabbed him in the spine. Coulda bashed his head in. I was so close to him.

He shifted his weight. He stole a glance or two behind him. He felt my presence but was too cowardly to actually turn and face this demon that was invading his personal space. I could have reached out and killed him and he was too polite to actually turn around and say, "Back up, buddy."

That was a win for me. I got right up on him and he let it happen.

I congratulated myself for having the restraint to not hurt him.

And thus, my game began.

It continued on like that. Just making people uncomfortable. Getting in their space. Letting myself get real close to them, so I could smell them, so I could see those little peach-fuzz hairs on their neck stand up. But never doing nothing.

Not one person said a thing to me. Not one person listened to that little voice that screamed in their heads, "This guy means you harm." I could feel their fear, and yet they did nothing.

Like all games, though, eventually you need to go up to a new level, or else you'll just get bored with playing.

I started going to stores—big box stores like Home Depot or Freddy's—and taking a hammer off the shelf. I'd stand behind people with a hammer in my hand, although sometimes it was a box-cutter or a screwdriver. In any case, there was always some rich fucker right in front of me, and I had a weapon of death in my hand.

I would visualize striking them. Just bludgeoning them or stabbing them. I could *feel* the rage boil in me, and I could *see* myself turning this person into a bloody mess on the floor.

Day after day after day, I walked into stores and held a life in my hand.

At the time, I felt this game was a good way to act out my anger without ever doing anything that might lead to trouble. Nowadays, I realize that it was only making what happened next inevitable.

***

Yes, I took Trixie.

But I paid for her. Just like every woman made me pay for them. If not with money, which it almost always was, then they made me pay by having to put up with their little games. Women ignore you, and then turn around and flirt with the guy beside you. And those guys... they ain't better looking, they ain't smarter, they're just richer and that's about it. God shines his blessing down on some men and says, "Women shall love you." Then he casts his gaze to other men and says, "But not you."

So, yeah. I paid for sex. I paid for Trixie. And as I fucked her in my bed, my thoughts went back to that donut. How Elizabeth had given me a gift for free and here I was *paying* to fulfill my most basic needs.

An anger rose in me, and yes, it was the anger I'd been feeling so much of since that day I met Elizabeth.

I dealt with the anger the same way I always did.

As Trixie humped me from on top, I reached my hand out to my nightstand. I didn't have a weapon planted or nothing. I didn't plan this. My fingers simply found the first heavy thing they could wrap themselves around—the neck of that green accountant's lamp.

Trixie noticed. I saw her eyes. They darted from my face to my hand and I could tell she was thinking *What the hell's he doing grabbing that lamp?*

Being a whore, I expected her to be a bit more wary, but the look on her face was just one of confusion, like she was wondering if the old man she was fucking had gone senile and couldn't figure out how to turn off the damn light.

As I held that lamp in one hand, and my other hand ran its fingers through Trixie's long, greasy hair, I could feel that power of God flow through me, just as it had in every one of those stores when I stood behind someone who didn't know any better. Maybe on a different day, that thrill would've been enough. For whatever reason, though, it wasn't today.

At that precise moment in my life, if she had been walking in front of my car, I woulda run her down. If she had been standing next to me on a cliff, I woulda pushed her off.

I didn't care. I didn't give no shit.

That little GFCI switch in me had been holding me back. Suddenly, it wasn't restraining me no more.

So I hurt the bitch. I bashed her face in.

And it felt good. So good. So right.

The restraint was gone.

***

It was as if I had gone up to a new level in my game.

My old ways of playing the game in my mind were gone. I couldn't just wander around a store with a hammer and expect to calm my demons with that no more.

The preparation of putting Trixie in the closet, and then moving her to the basement, well, all that thinking consumed me. It was a new hobby. A puzzle. It stimulated my mind and my emotions in ways I ain't never felt before. And boy, like those junkies lounging about on Burnside, I had found a high and I needed to feed it, so help me.

The game was simple: Who do I punish? And how do I not get caught?

My opponent?

The world.

The fucking world.

And after much thought, I knew who should be next.

The Mexican.

You see, Luce Contracting always paid its taxes. If I wanted to staff up for a job, I needed to hire workers. I had to insure them and pay employer tax and Social Security.

But I couldn't compete with the illegals.

So, I went on one of them classified sites—"Average Joe's Jobs." This was a place for people to post up ads for work they needed done around their homes, and then the "Average Joes" of the world would place bids for their services. Even after Luce Contracting went under, I found work on that site for a while. No matter the times, no matter the economy, people always needed help with their plumbing. Their electrical. Their concrete. Their drywall. You know the game.

And I was their man.

But then the Mexicans swarmed that site too.

They underbid us all. I don't know how they do it; they need to feed fifty fucking children. Or maybe they don't feed their kids and just leave them to scavenge in the schools that my tax dollars pay for. I didn't get a lick of investment return out of them schools. Never went myself. And my own flesh-and-blood barely applied himself after the "tying your shoes" and "learning your phone number" curriculum was over. Ain't that right, boy? Anyway...

I went to the library in East Salem. Opened an account with a fake name and address, and started using their internet. I went into Average Joe's Jobs and put up an ad. Something about wanting help ripping up that old shag carpet. And lo and behold, who do you think answered that ad? Who underbid every other outta work contractor in the area?

His name was probably fucking Jose, but I called him Average Joe.

Average Joe sent me his number, and so, I called him and scheduled the gig. He showed up that afternoon. He was a 30-year-old Mexican with a mustache. Talked the whole time. Good English too. He must've been confused and thought he was gonna get paid by the hour and not the job because he went on and on about his time fighting in the Honduran civil war, or some shit.

I didn't even know Honduras had a civil war. His stories actually sounded interesting, but at the time, I didn't care. I hated him. I fucking hated him.

As he ripped up that carpet, I stood behind him. He was a big guy, as a lotta these Mexicans are, so I knew I was gonna have to keep a good grip. I took a length of baling cord in my hand. Figured it was best if he was out of breath before I laid into him, so I waited for him to finish the job. I also figured that if he ripped up the tack board for the carpet then I wouldn't have to later.

Soon as he was on his knees, almost done ripping up tack board, and breathing heavy, I wrapped that baling cord one full loop around his neck. I pulled both ends tight, getting some good tension.

Oh, he fought. We tumbled to the ground. He was kicking and a flailing.

But I held on tight.

He got his hands on a chunk of that tack board and whacked me good a couple times with it. It scratched up my neck a bit. Nicked up my shoulder. But I wasn't letting go.

Within a few minutes, he gave up the ghost. He collapsed. I loaded his body on the toboggan and pushed him downstairs. Chained Average Joe up right next to Trixie.

But I wasn't done.

Next was Hitch.

***

Hitch was easy.

Next evening, in fact, I had to go get some milk at the store. The route goes past the freeway entrance and standing there, right on the on-ramp, was this kid. He was about twenty years old, probably about your age. He had a cardboard sign, just said "Portland." He had his thumb out too.

Now the true beggars, the homeless and such, I feel bad for. And I've been known to put a one, a five, even a twenty in their can if I think it means their kids will eat that night. And hitchhikers? I've picked them up on occasion.

But this kid?

This fucking kid?

I took one look at his ivory white basketball shoes, crisp blue jeans, and his brand-new backpack, and I said, "Fuck this kid." The gear and clothes he had must've cost a mint. But he had that shaggy hair and that full beard that just screamed, "Look at me! I'm rich. I'm privileged. Mommy and Daddy put me into good schools where I got good grades. I can do anything I fucking want, and yet I choose to do *nothing*." Fucking zero back to society.

Hitch was the kind of kid who would never do real work in his life. He'd never build anything. Never fix anything. And yet I bet he'd get through life without being smacked by the shit-storm that threatens to capsize the rest of us.

So, I turned myself around and pulled to the shoulder of that on-ramp. There's something about me that people just seem to trust, because that kid, well, he had no hesitation. No little hairs on the back of his neck standing up. No fumbling for an excuse to say no. He just threw his bag in the backseat and hopped right in the passenger side.

"Yo, thanks, bro!" is what he said.

I went on down the on-ramp and drove a couple miles down the freeway. It was dark and the other cars on the road were getting sparse. Kid started dozing off. Didn't even try to make conversation.

Just so happened I had a breaker bar under my seat. That's one of them long wrenches; the extra length gives you more leverage, allowing you to "break" off finicky, rusted bolts and nuts.

Well, I pulled that bar out and slammed it into Hitch's nose.

His whole face exploded in blood.

He screamed and leaned over, trying to catch the blood, I guess. He was probably pretty well concussed at that point anyway.

I swung again and — whack! — down he went.

He left blood all over the upholstery.

I guess I knew I was already in a place where I couldn't turn back, but there was something about seeing all that blood in the car when it really clicked for me—this was DNA evidence that I could never run from. I was in this forever.

I was emotionally committed before.

I was mentally and spiritually committed now.

***

I threw Hitch down the stairs and chained him up with the others.

And then I went out again.

Boy, I tell ya, the first one, Trixie, *that* was hard. The next was easier. And the next was easier still. It's just like any job.

I can't tell you how many times I went out for a job, and some slick asshole would try to nickel-and-dime me outta my rate because I did the job too damn fast. What they don't understand is that you ain't *just* paying for me to auger out your drain for fifteen minutes. You're paying for all my lifetime of experience in figuring out where the problem *is,* and knowing how to fix it quick. For these rich assholes, a simple plumbing job might take a whole weekend, if not more.

The more you do it, the better you get.

I'm a professional at household repairs.

And now, through training and experience, I was a professional collector of humans.

I could feel this change in myself and how I approached my work.

It wasn't willy-nilly no more. This time I was on the hunt. When I went out again, I was going out with the sole purpose of adding to my collection.

This time, I went straight to campus.

All them well-manicured lawns and trees and plazas and shit. These kids were living in a park. Tens of thousands of dollars a year of their parents' hard-earned money for them to get drunk and fuck.

When this education system shit them out the other end, they'd get management positions and would go on to be the bankers and the corporations that ruin the Luce Contracting businesses of the world.

They wouldn't even appreciate that leg-up they had. You got all this knowledge and all this opportunity a stone's throw away, twenty-four hours a day, and what did they do? They run away to off-campus apartments first chance they get because it's easier for them to fuck, drink, and party.

These were the kids whose closest brush with manual labor came when they had to turn the water on so they could flush their shit into my trench as I repaired their sewer line.

So, I drove around that beautiful campus that night.

I found a spot, hidden a bit by trees, in the woods near their football stadium. I saw there was a jogging path that went right through there.

I pulled off to the curb, jacked up my truck like it was broke, and pretended to be all old and feeble-like.

Within five minutes or so, this big dumb jock—a Good Samaritan—came jogging on by. Wasn't another soul in sight. Good Sam ran right past, but then kinda glanced back over his shoulder. His hero-instincts got the better of his fear-intuition, and he turned back around and jogged over to me.

"Need help?" he said as he jogged in place, checking his heart rate on one of those wrist thingies.

I told him I'd love some assistance.

He knelt down at the jack and inspected the situation. It should've been pretty clear to him that the tire wasn't flat at all, but I don't know if kids today can tell a flat tire from a dead battery.

"What's the problem?" he asked.

By then, I was standing behind him.

I had the tire iron clutched in my hand.

With him kneeling and me standing, the leverage was perfect. One clean hit from that tire iron to the side of his head. If you're gonna hit someone, do it strong and follow through. Don't hesitate. Don't pull back. Don't be weak.

I've truly seen bricks fall with more gentle, graceful landings than Good Sam did. He just crumpled down.

I actually thought I mighta killed him. The blow popped his eye and the pavement knocked out a couple his teeth.

But I checked and he was still breathing.

I hefted him over my shoulder and dumped him in the bed of my truck. I got that truck unjacked and down on the ground just before another couple joggers came on through. They didn't notice a thing.

I turned off Good Sam's phone and tossed it in the nearest garbage bin. Covered him with a tarp, and off I went.

So, let's see, that's Trixie... Average Joe... Hitch... and now Good Sam. So that's four of them.

The next batch was a two-fer.

***

I went out again the next night.

There was some part of me that felt like I could do this forever. Night after night for the rest of my life. Whittling down the privileged and incompetent of the world, until only the honest, hard-working folk remained. I was like Death itself, patrolling the town, getting to choose whom to claim and whom to absolve.

I drove around until I saw them.

Chink-Man and Chink-Woman.

Although for all I know they were Japanese. Or Vietnamese. Or Koreanese. All them look the same to me anyway.

They were walking toward some Italian place off Liberty for dinner. They were young. They were cute. They were obviously in love. The way their arms were wrapped around each other as they laughed and kissed while they walked.

How adorable.

It was like they were straight out of some syrupy movie.

The parking lot at the restaurant was full, so Chink-Man and Chink-Woman parked across the street at some insurance office or something. It was closed and there was no one else parked there. They jogged across the street, hand-in-hand, and went in for their dinner date.

I looped around the block once, making sure there were no security cameras watching me. There was nothing. So, I pulled up into that empty lot and stopped right next to their car. I got outta the truck, made sure no one was looking, and crawled under Chink-Man's car.

That parking lot was dark. Lotta shadows. No one could see me unless they were real close and staring right at me. Otherwise, I was just more darkness in the world.

And I waited.

And waited.

And waited.

You kids today couldn't do like I did. Five minutes of being in one place and you'd be lighting up your phones and checking them. But I've learned patience through a long life of having to calmly and quietly wait for everything.

Must've been more than an hour before they stumbled outta that restaurant. I could see 'em from my spot. Looked like Chink-Man had polished off a whole bottle of wine with dinner, all by himself. He was swaying, stumbling around, talking real loud. Chink-Woman seemed more sober. She helped support him.

I made my plan for how I was gonna do this.

Chink-Woman used her remote thing to unlock the car.

Chink-Man stumbled on up to the passenger side.

So, I took my box cutter, grabbed his foot, and sliced his Achilles tendon. He screamed and went down.

I was on top of him quick.

My right hand just latched onto his throat. A good, firm grip. He wanted to scream more, believe-you-me, but he couldn't get the air through, I was crushing his windpipe so tight. My left hand pressed the box cutter into whatever folds of his neck I wasn't currently crushing.

Chink-Woman rushed around to our side of the car. Curiosity must've made her do it, 'cause her best instincts would've been to run back to the restaurant, screaming to high Hell. That's what I feared, actually. It flashed through my mind that maybe I had gotten greedy, trying to take two.

But luck was on my side. It was like that a lot. So many things could have gone wrong for me, but they never seemed to.

Chink-Woman ran to see what was happening. And that let me take control.

"Do not scream," I said, real nice and quiet-like. "Walk to that pickup and lay facedown in the bed."

That's exactly what she did.

It gave me time to gag Chink-Man and zip-tie him up. Then I went over to that pickup bed, bashed Chink-Woman a couple times in the head, and she was out.

I looked around. Restaurant was quiet. Street was quiet.

Nobody saw nothing.

I turned off their phones and threw them down the sewer drain.

Then I covered them with a tarp and drove off.

CHAPTER 22

As I left the parking lot, I was kicking myself for being so foolhardy as to take two right off a public street. Anyone could've walked out of that restaurant at any time. Any car could've driven by and seen the struggle. Chink-Man could've yelled louder. Chink-Woman could've run for help.

As a builder it's good to have a plan. And it's good to follow the plan. If you need to make alterations, well, you don't do it on the fly. You don't cut corners. And when you're building something, you don't do two-for-ones. If I needed two boards cut to the same length, would I stack 'em on top of each other and run one saw blade over them? Heck no. So, why was I grabbing two Chinks in one trip? Must've been outta my mind.

I swore right then, I was done. Too many risks. I had what I wanted.

And wouldn't you know...

At that moment, God smiled down on me and said, "You can have one more."

Because as I drove my Chinks home, I went right past the West Creek Apartment Complex. And who should be standing in front, waiting for a ride... but Elizabeth.

I pulled to a stop in front of her. No looping around the block. No planning out my moves. No checking for cameras, although there were none anyway.

This one was Divine Intervention.

I stepped out of the truck.

She had on one of those hooded sweatshirts and jeans. Nothing fancy. Not for her. She wasn't a dolled up kinda girl. Functional and casual.

She seemed to be on edge at first glance of this strange man in a truck who had stopped in front of her. But I stepped into the light and I could see the recognition flash through her eyes.

"Walter?"

She remembered my name. Good start. I smiled back at her, real friendly-like. "Where you headed?" I asked.

"Um, Portland. A cab's coming to take me to the bus station."

"Let me drive you. It'll be faster."

I motioned to my truck, but she made no move to join me. Instead, her hand actually went down to her purse, and she clutched it tightly.

"I'm okay. I already called the cab. Thank you, though."

"It's no inconvenience. Get in," I said.

"No. I'm fine."

I think my smile was getting strained at this point. I stepped toward her. I was only a few feet away when I said, "Get in the truck."

It definitely came out as more a threat than I intended.

I saw her hand defensively reach into her purse. Might be a cell phone she was digging for. Hell, could've been a gun for all I knew. So, I put my hands up and stopped walking forward. I showed her that I meant no harm.

"Whatever makes you comfortable," I said.

She relaxed her posture a bit. But I was already close enough.

It took three quick steps and I was on her. She reached into her purse as I grabbed her arm. Her purse fell down on the pavement, spilled all over the place. She had a can of pepper spray in her hand, but I was holding her arm tight. She tried to aim the little cannister at me, but it just sprayed harmlessly in the air.

I twisted her arm hard and she dropped it.

Her next move was to try to scream for help. But I clamped my right hand onto her windpipe and choked off her cries before they could escape her mouth. I drew my knife from my belt and pressed it firmly into her neck, making sure she could feel it dig in just a bit.

"If you scream, I will kill you," I hissed in her ear.

She managed to croak out, "No... no... no..."

It took some tugging and pulling but I got her over to the passenger side of my truck. I twisted her arms behind her back to zip-tie them. This meant I had to let go her neck. She immediately started kicking and flailing.

"Help! Help!"

I had one of those U-locks from an old bike handy for this. Had to bend her down at an awkward angle as I slid that puppy over her neck and locked her throat to the armrest. The only way she was getting out of that one was if she took apart the car door or took apart her own head. That U-lock pressed up against her throat and she couldn't really scream much anymore. My truck had those old pop-up locks, so I unscrewed those in case she tried to open the door herself.

Then I covered her head with a pillowcase and closed the door. I strolled back to the sidewalk, trying not to look like I was hurrying too much. I scooped everything up into her purse, then walked back to the truck and drove away.

CHAPTER 23

Isaac crouched forward in his seat, completely transfixed. His mouth hung open and his eyes barely blinked, hypnotized under his father's spell.

Walter noticed. His eyes returned to Earth from whatever far-off universe of memory he was gazing into and looked across the table at his son. The calm, storytelling father and the wide-eyed son. It might have been a dad telling a seven-year-old about the time he killed a bear in the wilderness.

"Mind if I ask you something?"

Isaac blinked, the spell suddenly broken. "Uh, yeah. Sure. What?"

"That way you're looking at me... What's going through your mind right now, boy?"

"What do you mean?"

"You angry? Disgusted? Or you getting hard?"

Isaac cleared his throat and shifted his posture. "What the hell, Dad?"

"You know I ain't a perv, but I am curious. I don't respond to the letters that guys send me in here, but I do read them. Whole lotta envy. Whole lotta pent-up, weird sex shit out there. But one thing I can swear to, sex had nothing to do with this."

"Or course. It was just idle misogyny and racism."

"It was anger. All seven of them represented a fucking boot that had been stomping on my face. Hell, they stomped on my dad's face too. I betcha even you've felt their heel grinding into your cheek once or twice. I may have tumbled from the high road, but them's the ones that pushed me."

"Sure, Dad."

"Don't dismiss me, boy."

It wasn't an actual apology, but Isaac gave a little bow of his head in a sign of contrition. Walter's postured puffed up, and his chin raised, accepting this as respect.

"Let's back up," Isaac said. "You grabbed *seven* young, healthy adults *in public?*"

Walter shrugged. "They sure as hell didn't volunteer."

"And you just used hand-tools? No guns?"

"I don't even own a gun. Never have."

"Bullshit."

Walter crossed his arms. "Excuse me?"

"Grandpa killed himself with an old bolt-action rifle. I think it was a thirty-ought-six. You always told me that story as some sympathetic 'look how shitty my life was' lesson. You hid that rifle in your closet. Up on the shelf. Behind your suitcases."

"What were you doing in my closet?"

Isaac couldn't help but grin. "I was a kid. You worked all summer. I practically lived by myself in that house. If there was a gun, I was gonna find it."

Walter nodded. "Well, I hocked that old thing back when you were in high school. Hadn't been fired or cleaned in a generation. So, no, I didn't use no gun to get those kids into my house. Just good old-fashioned elbow grease." His eye twinkled a bit at the memory. He seemed thoroughly impressed with himself. "It has crossed my mind that God had every opportunity, and then some, to put a stop to this boulder before it really got rolling. But He didn't. Can't put my finger on what that means, exactly, but it must mean something."

"Maybe it just means that we live in a society where people implicitly trust an old man. Or maybe we live in a society where people are lazy; they think they hear a scream for help, but don't really follow up on it."

"Could be. I ain't a philosopher; I didn't go to college." His eyes mocked Isaac as he said that. "I never had such opportunities. *My* father never set me up for that kind of success."

"So, you had seven people chained up in your basement. What was your plan?"

"Didn't have one."

"And you didn't rape them?"

Walter's eyes narrowed into a glare. He seemed truly insulted by the question. "I just said I didn't, boy."

"Come on."

"Never. I told you—I ain't no perv."

"This Elizabeth obsession is a bit—"

"You keep heading down this road and you're gonna run smack into a dead end. I won't put up with this. Not from you." His voice began rising. The blood rushed to his pale cheeks, turning his whole face pink. "Not from the one person who should know me better. The one person who owes me their respect. You gonna sit there and call your own father a sex fiend? These kids were punished for the sins of *your* generation. If I wanted to put my dick in something, I could just keep paying hookers. No. This was a mission to right the wrongs of this world. Each of them represented all that is wrong. Get that through your skull!"

By now, Walter was breathing hard. The veins in his forehead stood at attention.

For a moment, Isaac felt like a child getting lectured. And just like a child, he crumpled. He put his hands up for peace. "Okay, okay. I'm sorry. I'm sorry. I didn't mean anything."

Walter immediately calmed down. The earthquake had rumbled through one side of him and out the other, and now he was again at peace.

"Tell me about life down there," Isaac said.

"I wasn't down there that much, actually. There was a smell. They stunk. I didn't care for it."

"So, you just planned to let them rot?"

"No, no, of course not," Walter said. "Why would I do that? What would be the point? Oh sure, there were certain logistics to it all. But I subcontracted out most of the responsibility to Elizabeth."

"Subcontracted? To Elizabeth?"

"She was the last to join. She got the spot closest to the door. That meant it was closest to the length of hose that I ran down from the kitchen. It was her job to use that hose to keep some semblance of sanitation down there. It was a big responsibility. If someone took a piss or a shit, she'd be the one who'd have to wash it down toward the back grate. That hose was also the only water supply. So if Trixie or Average Joe or Hitch got thirsty, it was Elizabeth's job to spray the water in the air so they could drink. That's a management-level position down there. If you didn't have good hose control, you're gonna get everyone all wet, and it ain't gonna dry too quick down there. It'll make for some cold, damp nights. She did admirably well."

Walter thought for a moment, and decided to reconsider, upping his praise. "In fact, I've employed a lot of people in my line of work, yourself included, boy. Hell, I gave you a couple jobs to do with a hose. You had to fill the cement mixer and you overwatered it, came out all runny. Another time, I had you hose off a job site. Well, you got all lazy and sprayed water for ten seconds, then walked right off the job."

"I was, like, nine. And you weren't paying me."

"I paid you in a roof... bed... heating... electricity... food... Would it have killed you to say, 'thank you'?"

"Yeah, yeah. Thanks."

"I paid you a hell of a lot more than I paid Elizabeth. I gave her a job with a hose and she took it to heart. Nary a drop of water fell outside its intended area. She took good care of those kids."

"She was your slave."

"As I just said, I paid her."

"How?"

"As long as she served me well, I treated her like a queen."

"I can't even tell when you're joking anymore."

Walter smiled in return, as if he were in on the joke, but the smile lingered on his face long past when Isaac's smile had vanished. He was apparently truly fond of the memory. "She would eat my left-overs. And if there weren't any, I gave her some pizza rolls or something. The rest ate dog food. She had access to water. The rest had to beg to get sprayed in the face. She got four squares of toilet paper a day. The rest used their clothes or had Elizabeth rinse their fannies off with the hose. So, yeah, she appreciated everything she had. If she didn't do her job, she would lose her privileged place. And she knew it."

"What would it mean to lose your privileged place in that house?"

"You'd be open to punishment."

"The papers said you tortured them."

"*Punished*. There was always something to punish them for. If they looked me in the eye. If they talked among themselves. If they didn't heed my rules. They got punished. Elizabeth had to report on them. Sometimes, I would simply ask her for a referral. 'Who gets punished today?' If she didn't comply, then she would be the one to get punished."

"How did you punish them?"

"Various ways."

"Tell me what you did."

Walter's face lit up at what must have been one of his prouder memories. "The key was simplicity. No need for nothing too complicated or weird. In fact, it became my *new* favorite game to play, now that I had grown tired of my previous game."

"You seem to like your games."

"You know I do. You know I was always into puzzles and mind games and stuff."

"No."

"Well, I do. Love 'em to death. Playing games for the mind keeps you fresh, keeps you young. Keeps the Alzheimer's away. And let me tell you, that's the disease I fear most. I watched my grandma get Alzheimer's, or dementia, or something when I was young. I hate the movies that depict it as some kinda peaceful, 'your mind is living in the past' disease. It's a horrible way to die. Grandma would just lay in bed and moan and scream. It robbed her of who she was."

"Dad?"

"Yeah?"

"The game you would play?"

"Oh. Yeah. See, I would walk around the house, looking at various objects. Things. A book or an iron or a toothbrush. Then I would think to myself, 'How can I take this weak object and make it powerful?' I wanted to make it scary.

"For example, take a cotton ball. Nothing softer or as innocent as a cotton ball." His eyes turned dark. "But then you douse that cotton ball with lighter fluid..."

He looked off, not completing the thought.

Isaac hung on his words, his mind raced trying to think of what he would do with such a cotton ball. "And?"

"Why, I'd shove that lighter fluid little ball up each of their nostrils. Wedge it in real good. Then make Elizabeth choose who got the—" He mimed lighting a cigarette lighter.

Isaac's mouth hung open. "Jesus, Dad."

Walter took a deep, almost aroused breath. "Oh, how it lit up. Real bright. You could see the veins in his nose, just for an instant, before he flailed around so much I couldn't make nothing out. Looked like his whole head was gonna burst into flame. And that basement, it was so dark all the time, but the way the light danced..."

His eyes looked down at Isaac. "She chose Hitch, by the way. If you were at all curious. She sure as shit wasn't gonna choose herself."

"And that was it? You just invented new fucked up ways to be cruel to people?"

"It wasn't always smooth sailing. Especially in those first few days when they hadn't yet been fully broken..."

CHAPTER 24

It was mealtime. I remember that.

I had bought a twenty-five-pound bag of dried dog chow. It only cost me twenty bucks at the store, and I figured it could last me a month, maybe more. I contemplated stocking up. I had the space.

Those bags have directions on if your dog weighs X number of pounds, then he'll need X cups of food per day. It was confusing, as I couldn't exactly convert it to human, so I just eye-balled it. I never told you this, but that's what I always did with Buddy, anyway. That's why your dog got so fat. But, then again, if you cared, you woulda been the one feeding him.

Anyway, I poured a bunch into one of them big mixing bowls. I also took out a box of frozen pizza rolls for Elizabeth. Those were your favorite, I recall. It seems like for three years, that was your breakfast, lunch and dinner. Pizza rolls. I figured if those had enough nutritional value to keep you alive, then Elizabeth should be fine.

I unlocked the basement door and carried the food down those creaky steps in the dark. When I got down there, I tried the light switch. Nothing.

"The bulb died," Elizabeth's voice said out of the blackness.

I couldn't see anyone or anything, but it all seemed to be in order. There was a little bit of light coming down from the kitchen, and I could sorta make out everyone's shadows. I figured they couldn't get through their chains anyway. And if they did, where would they go?

"When did this happen?" I asked.

"I... I don't know. Yesterday, I think," Elizabeth said.

I might've punished her for the incomplete answer, but then again, down there in the pitch dark the concept of days and time was something that existed in their previous lives. It was a memory. I'm sure it was as foreign to them now as being inside their mother's belly.

In that way, they had been reborn in my basement.

Well, I handed the dog chow and the pizza rolls to Elizabeth, and I trudged back upstairs. I went to the kitchen drawer and grabbed a new lightbulb. I had stocked up on incandescent the moment I caught wind that the government was going to make us all switch to those god awful, pig-tail monstrosities. As if they don't got better things to do than tell us what kind of lightbulbs we can use.

With a bulb in hand and a lamp on my head, I went back downstairs.

Using the light from the headlamp, I took a moment to glance around at my properties. They all seemed to be in good order. Seven of them. Still in their places. They all were silent, just sitting there, staring at their laps like good children.

The light, if you recall, was mounted to the ceiling right smack dab in the middle of the basement. I had positioned the kids around the walls in a U formation, and I'd have to walk right into the center of them to get to the fixture. I didn't like doing that, which is why I mostly handed things off to Elizabeth. But maintaining proper illumination was one of my few responsibilities, I guess.

As I stepped toward the center, I glanced up at the light. The bulb had been shattered. I suddenly realized that this was no accident. My mind knew I was walking into a trap before it could communicate with my feet to stop moving.

"Now!" Elizabeth shouted.

Elizabeth was on one end of the U and Good Sam was across from her on the other end, and between them, they held a length of the hose. I don't know when she did it, probably the night before, but Elizabeth had gotten enough slack on the hose that she was able to gnaw through it like a rat through cardboard. She had ripped off a good seven feet of garden hose and now, on her command, she and Good Sam pulled that hose tight.

It caught my ankle perfectly.

I fell facedown. Hard. Right in the center of that concrete floor.

And just like that, they were on me.

With as much slack as their chains would allow, they were kicking. They were grabbing. They were clawing. They were trying to scrape out the flesh from my face.

And the noise. The sounds they let out as they went for me, why, they weren't human sounds. Hell, I never heard a dog make such sounds. They were screaming. Shrill, howling screams.

My first thought was to curl into a ball. Protect myself long enough to get to my feet and run off, or maybe even crawl on out of there. They still had chains holding them back, you know. But they were wild. Those chains must've taken out a few inches of their flesh, they pulled them so tight to get their grubby claws on me.

Someone would grab my ankle, and I'd have to kick them off.

Someone would grab my wrist, and I'd have to twist it free.

Someone pounded that metal dog food bowl into the back of my head, and I'd just have to take it.

They whaled on me with it, over and over. In truth, I didn't even notice at the time. The welts and the pain came later. I just knew I had to fight or die.

I tried crawling away. But Chink-Woman had gotten a good firm, fist-full of my shirt collar. I don't know where she found the strength, but she yanked me back hard. I fell down again.

The next thing I know, she's got both hands wrapped hard around my neck. Her grip was tight. I couldn't breathe.

The shrill, wild hollering then turned to screams of encouragement.

"Kill him!" shouted Good Sam.

"Do it, Grace! You got him!" Trixie was yelling.

Elizabeth, meanwhile, kept her composure. She kept her eye on the plan. She started shouting, "Get the keys! Someone get his keys!"

I could feel them reaching toward my pockets, some using their feet or whatever they could reach best with.

Chink-Woman squeezed my neck with everything she had. My vision was going black. I tried to get air in, but I couldn't. The weaker I got, the more the screaming and the noise and the kicking and the clawing got blocked out, although I'm sure their intensity didn't flag one bit. I just didn't have the strength to notice anymore. I was about to give up the ghost.

But I did hear Chink-Woman. She wasn't screaming. She was hissing. "Die... die..." she said in that low, cunt voice of hers.

That's when I decided I wasn't going to let them kill me. I wasn't going to let them win again. All my life I been rolling over and letting them squeeze the oxygen straight from my lungs. Again and again and again. But down here? Down in my basement? Here, *I was God.*

God does not die at the hands of his subjects.

I grabbed Chink-Woman's right pinkie. Wrapped my whole hand around that one little finger of hers. And I yanked it. I yanked it so hard that despite all the shouting and commotion, every single person in that basement heard the deafening snap it made. And then they heard Chink-Woman scream. I ain't never heard such a scream.

She didn't have no grip left in her after that.

She let go my neck and I gulped up the air. It filled my lungs. My body. My soul. I was rejuvenated. I was back.

"Don't let him go!" Good Sam shouted. "Grab him!"

I tried to scramble away. Chink-Woman still had some fight left in her. Her good hand grabbed hold of my belt. She held on for dear life.

Elizabeth started yelling, "Hold him! Someone help her!"

It was Chink-Man then who managed to grab hold of my foot. Wrapped his fingers around my shoelaces. By now, my headlamp had fallen off somewhere back in the scrum. I was groping in the dark for something to hold onto. Anything. Chink-Man and Chink-Woman were teaming up to drag me back into it all.

Then my fingers—clawing at that cold, damp concrete floor in the dark—latched onto something. The grate. The metal drainage grate. I pulled out a section of that grate, flipped onto my back, and swung it blindly into the blackness of the room. As hard as I could.

It didn't travel far before I heard and felt it bury itself into human flesh and bone.

Chink-Woman stopped tugging on my belt.

She stopped doing anything, actually.

I don't know if anyone else could see what happened in the darkness, but they all seemed to know. It went so silent in that basement that I was sure I could hear the blood pumping out the dent I had just made in Chink-Woman's head. I was able to kick my foot away from Chink-Man's grasp, and I scrambled to my feet. It was about time, but I was finally out of their reach. No one could touch me.

"Oh, we're gonna have some fun now," I told them.

I wish I could've seen their faces. But I'm thankful they couldn't see mine. I recall I was quivering. I was breathing heavy. I was scared and I was furious.

I hugged that wall and stayed just out of their reach. I made it to the stairs and I got outta there quick.

Only sound I heard was Chink-Man, crying and calling out Chink-Woman's name, "Grace? Grace!" But soon I couldn't even hear that anymore. All I could hear were my own feet, clomping up those stairs.

And I could hear the voice in my head. It was planning what to do with this latest development.

CHAPTER 25

Walter nodded quietly to himself for a moment as he stared off, as if contemplating his own story. "Truth be told, I had always intended to fasten down that drainage grate. It had bugged me this whole time too. The Trixie-closet situation had rushed me, and I just plumb ran out of hours in the day. As you, I'm sure, are well aware, I don't like cutting corners in my gigs, and a loose grating seemed like it was just begging to cause me headaches in the future. For some reason, I never got around to it. I'm starting to think that maybe a higher power told me not to fasten that grate. God knew it would come in handy. It would save me. Something was protecting me through all this."

Isaac took a deep breath. "I don't think there was a higher power protecting you, Dad."

"If not God, then maybe it was the other end of the coin."

"I think Satan's got better things to do with his days than to make you too lazy to fasten down a drainage grate so that you could use that grate as a weapon when your life depended on it."

"I gotta disagree with you, boy. I think that's exactly the way Satan might've played this one out."

"Fair enough."

"I mean, there was some sort of darkness went into me that made me do all this, wasn't there?"

"I guess."

Walter raised an eyebrow. "You don't sound too convinced."

"I don't really care to have a theological debate about where God and Satan were while you were doing this. And I know you don't give a shit about that either. You never did. Anytime you'd go into that Mennonite secondhand store, all you'd do is call them retarded for having any sort of belief structure."

"Apparently you can't use that word no more."

"No, you can't. But that's the word you would use."

"That's because he's retarded for having a belief structure." Walter laughed. "Jokes on me, anyway. One of the detectives came down to talk to me once. I asked what happened to all my tools. I suspected they'd go to you."

Isaac leaned forward, interested. "I never got them."

"Course not. He said they donated them all to charity. I finally squeezed the details outta him. Guess where they went."

"Where?"

"That damn retard's secondhand store!"

Isaac couldn't help but grin at the realization.

Walter continued, "Fucking Mennonites. If they actually picked up a newspaper or turned on a TV, they'd know those tools were worth a pretty penny. Now that's what I call value-added. So, yes, believing in God and Satan has made them mentally disabled."

"Let's get back to the basement."

"What about it?"

"Did you punish them? For the escape attempt?"

"Well, it ain't so much about punishing their failed escape as about stopping their next one. That's the key. Don't dwell on the past. Plan for the future."

Isaac chuckled. "Yeaaah. If there's one guy who doesn't dwell on the past, it's you."

Walter cocked his head to the side, apparently not understanding what was so funny. But he shrugged and continued, "I figured they could only plan escapes if they could communicate. So, I could stop them from escaping if I could stop them from communicating."

"Did you gag them?"

"Gags are temporary. As I said before, one thing a builder is always striving for—"

"—is permanence."

"Good boy. Ain't no better use of time than brainstorming a permanent solution to a recurring problem."

"So, what was your permanent solution?"

"I had Elizabeth scrape out their eardrums with a flathead screwdriver."

The blood drained from Isaac's face. He couldn't help but tremble at imagining it. "What?"

As if trying to make it easier for Isaac to comprehend, Walter mimed holding a screwdriver in his hand. He held his other hand into a circle, as if it were an ear cavity. Then, with his "screwdriver," he violently scraped, gouged, and swirled it inside the "ear."

In an impulsive reaction, Isaac's hands went to his head and clutched his ears, shielding them from the mere possibility that a screwdriver could be jammed into them. His skin crawled at the thought. It was such a simple concept that it shouldn't have felt out of place with the other horrors Walter regaled him with, but the thought made Isaac want to stand and move his muscles.

"I plopped that flathead down in front of Elizabeth and told her she had to do it. Both ears on all of them. That's what they deserved for violating my trust."

"She didn't."

"She took some persuading."

"How do you 'persuade' someone to do that to six people?"

"That there's a good question. And I hit upon a pretty good solution. I cut the head off an extension cord, separated the wires a bit and scraped the sheathing off. I used twelve-gauge cord because the smaller the number, the thicker the wire, and the thicker the wire—"

"The more amperage it holds," Isaac said.

Walter couldn't help but beam, "Good boy. I taped the wires to the ends of a metal dinner fork. I wanted terminals for the electricity to arc between. Then I taped the whole shebang to the end of a broom handle, 'cause I sure as hell wasn't getting close to the business end of that thing. Once I plugged it in, I had me a homemade cattle prod."

"But wouldn't it trip the breakers?"

"You know your electrical wiring. Good for you. And we both know what can shut off the circuit when too much juice passes through."

"A GFCI switch."

"Yep. I took the GFCI switch out of the bathroom, connected it to another cord, and *that's* what I plugged into the house. Every time I used the cattle prod, it would give one good shock before the GFCI detected the runaway current and clicked off. I just hit the reset button, which I kept right by my thumb, and wham-bam-thank-you-ma'am, she was ready for another go. I liked this because it wasn't frying the house circuits. It also kept the shocks nice and short, so I didn't have to worry I'd kill 'em or something."

He smiled at the memory.

"I jabbed that thing at Elizabeth again and again. She took it for a good thirty minutes or so. I had to actually go upstairs and grab a chair so I didn't have to keep standing while we played this game. Standing hurts my back after while. But I had plenty of time on my hands, and it wasn't like I was running outta electricity any time soon. So, I just kept at it. She screamed and she kicked and she started sobbing."

He closed his eyes. He was so engaged that his hand made involuntary jabbing motions, as if he was re-experiencing it all and it brought him an immense satisfaction.

"It took some time, but her hand wrapped itself around the handle of that screwdriver. I unlocked her. Oh, how the others hollered at her to fight me. But her legs and arms were weak. She hadn't stood in a month. She was finally broken. I remember her looking at me. For the first time I didn't see hate or fear in her eyes. Just... nothing. Acceptance, I guess. She threw herself on Hitch first. She gouged out his ear drums. He tried to fight back, but all that good food I fed Elizabeth made her stronger than him. She scraped out his ears. She went down the line and did them all. Each one she did, I could see the light dim a bit from her eyes. Until there was nothing. Blackness. Even then, she had Average Joe and Good Sam to do. And she did them. I bet it hurt like Hell."

The room went silent. The only sounds were Walter's excited breaths.

A buzzer went off, snapping Walter out of his trance.

"That's time," Teddy said, the first time that a voice that didn't belong to a Luce had been heard in hours. Isaac turned to Teddy, seemingly jarred by his presence and just now realizing that the mammoth man had, in fact, been standing over Isaac's shoulder this entire time.

Teddy seemed to sense the disruption he had caused. "I'm, uh, I'm sorry. I gave you a triple time allotment, which we never do. It's way against the rules. But I gotta get him back for chow."

"That's alright," Walter said as he pushed himself back from the table.

"I can set you both up with another session tomorrow," Teddy volunteered.

Walter looked at Isaac with a hint of nervous expectation on his face.

For once, Isaac didn't hesitate. "Yes, please."

A glow seemed to emanate from Walter's expression as his lips turned upwards in a grin that spread well-worn wrinkles throughout his face.

It wasn't much of a smile, and yet Isaac realized he had so rarely seen such looks of true satisfaction on his father's features before. Walter looked as though he had been genuinely touched. "I'd like that very much, boy. I think this is a real important thing we got going on here. I'd hate for anything to blunt its momentum."

"Agreed."

The door buzzed and opened with a clang. Two guards stepped in and flanked Walter.

"As always, you may share a brief hug," Teddy said.

Isaac rose and walked around the table. Walter's eyes went wide with confusion as Isaac opened his arms and wrapped his father in a hug. Walter's restraints prevented him from fully embracing his son in return and so, he stood. Tears welled in the old man's eyes.

"I've never felt closer to you, boy," he said. "It feels good that, after all these years, you and I have something to actually talk about."

Isaac released. The two looked at each other.

"See you tomorrow, Dad."

"See you tomorrow."

Isaac watched as his father gave him one last longing look before turning and allowing the guards to escort him away.

The moment the door closed behind him, Isaac's wistful smile vanished. His face turned cold as he looked back at Teddy.

"What do you think?" Teddy asked.

"He's way more racist than I remember."

"Well, that's great. I mean, it's not great that he's a racist and a woman-hater, but it means his guard's down. We're getting some honesty." Teddy slapped Isaac's shoulder.

"Or he's just playing around. Seeing what sticks," Isaac said.

"Nah. You don't make up stories like this."

"Maybe."

"Well, I think this is great material. You talk to your buyer?" Teddy asked.

"He's kicking it upstairs. They're putting an offer together."

"Joan Larkins is still interested. Her offer is on the table. Maybe I can set you guys up with a—"

"No."

Isaac stepped to the door and waited for Teddy to let him out.

"Come on, Isaac. Just give her a chance. No one in the world is more invested in this story than Joan, I guarantee ya."

Isaac faced the door. "I got things to do tonight."

CHAPTER 26

"Here's the challenge," Lauren said, keeping her voice level and professional, as if she were in a heist thriller, outlining the elaborate challenges and security methods that must be overcome. "The guard starts his patrol at 10 p.m."

Isaac followed where she was pointing.

They were both seated inside his car, staring through the windshield. It was night. His lights were off, and he tried to make out the world beyond. They were parked along the outer fence of an old Gothic cemetery. He could see the headstones, spires and stone angels on the other side.

"A little backstory—the flower vases are built into the headstones here, and they're made out of bronze or iron or some shit," Lauren said. "Anyway, people used to pry them off the gravesites and sell them for scrap."

"Dick."

"Totally. Anyway, relatives of the fallen get kinda pissy when you disrespect their brethren, so the cemetery had to hire a guard," Lauren said. "As long as he doesn't hear anything suspicious, then his patrol goes off like clockwork. The place closes to visitors at sundown. Then, every hour on the hour, he leaves his booth at the front gate. He gets in his little golf cart and putt-putt-putts his way up the paths to the top. And then back down again. Every hour on the hour."

The cemetery was built on a hill. A narrow road wrapped around the hill, climbing toward the summit. Isaac barely made out the pathway in the darkness, but he nodded anyway. "I'm with ya. Are we stealing headstones?"

Lauren gave him a look. "Uh, if you want. But that seems like a good way to get a gypsy fuck-you-curse."

"Then what's the plan?"

"The moment he starts his patrol, we hop the fence, book it up the hill, high-five Virgin Mary—"

Isaac looked out the windshield. Although most of the cemetery was shrouded in darkness, at the summit of the hill—plainly visible and reflecting back the moonlight—was a large, stone statue of the Virgin Mary. She looked down the hill, almost directly to where their car sat. She seemed to be looking at Isaac. Her arms were outstretched with her palms up, welcoming all and waiting to offer absolution to any heart that requested it.

Lauren continued, "... then you turn around, race back down the hill, hop the fence. First one in the car with the door closed wins."

Isaac nodded. He gets it. "And if the guard sees us?"

"Fail."

"Jesus. When I was in high school, we'd just steal watermelons and throw them off bridges."

"How bourgeois. Oooh! Here he comes!"

They slumped down in their seats, keeping their heads below the level of the windshield and out of view. Just as Lauren said, an old security guard, picking up a few extra bucks at night to supplement his retirement, came around the corner in his golf cart. He passed in front of them on the inside of the fence then disappeared around the bend as he wound his way up the hill on the narrow cemetery paths.

Isaac and Lauren poked their heads up and looked out. The coast was clear.

"I forgot to mention one rule," Lauren said as she cracked open her door.

"What's that?"

"You must present yourself to the Virgin in your purest form. Naked."

With that, she rolled out of the car and quietly closed the door behind her.

Isaac hurried to follow her lead.

Lauren jumped up and grabbed the top of the wrought-iron fence. She pulled herself up with a speed, strength and dexterity that made Isaac marvel. She balanced on the top cross bar, steadied herself, and then jumped down to the ground.

Isaac wasn't far behind. He pulled himself up, but he took a little more care to gently lower himself down.

And the race was on.

They took off at a sprint, charging their way up the hill. Lauren pulled her shirt off as she ran. Without breaking stride, she draped it on a stone cross.

Isaac tried to pull his shirt off, but it became stuck around his head. The momentary blindness caused him to smack into a headstone and tumble to the ground.

Lauren paused and ran in place as she pointed and laughed at Isaac. Or, at least, *stifled* a laugh in the silent cemetery.

It didn't take long for Isaac to pull his shirt off and toss it to the ground. He looked up at Lauren, a few feet away. The moon reflected off her bare shoulders.

"Put your clothes on the headstones or you'll never find them on the way back," she said with a laugh.

"How many times have you done this?"

"Enough to go pro," she said as her left hand reached behind her back and in one swift moment unclasped her bra. It fell from her chest.

Isaac held his breath as he watched. The angle of the moon was just right so that it backlit her, casting her front in shadow. He strained his eyes, waiting for his night-vision to kick into another gear so that he could make out the details of her silhouette.

But before he got the chance, she turned and took off at a sprint again. Isaac re-engaged his pursuit. He kicked off his shoes, only to promptly stub his toe on a metal vase of flowers. "Ow! Fucking remembrances."

Suddenly stopping her sprint, Lauren waved for Isaac to hit the deck. "Down, down, down!"

Isaac followed her lead and ducked behind a stone spire.

At that moment he heard the sound of an electric motor. The guard putt-putted around the corner in his golf cart, shining his flashlight between the rows of headstones.

Up the hill from Isaac's position, Lauren, completely topless, wrapped her arms around her breasts and performed an exaggerated commando-roll from her exposed position to a secure hiding place behind a stone angel. Isaac stifled a laugh at the sight of this near naked girl, her hair flopping around, performing an action-movie maneuver.

Now well-hidden from the guard, she sat up and leaned her back against the angel. She pulled off her shoes and socks. She laid her socks into the angel's outstretched hands and propped her shoes onto the tips of its wings. Isaac could only smile and shake his head. *The balls on this girl.*

The guard drove around the corner and out of sight, which prompted Lauren to immediately hop to her feet. She turned and faced down the hill toward Isaac, and then stretched out her arms and began to shimmy in the dark, letting her breasts bounce around in the night air.

Isaac gulped.

Lauren then flipped him off with both hands and continued running up the hill. Isaac raced to catch up.

After a few strides, they both had to pause and hop on one leg as they pulled off their pants. Lauren hung hers on a spire while Isaac draped his on a cross. With their eyes locked on each other and Lauren maintaining a slim lead, they bent down and removed their underwear, also draping those on the gravestones.

They stood for a moment, separated by a few feet, and grinned at each other standing naked in the moonlight.

"Oh shit! Get down!" Isaac said in an urgent whisper, pointing to the road just behind Lauren.

In a panic, she dropped to the ground.

Isaac let out a laugh and burst up the hill in a sprint, racing past Lauren's prone position. She looked around, realizing nobody was coming and that she had been fooled.

Keeping her voice low, she hissed out at him, "You mother-fucker!"

Then she jumped to her feet and ran after Isaac. It was neck-and-neck as they raced up the hill.

They crossed the road and approached the summit.

With a final burst of speed, Lauren caught up to Isaac. They both jumped up, reached out their hands, and high-fived the statue of the Virgin Mary.

Lauren rounded the statue's wide base and began to race back down the hill when—

"Watch out!" Isaac grabbed her wrist and pulled her back toward him behind the Virgin Mary statue. He wrapped his arm around her and tackled her to the ground.

Just at that moment, the electric golf cart rounded the corner and glided to a stop. The guard held onto the golf cart roof to support himself as he hoisted himself out of the seat. He stumbled around, too drunk to walk a straight line. He staggered toward the Virgin Mary statue. With one hand supporting himself against the statue, his other hand undid his fly.

In the bushes behind the statue, hidden just feet away, a naked Isaac and Lauren held each other. They struggled to keep the laughter in their mouths at the sound of the guard's urine splashing at the base of the statue. As they looked in each other's eyes, the sight of the others' facial contortions, trying to stifle laughter, made it even more challenging to remain silent.

Unable to bear it anymore, Isaac raised his head. He peeked around the statue's base to check on the guard. "For fuck's sake," Isaac whispered.

"What? Is he still there?"

Isaac turned and faced her, a smirk on his face. "He's back in the cart. And he just lit up a joint. He's just sitting there."

Lauren sniffed the air. It was true, the sweet smoky smell wafted over the area. She smiled and let out a silent chuckle.

"We might be here awhile," Isaac said.

They looked in each other's eyes. They weren't laughing anymore, just smiling. They gazed at each other, their faces lit by the moon.

"Well, what the fuck can we do to kill the time?" Lauren said as she slowly ran her hand along Isaac's flank. Her hand migrated down to Isaac's waist. Then she reached over toward his crotch.

"No fucking clue." Isaac traced his hand along the side of her face, over her bare shoulder, and down her ribcage. He paused when he reached her waist. His hand stayed there for a moment.

"I told you, I'm eighteen. I'm legally capable of making bad decisions," she said as she grasped his hand and angled his fingers inside her. She let out a soft moan. "Just don't tell my dad," she said.

He grinned. "Don't tell mine."

They both leaned in and kissed.

CHAPTER 27

Teddy turned off his car.

He pressed the button on his remote. With the loud creaking of dying springs, his garage door jerked closed behind him. He grabbed his empty lunch bag from the passenger seat and, with a weary sigh, stepped out of his car.

He walked in the house.

Every light was on.

He cursed under his breath as he trudged from room to room, turning off the switches one by one. He momentarily tried to calculate how much money Lauren had wasted by leaving all these lights on, but the mental math was, and always had been, too much for him and he gave up.

It upset him that she continued to ignore his rules. Maybe he would lecture her when she came home. But maybe it was a waste of a lecture. He didn't want to play the "I'm your father and you'll obey me" card for something as trivial as light switches. No, he'd save up his lectures for when she turned 21 and began to drink.

She wasn't drinking already, was she?

Nah. She was a good girl.

He lingered outside Lauren's closed bedroom door. Was she home already? He'd love to hear how her day went, although he wouldn't get more than a "Fine" from her.

"Lauren? You home?" he called out as he knocked on her door.

No answer.

He opened it and peered inside.

Empty.

His eyes caught something. Her backpack. Thrown on her bed. Some books were strewn over the covers where she had apparently been working on a math problem set.

Teddy pulled out his phone and checked his texts. Yep, it was just as he thought. At 6:13 p.m., she had texted him, *"Studying for calculus midterm at Becky's. Be home late."*

It wasn't a lacrosse game or a Model U.N. meeting. She *said* she was studying math. But she left her books at home? Lauren wouldn't lie to him. Maybe it was a different class and she made a mistake. Or maybe she was using Becky's calculus book to study.

Or maybe it was a boy.

He pushed the thought out of his mind.

She was eighteen. She could have a boyfriend. She was responsible. Teddy didn't care. Teddy was a cool dad.

Right?

And Lauren respected his coolness.

Right?

Instead of answering those questions, Teddy went to the kitchen to fix himself some dinner. He pulled a tub of stew he had made earlier in the week out of the fridge, spooned some into a bowl and put it in the microwave.

As he waited for the two minutes of heating to pass, he checked his phone. Nothing new there. With less than thirty friends he followed on social media, it wasn't as if he was inundated with status updates. Scrolling over to his news app didn't kill much time either. Nothing happened in the world that he cared to read about. He knew that kids could fritter away hours on these devices, but he couldn't for the life of him figure out on what. Searching the ends of the Internet didn't kill enough time for Teddy to heat up a bowl of stew.

With no other diversions presenting themselves, he opened the most recent audio file. Walter's detached, yet folksy, voice drifted out the phone's speaker and through the kitchen. Teddy scanned forward. He pressed play. Walter's voice described in detail how he forced Elizabeth into his truck and slid the U-lock over her neck.

Teddy listened.

His muscles clenched. An anger rose as he listened to Walter brag about restraining that girl. Teddy wanted to punch the wall. He wanted to punch Walter's face. He wanted to make his own cattle prod and find every sensitive spot on Walter's body with which to use it. He wanted to hurt the man who would hurt those kids.

The chunks of meat in the stew popped and exploded in the microwave. Teddy glanced over and realized that he had accidentally set it for twenty minutes instead of two. He cursed himself as he popped the door open, receiving a face-full of steam in the process. Splattered chunks of stew clung to the microwave walls. He'd have to clean that now. Yet another thing he had to do. Lauren sure wouldn't take the initiative to clean the microwave, nor anything in the house for that matter.

He set the hot bowl on the table and sat down for dinner.

Ding-dong! His doorbell.

Of course.

It was probably a Jehovah's Witness or one of those "I was passing through and saw your driveway needs repairs and I happen to own a company..." guys. Whatever the case, they always timed their visits right when they expected people to be home, weary from work, and finally relaxing. He could ignore it.

Ding-dong!

Maybe it was Lauren. Maybe she forgot her key and was locked out. Teddy set his spoon back in his bowl and trudged to the door. He opened it and—

"Joan?"

A tall, middle-aged woman stood on his front step. She wore slacks and a hooded sweatshirt, apparently an attempt to blend in with the lower-class neighborhood she was visiting, but it didn't hide the "Gucci" on the frames of her glasses. Or the Tesla symbol on the grill of her car.

It was Joan Larkins, attorney-turned-independent-film-producer.

"You didn't have to come here," Teddy said.

"Would you rather there be phone records? Or emails? Or texts?"

"No. No, but we shouldn't be in touch. I mean, it's all taken care of."

"Is it?" Joan smiled at Teddy, but there was displeasure in that smile. "I hear he's fielding his own offers?"

Teddy gulped. "Yeah, I'm real sorry. He threatened to pull out. I figured you'd want us to keep going."

"I see. But if he's fielding offers, does that mean he has something to sell?"

"I, uh... I—"

"You sent him a copy of the recording."

"It was the only way to keep him on board."

"Which means there *are* recordings."

Teddy looked away. He was twice her size, but her glare made him wilt. He fidgeted in the doorframe.

"It, uh, it seemed like it would be a good idea to, uh, have them handy. You know, in case he ever asked to hear 'em. Which he did. So, I think it was smart of me. Otherwise, he wouldn't come back, and Walter would just be sitting in a cell. And, then, you know, what would you—"

"It's fine, Teddy. It's fine." She took a deep breath, allowing her glare to dig into him for a few moments longer. "Are we on schedule?" she asked.

"Yep. I talked to my guy. He's in."

"When?"

"Tomorrow. They're meeting again."

Joan nodded, satisfied. "I'll be here tomorrow night. And then we'll never see each other again."

She turned and walked back to her car, but then paused and looked at Teddy. "You made the right decision for you and Lauren. Congratulations on Columbia. It's a wonderful school. You should be proud of her. College is expensive but worth it. She'll have a great time. She'll meet great people. She has a bright future."

Joan climbed into her car and started the engine.

Teddy shut the door. He went back to his dining table and plopped down in front of his stew. He sat there for a minute, staring off, making no effort to eat. He wasn't hungry anymore.

He pulled out his phone.

He opened a locator app. Up popped an icon with a picture of Lauren's smiling face. The GPS searched for her and then zoomed in on a map.

Teddy raised an eyebrow. Was she at the *cemetery*?

At night?

Huh?

CHAPTER 28

Isaac struggled to contain himself.

He wanted to go faster, like the jackhammer porn stars that he was used to watching. In fact, he now realized that every sexual encounter he'd ever had (and there hadn't been many) wasn't much different than masturbating; he had just swapped in a vagina for his right hand. It was always fast and messy. Just friction.

But with the security guard only a few feet away and blissfully ignorant, Isaac was forced to go slow. The strange thing was he liked it. He liked pausing between the thrusts, taking the time to look at Lauren's face in the moonlight. She was swallowing back her moans, trying to stay quiet. Isaac was too.

They would kiss in the pauses between the thrusts. They would take time to touch each other, running their fingers over each other's faces and bodies.

They both *wanted* to go faster, but couldn't. Being forced to be gentle made them want to be wild. It made each moment stretch out and become all the more special and erotic. It was the first time Isaac had ever experienced sexual tension *while* having sex.

When he finally came, his entire body clenched. He could feel the moment everywhere. Lauren wrapped her arms around him and held him close. He could feel her body quiver as the waves of ecstasy flowed through her.

They held that position.

They held each other.

Their bodies remained tense.

Isaac finally propped himself up and stared at Lauren's eyes in the moonlight. It was the most perfect moment of his life.

Then, a ringtone shattered the silence. It blared out across the serene cemetery, the manmade noise completely out of place amongst the fields of serenity.

Lauren put a hand to her head and grimaced. "Ah, cock-n-balls," she muttered.

"Your phone?"

She nodded.

"You didn't turn it off?"

She shook her head.

"Because you turned it off last night and you can't play the 'my battery died' card twice."

She nodded.

Isaac crawled off her. On their hands and knees, they peeked around the statue.

The guard had dropped his joint and was shining his flashlight down the hillside. "Who's there?!" he shouted. "You're trespassin'! Come on out!"

His light swept over the tombstones.

It finally found the culprit. The light stopped and shone on a stone cross. The guard stepped forward and peered down the dark hill at the stone cross, trying to figure out what was making that noise. Lauren's jeans hung from the cross. Her pocket lit up and vibrated from the phone inside.

Behind the Virgin Mary statue, Isaac looked at Lauren. "What now?" he asked.

She grinned and shrugged. "I lose."

With that, she jumped to her feet. Isaac hurried to follow.

The guard, startled by the noise, turned around just in time to see two naked people rise up out of the bushes, charge past him, and take off down the hill.

"Hey! Stop!" he yelled as he jumped in his golf cart and started the engine.

The chase was on.

Isaac and Lauren ran.

They ran at a full sprint before having to screech to a halt so they could grab their underwear from two headstones. They pulled them on before sprinting to their next discarded piece of clothing.

They crossed the road and continued down the hill just as the golf cart rounded the corner.

Lauren ran up to the stone cross that held her pants. She yanked the phone out of her pocket and answered, "Hey, Dad!" She hopped on one foot as she struggled to pull on her pants while cradling the phone to her ear. "Yeah, we were studying, but just took a trampoline break. Didn't hear you call."

Still on the phone, she raced down the hill again. "Anyway, I'm coming home now..."

She realized that she just ran past her bra and had to double back to grab it from a headstone. With no time to strap it on, and needing her hands free, she simply shoved it down her pants and continued running.

"Gotta go!" she said as she hung up.

Isaac glanced over his shoulder to check on her.

He watched as Lauren came off the hill and onto the pathway. She wasn't looking. Her attention was on her phone, fumbling to shove it back into the tight pocket on her jeans. In that momentary lapse of focus, she stepped onto the pathway and smacked into the on-coming golf cart.

It wasn't a big collision, but it knocked her off her feet.

Isaac slid down on the grass and rolled behind a headstone.

He poked his head out and watched. The guard was already out of his cart, standing over her with his light. She was cornered.

"I'm armed! Come on, get up. Slowly!"

Lauren did as ordered. She climbed to her feet and stood there on the pathway, her arms wrapped around her bare breasts.

Isaac could see it clearly. The guard's flashlight shone directly in Lauren's eyes, causing her to squint and turn her head away. The man's other hand grasped down at his utility belt, clutching whatever weapon he carried.

"Hands above your head," the guard commanded.

She hesitated.

"Do it now. Or else," the guard said.

Slowly, Lauren removed the only thing shielding the man's gaze from her breasts. She raised her arms and rested her hands on her head. Isaac could see her face scrunch up into a grimace at being so exposed and violated by this man's wandering eyes.

A silence overtook the cemetery that was so total that Isaac could plainly hear the old man's quickened breathing. The guard's light held for a moment on Lauren's eyes. Then it began traveling down. Across her nose, still glistening with beads of sweat from the night's excitement. Then down to her chin where her lips quivered in fear against her tightened jaw. Then her neck, involuntarily gulping.

Finally, the light settled on her breasts. The light sat there. The man saw no need for it to travel further. He stared. And stared. And licked his lips. And stared some more.

Isaac dropped his clothes and burst from his hiding place and sprinted toward the scene. He had no plan. But he wanted to hurt that man. He wanted to jam a screwdriver in his eyes or insert a flaming cotton ball in his nose.

Despite making no attempts at silence, his bare feet made no sound on the grass. He ran up behind the guard who was too distracted to notice. But as Isaac got within two strides of grabbing a brick off the ground and bashing it into the backside of the man's head, his eyes caught Lauren's. She saw him approaching, coming to her rescue, and a giddy grin overtook her face. It was a grin that seemed to say, "Well, this night took a weird turn, but we're still having fun, right?"

The hate melted from Isaac and was replaced by mischief.

Without breaking stride, he ran up to the golf cart and grabbed it by its undercarriage. With all his strength, he lifted one side of it, as if he were a body builder doing a clean-and-jerk.

He let out an exaggerated animalistic scream, "RAWWWR!" as he flipped the golf cart on its side.

It crashed onto the pavement.

The guard turned, shining his light around. "Hey!" was all the guard could think to shout as Isaac wagged his dick at the man.

"Run!" Isaac yelled as he took off back down the hill.

Lauren, now giggling, ran after him.

The guard pulled out his can of mace and shot it toward them, but the spray dissipated harmlessly in the night air.

The guard took a few strides in pursuit, but only made it five feet before slowing to a walk and gulping in much needed breaths of air.

Isaac and Lauren ran off down the hill, increasing their lead over the hapless guard. They paused to pull on their shirts, and then their shoes. When they reached the fence, they both pulled down their pants and slapped their asses at the guard.

Then they hopped over the fence and disappeared into the night, giggling and hooting.

CHAPTER 29

Teddy hunched over, rocking slowly in his favorite recliner. He rocked it back and forth, not even considering the option of kicking his feet up and reclining. It wasn't that he was too deep in thought; it was the opposite. He was empty. Completely vacant.

He heard her feet walking up the driveway. He knew he hadn't heard a car engine, or a car door, or the usual giggling goodbyes that she would give to Becky or her other friends. No, she must've told her ride to drop her off around the corner. Which meant she didn't want him to see who her ride was.

Must be a boy.

A few moments later, the front door quietly opened.

Lauren slinked in.

Teddy watched her. It was obvious to him that she was trying not to make a sound, trying not to give an indication of the exact hour of her late arrival. With skilled practice, she silently closed and locked the front door.

Then she turned. She jerked to a halt at the sight of Teddy. "You're still up?" she said with surprise.

He nodded. "Done studying with Becky?"

"Uh, yeah. It was good. I got a test tomorrow, but I think I'm ready."

"That's good." He debated calling her out on her lie, but he didn't have the energy. He didn't want the confrontation. He didn't want to be the bad guy. He had spent all his daughter's life *not* being the bad guy to her. He wasn't sure he was up for the role. Would it break every bond he had created with his daughter? Were those bonds already broken? Maybe this was part of kids growing up. Or maybe this was what it felt like for a child to disrespect their parent.

He knew the feeling of disrespect well. From the prisoners who spit at him and called him "retard" and "cunt" and "faggot" to the coworkers who forced him to do the shit jobs because they could.

Was his daughter, his only child, one of *those* now?

He looked up at Lauren, seeing her in a new light.

She yawned, kicked off her shoes, and started to walk toward the hallway. "Anyway, we both need our beauty rest. 'night, Dad."

He wanted to tell her that he knew she was out with a boy, that he knew she was lying to him. He wanted to confront her. But the words didn't come. They rarely came to Teddy. He knew that if he challenged her, she'd simply flip it around with some wisecrack and then trot off to bed, leaving him sitting in his chair with his power and authority forever weakened.

He needed to be strong. He wanted to tell her how much he had sacrificed for her and how much he deserved her respect.

But she was walking away, and he was losing his chance. And so, he said the first sentence he could properly form.

"Your mom screwed us, Lauren."

She stopped. She looked at her dad. "Yeah. I know."

"We would've been comfortable, but—"

"It's cool. She's a financially-unscrupulous c-word."

"Everything I do is for you. It's what a father is supposed to do. It's all he's supposed to do."

"Uh, thanks."

"I'll always provide for you."

"You're doing a bang-up job."

He looked up at her.

She seemed to realize how her last statement sounded. "That totally was *not* sarcastic. I know everything I say *sounds* sarcastic, and that's my problem and I will see to improving that, but I did not mean that to be sarcastic in any way, shape, or form. We're doing fine. *You're* doing fine.

We're happy, we're healthy, we got a good thing going. So, buck up, skip." She paused and looked at his expressionless face. "Again, that last bit sounded sarcastic. Didn't mean it. Working on it."

Teddy continued to stare off. In theory, he was looking at her, but his gaze now went through and past her.

"Dad? You okay?"

His head bobbed up and down in an almost imperceptible nod.

Lauren inched her way to the hall. "Cool. Then, uh, I'm gonna go do my part to help the family finances. Gonna work on some scholarship essays. Maybe apply for a job. Stripper pays well... drug dealer... high-class escort..."

Teddy wasn't listening. He just stared off.

Lauren backed her way out of the room.

CHAPTER 30

For perhaps the first time in his life, Isaac awoke early and refreshed. No wailing alarm clock. No pounding headache that demanded attention. No urgent need to get up and urinate, lest he ruin his mattress.

His eyes drifted open and he felt...awake. Alive. Rejuvenated.

He climbed out of bed and immediately went to his computer, as he always did. A row of notifications awaited him. Since he last checked his accounts, he had sold a pry-bar for $199, and a hacksaw for $249. There was also a string of direct messages. Mostly they were from people seeking deeper evidence of authenticity.

Isaac was about to click on the first message and work his way down the column, but something stopped him. Instead, he clicked over to his photos. There, amidst his glamour shots of tools on the red velvet pedestal, was his photo of Lauren, waving the hammer and making a goofy face in front of Isaac's childhood home.

He smiled as he stared at the picture. Then he closed all the windows on his screen, not answering a single message.

Isaac showered, dressed, shaved, ate breakfast, and went out to his car. For once, he didn't feel rushed.

He pulled out of Woodburn and onto I-5, beginning his familiar commute to WAVECLIFF.

Oregon blessed its citizens with sunshine on only a handful of spring days, but when it did, there wasn't a more beautiful sight on Earth. Months of drenching rain created a vibrant green tapestry that reflected back and glimmered in the sun, standing out against the blue sky. Even when traveling on the state's largest freeway, the world felt fresh and new.

Isaac drove through Salem, riding alongside the blooming shrubs that obscured the concrete medians.

He parked his car, climbed out, and stood, soaking in the glorious Vitamin D. Even WAVECLIFF looked rejuvenated today. Bright yellow wildflowers shone against the concrete backdrop.

With some extra energy in his step, the kind that can only be generated by the sun, Isaac strutted toward the Guest Entrance.

He passed through security, checked in at the front desk, and sat in the waiting room with the mothers, wives, girlfriends, and children. He idly watched a little boy, maybe 5 years old, push wooden shapes across the wire track toy. The boy seemed bored. Isaac thought of all the places he had encountered that same toy as a child. It was a fixture of the waiting rooms of dentist offices, doctor's offices, the DMV, and, apparently, prisons. The toy hadn't evolved or changed at all in Isaac's lifetime. He wondered if any child, at any time, had ever *enjoyed* playing with it.

Probably not. What fun is it to push a wooden block around a pre-determined track?

Of course, all the smart phones were in lockers and unavailable to occupy an attention-deficit mind.

As Isaac watched the child near a breakdown from pure boredom, a corrections officer entered the waiting room.

"When I call your name, please present your state-issued ID to the clerk," the officer announced. "Once your ID is verified, you will be given a hand-stamp. At which point, form a single-file line along this wall." He held up a list and began reading off names. "O'Reilly. Garcia. Carlson. Luce. Bennett. Allen."

Isaac wasn't even paying attention. Everyone else in the room rose and went through the proper procedures before standing along the wall. Even the young boy playing with the blocks—whose grandmother had to drag him away from the toy he didn't even enjoy—knew the routine.

Meanwhile, Isaac sat.

He stared at the blocks on the wire track. He thought about walking over and playing with it, just for old time's sake. After all, this toy was meant for boys visiting their incarcerated fathers. He chuckled at the thought.

"Last call for Luce," the corrections officer announced.

Isaac turned. *Was that his name that was being said?*

The officer checked his list. "Isaac Luce visiting Walter Luce."

Isaac stood and raised his hand. "Um, that's me."

The officer gave him an annoyed glare. "Then why aren't you in line?"

"I'm supposed to have a private room. Teddy Anderton set it up."

The officer looked down at his list. Then up at Isaac. Then down at his list again. His motions were robotic and repetitive, either trying to make a show of not caring, or, perhaps, he actually just didn't care. "Isaac Luce visiting Walter Luce?"

Isaac nodded.

The guard shrugged. "Either come with me, or you'll have to return to your vehicle. But you can't wait here," he said as he swiped his badge at the door. He turned to face his visitors who were assembled against the wall, and announced, "You will follow me. You will walk single file. Please hold children by the hand."

Not having much choice, Isaac hurried to the clerk's window and handed over his ID. He received his hand stamp and managed to join the group just as the last person proceeded through the door.

The guard guided the group through twisting checkpoints, corridors, and narrow chain-link pathways. Their feet followed along with a yellow line painted on the concrete floor, leading them from Point A to Point B. Some of the children had traveled this route so frequently that they now made a little game of balancing on the yellow line running the center of the path, refusing to let their little feet fall on either side of it while keeping up with the brisk pace of the group.

It was a different route than Isaac had ever taken. The walls on this route were freshly coated in calming gray and beige paint. The signage was clear and informative, warning guests of the various rules and reminding them that they were under surveillance at all times. The echoing noise of the prison seemed more jovial along this route. Isaac could make out laughter mixed with the loud hum of daily conversation. There were none of the screams of pain, or shouts of anger, or barking of orders that he had grown accustomed to hearing.

Even the smell felt different along this path. Isaac couldn't detect those dank embedded whiffs of urine and feces that had seemingly penetrated the concrete walls of the deeper bowels of the prison. Here, there was a strong bleach scent. A freshly scrubbed and sanitized pathway for the prison's visitors.

The walk ended quickly. A few security doors, and one or two turns, and they were there.

They passed through a doorway and entered a large, concrete room with a wall of grimy, scratched glass. Divider walls with telephones mounted on them created small visiting booths.

Isaac looked around at the familiar set-up. This was the General Population Visiting Room. It was the kind of room he had seen in movies and on TV, where inmates and their guests spoke to each other by phone while being separated by glass.

He walked over to the corrections officer.

"Excuse me," Isaac said. "There's a mistake. I'm supposed to have a private room."

The officer *again* made a show of reading his list. "Isaac Luce visiting Walter Luce?"

"Yes. But Teddy Anderton gave us a private room. Check with him. My father is a V.I.P. here."

The officer cocked a bemused eyebrow. "V.I.P., hmmm?"

"Or whatever you would call it. He's on Death Row. He's famous. I know you know who he is."

The officer's face said it all. He wasn't impressed.

"He barely agreed to meet with me in the private room. There are death threats against him, or something. He's not going to come to *this* room. Please. Talk to Teddy Anderton. This is a mistake."

The officer nodded. He understood. He got it.

Then, he pointed to a chair in one of the booths. "Isaac Luce." He pointed to the chair on the other side of the glass wall. "Walter Luce."

Isaac sighed. There was no arguing with this guy. He folded his arms and took his seat. "He won't come. Not here."

He sat and waited.

After several minutes, a door buzzed.

A line of inmates in blue denim shuffled in and took their seats across from their loved ones. Hands pressed against glass, reaching for contact even through the thickness. The phones, shiny from being polished with the oils of years' worth of faces, were held tightly to ears. A hum of conversation grew and grew as inmates and guests were reunited.

The door closed behind them. All the inmates were seated and talking.

Isaac looked at the clock. Was he going to have to wait here alone for an hour. Or were they going to kick him out?

But then—*BZZZZZ*. The prisoner's door unlocked again and swung open. Guards led one final inmate into the visitation room.

The old man shuffled in.

Walter pulled out his chair and sat across from Isaac.

CHAPTER 31

Isaac and Walter stared at each other through the glass.

They simultaneously extended their arms to delicately grasp the nearby phone. They were so synchronized in their awkward movements that an outside observer might think they were mimes performing a rehearsed bit. The two men carefully held the phones to their heads, being sure to not actually touch flesh-to-plastic.

"Do they clean these things?" Walter said, his voice coming through so loud and so clear on Isaac's end that it sounded unnatural.

"We're supposed to have a private room," Isaac said.

Walter sniffed his phone. "Smells of bad breath and semen."

"Where the hell is Teddy?" Isaac said as he craned his neck, looking among the guards and toward the doors for any sign of their chaperone.

"Ain't seen him."

"He's supposed to be here. Hold on. I'm gonna ask someone." Isaac began to rise. He couldn't wait to get out of this common room full of common criminals. Didn't they know his dad was famous?

"Sure thing. I reckon it's best if we don't say nothing until our tape recorder shows up anyway," Walter said, staring off.

The words made Isaac settle back into his seat. He looked at his father. "What did you say?"

"Please. I know you think me a monster. But a moron? An idiot? You think I ain't got the eyes to see that you and Teddy got some sort of deal worked out between the two of you?"

"I don't know what you think is going on, but—"

"Give me a break. The way you speak all nice and slow when he's near. The way he hovers, puffing his chest out right in between us. Then, when I actually thought to look, it's clear as day. That ain't an extra button on his uniform. It's some kinda microphone. He's been taping this whole thing. I've just been wracking my brain trying to figure out why. It's not like the D.A. needs a confession. The only thing I can figure is that someone's paying you for them. And it's probably a pretty penny if it got you in here. Am I right?"

The two men stared at each other. Isaac made no move to deny.

Walter shrugged. "I don't mind you making a little money off me. You know, I ain't gotten you a Christmas or a birthday gift since you were eighteen. I figured this could make up for lost time. Just be straight with me. How much you getting?"

Isaac took a moment. Then he said, "I think it'll end up being about a hundred and fifty thousand."

The old man let out a whistle and raised his eyebrows. "Well *that's* worth waiting for. I guess I won't see any of that."

"Doubtful."

"It's nice to know, though, that I can still provide for you. Things being as they may. At least I ain't a total albatross 'round your neck."

He settled back into his seat. The two men looked at each other, neither having anything to say. The hum of the conversations around them drifted into their earpieces. Conversations of love. Of commitment. Of sorrow. Of longing. Isaac and Walter sat in silence while the rest of the world satisfied their needs for human contact. Finally—

"You know, I looked that up recently. Albatross," Isaac said.

Walter raised an eyebrow, ready to listen.

"I don't know why I was searching it," Isaac said. "I guess I just spend all my time on the Internet just doing stuff. Anyway, I didn't know this, but the albatross is a bird, and it's actually a good thing. In nautical mythology, or whatever, it's a good omen for an albatross to follow your ship."

Walter nodded, following along with the story, although his eyes were glazing over.

Isaac continued, "But according to some legend, or poem, or something, this one time, an albatross was following a ship and a sailor shot it with a crossbow. By killing the bird, suddenly the ship was cursed. I don't remember what 'cursed' meant. Maybe they were starving or didn't have wind or something. Anyway, everyone else was pissed and they took that dead bird and they hung it around the sailor's neck. Kind of a Scarlet Letter sort of thing."

"So everyone then will know, 'Hey, this asshole shot the bird and now we don't got no wind,' or something," Walter said.

"Yep. So, he had to wear this albatross around his neck." Isaac looked off, thinking. "I forget where the story goes from there. If they get their wind back, or if the albatross is so heavy he drowns, or whatever. Anyway, that's what an albatross is. It's both good luck and bad."

"Fascinating."

Both men nodded, feigning interest in the story.

"What else can we talk about?" Walter asked.

"I don't know."

"Anything new with the Blazers?"

"It's the offseason. And they traded their draft pick. They also don't have the salary space to sign a free agent, and all their players are too over-paid to pull off a trade. Essentially, they're stuck being mediocre for the foreseeable future."

"My kind of team."

They both forced a chuckle, then sat in silence again.

"If not basketball, then what else did we used to talk about?" Walter asked.

"We didn't."

Another silence overtook them.

T.J. PAYNE

"I met a girl."

"Oh?" Walter leaned in, showing genuine interest.

"She's fun. Smart. Got into Columbia."

"The country that makes cocaine? Or the river?"

"The college, Dad. In New York. It's like an Ivy League. Really hard to get into. You have to be really smart. And she is."

"So, she's in high school."

"She's eighteen. She was held back a year because there was some messy business with her mom leaving and taking all their money. But she came out fine. And she's older than everyone else in her class and really mature. She wants to be a journalist."

"I'm happy for you."

"Thanks."

"I hope you hold onto her. I never had much luck keeping the ladies around. I mean, not without a sturdy length of chain and a good lock."

Isaac chuckled.

Walter looked at him. "What is it?"

"I made that same joke recently."

"Great minds. Like father, like son."

"Indeed."

The conversation again lulled itself into an uncomfortable silence. For as long as Isaac could remember, the old man had been a deep and noisy breather. Ordinarily, Isaac ignored it. But with the phone system, those deep, scratchy breaths were being amplified into Isaac's ear.

"If there's no other topic that you want to discuss, then let's just jump into your act. No need to wait for Teddy."

Walter's eyes narrowed. "My *act*?"

"Never mind."

Walter gave Isaac a familiar glare. The glare that his face contorted into when he felt disrespected. "Spit it out, boy."

"So much of your story is bullshit anyway. But you seem to enjoy telling it. And it's good for business, so I won't stop you."

"And what, pray tell, is *bullshit*?"

"Everything. Your entire legend."

"Care to give me some examples?

Isaac folded his arms and leaned back in his seat. "Tell me—what tool did you use to finish them off in the basement?"

"A sledgehammer."

"Yep. That's what everyone says."

"Who's everyone?"

"The news reports. The first responders. All three books that have been published about you. They all say you bashed their heads in with a sledgehammer. Not some four-pound, stub sledge, either. No, everyone is very clear that it was a ten-pound sledge with a thirty-four-inch fiberglass handle.

"One of the local news stations had a field reporter demo that sledge on a watermelon. Exploded everywhere. There was a big uproar because the watermelon obviously was meant to represent a human head collapsing. That started this big debate on whether or not the media was glorifying what you did down there.

"Of course, by debating it, the media *ended up* glorifying what you did down there. That clip of the local news reporter got national coverage. Everyone in America saw it. They all know that The Handyman abducted seven young, strong people. He chained them in his homemade torture basement. And then he tormented them with household tools.

"When The Handyman finally grew tired of them, he went down there with a ten-pound, thirty-four-inch sledge, and bashed their heads like watermelons. It's very vivid. Unique. People either go squeamish when they hear it, or they nod and go, 'Gee, that's badass.' It's part of your legend."

Walter sat quietly, his arms crossed and his eyes lolling toward the ceiling, seemingly bored by the conversation. "Your point?" he said.

"A claw hammer, like what you used at the dorm, I can believe. But a full sledge? In the basement? Now you're getting caught up in your own myth."

"I don't for the life of me see where you're going with this."

Isaac drew in a long breath, waiting for Walter to fill in the gaps and complete the thought himself. After it became apparent that his father had no idea what he was leading toward, Isaac said, "At about the time I was finishing up high school, you were doing a roofing job—for which you're not licensed, I might add. You lost your footing and fell. You caught yourself on the gutter, but your weight carried you over and you tore all the tendons in your left hand."

Walter couldn't help but glance down at his hand. He flexed his fingers at the memory.

"You didn't go to the ER because you weren't insured for that work. I think you were also worried that someone would find out how many licenses you pretended to have but didn't. Hell, you were lying about your credentials and underbidding legitimate contractors long before those 'illegals' started doing it. You just blamed them because it was convenient."

"Careful, boy."

"And so, you went right back up there and completed the job."

"It's called 'work ethic.' Your generation could learn a thing or two about it."

Isaac made a show of sighing loudly, although in truth he wasn't too annoyed that his father was playing dumb. He had grown used to this. "My point is that although there is no medical record of your injury, you and I both know that a thirty-four-inch sledge requires *two* hands to swing. You do a good job of hiding it, but your left hand is useless."

"It's fine."

"It's probably the main reason Luce Contracting went under. With only one good hand, you couldn't do about thirty percent of the jobs you said you could. Your work went to shit. You probably qualified for disability, but you were too proud to ever apply. That would violate your tough guy image." Isaac's mouth curled into a smile as he leaned toward the glass. "I might be the only one who knows that you're nowhere near as tough as you believe. You never were."

Walter tensed his shoulders. His chest rose and fell with rapid breaths.

"You may not respect me," Walter said. "But those kids in my basement did. They feared me." He cradled the phone on his neck as he held his hands up to the glass partition. "They knew what these hands were capable of."

Isaac didn't back away. He only shook his head in a slow, patronizing movement, as if he were looking at a rabid dog that was tied down but still trying to snap at him.

"There was no way you strangled Average Joe with baling cord," Isaac said. "Or wrestled Elizabeth into your car with your bare hands."

"That's exactly what I did, *boy*."

"You totally used grandpa's rifle. You abducted them all at gunpoint. Which, frankly, isn't as badass."

Walter chewed on his lower lip. He drummed the fingers of his right hand on the table.

"You can admit it, Dad. Teddy's not here. No one's recording this. It won't go on your permanent record."

Walter looked down at his left hand. He tried to clench his fingers into a fist, as if trying to will his own narrative to be true. But he couldn't. His fingers wouldn't fully close. They came close, and anyone watching from a distance might think it a fist. But Walter and Isaac both knew that a person could slip a pencil into that gap between his fingers and his palm.

The old man's eyes fell. His breathing slowed, and his body relaxed. A deep sadness seemed to settle over his features as his right hand massaged the tendons of his left arm. Isaac stared at his face, but the old man seemed unwilling to meet his gaze.

"But you sat there," he finally said. "You didn't blink. You held your breath. You listened to it all. I've never seen you look at me like that before."

Isaac gave a half shrug. "It will sell better. Anything to perpetuate the legend of The Handyman."

Walter's eyes finally looked up and met Isaac's. "What do you think of me? What do you *really* think of me?"

"Does it matter?"

"Yes, goddamnit. I'm your father. It matters. *I'm* the only reason you're anything. I'm the only thing that kept you out of the gutter. And I would like some goddamn appreciation for all that I gave you."

"You got it, Dad. Thanks for everything."

"If it wasn't for me, you'd be living on the streets of Downtown Portland, panhandling on the bus to pay for your booze or heroin. That's if you lived that long. Odds are you would still be chained up in your mom's bathroom, eating dog food and drinking from the toilet."

The smile vanished from Isaac's lips. His body tensed. His eyes darted at his father.

"We said we wouldn't talk about Mom."

"I spent my life tip-toeing around your poor feelings toward that fucking degenerate cunt. No more."

"She tried to save me from you."

"Bullshit. You only exist because she wanted money outta me. She was a shitty secretary who couldn't file or type or add worth a damn. And still, apparently, I didn't give her enough salary. She wanted more. And she was willing to give me *anything* for it. I was never good with the ladies, but your mom was just so pathetic and easy, it was impossible not to. I am a man, after all. And she was a woman who needed money."

"Stop it."

"So, every night as we locked up shop, in exchange for a few bucks, I'd have my way with her. Remember how when you were young—and it was summer break, and I had nowhere else to dump you—I'd sometimes bring you into the office, sit you down at my desk, and let you play with the paper, pens, and staplers, making some kid shit? Remember that desk? That's where you were conceived. Because I was fucking your mom on it every night. And I had no illusions that she was into my looks or nothing. No. She fucked me for money. And not much money at that.

"When the inevitable happened, she made sure I knew it. She made sure I knew it was a boy. She spent all nine of those long months threatening to abort you. She'd run off, not come into work, and then call me up, all in tears, crying about how she was at some abortion clinic right then and there. If only she had more money, then maybe she could hold onto you a little while longer.

"I knew these were lies, but what could I do? That was my son she was threatening. I'd beg and plead for her to come back. She didn't have to come to work no more. She could live in my house. I put a new mortgage on that home so I could buy her new clothes, a new car, anything she wanted. Just to keep her satisfied because the moment she wasn't, she'd run back to the abortion clinic. And if she wasn't threatening abortion, she'd threaten to start hitting the pills.

"Oh boy, was she a junkie. I kept her clean as possible, but I reckon she snuck a few hits in on the side. I admit I was fairly relieved when you actually managed to come out with two eyes, two arms, two legs, and a working brain."

T.J. PAYNE

Isaac tried not to betray any emotions, but he could feel his jaw clenching and his teeth grinding. He thought about interrupting but worried it would give the old man the fight he was obviously pining for.

Walter continued, "The moment you were outside that woman, breathing in the air and crying your lungs out, well, I think she saw her power over me slipping away. She started hitting the pills real bad at that point. Said it was for the labor pains. I didn't much care. If drugs and booze could get her to shut up and sleep, well, then they were all right in my book.

"Besides, it's not like I needed her for anything. I was the one did all the changing and feeding and holding you. And, boy, you were a colicky son-of-a-bitch. Every night, 1 a.m. to 4 a.m., you would cry bloody murder. And I'd hold you and bounce you. And, yeah, I'd try to get whiskey down your throat to put you to bed. Lock me up, why don't ya."

The old man stared off. His eyes glistened, and a smile spread on his face. The memories had started off as complaints, but there was a fondness emerging beneath Walter's wrinkles and scowl. A joy from another era. These seemed to actually be good memories for him.

"You know what my first real 'Handyman' repurposing of a tool was?" Walter said. "When you were a baby, I built a wooden box with a wooden base. I put a power sander in that box and just let it run all night. Damn thing, I'm sure, was a major fire hazard. And I know they now got white noise machines on phones and what not. But at the time, it was the only sound that could shut you up. You grew up sleeping with a power sander humming nearby. If that ain't the childhood of The Handyman's son, I don't know what is.

"That life only lasted a few months, though. I had you by my side twenty-four hours a day. I'd take care of you all night, then bring you to the office during the day. Lordy, I didn't get a wink of sleep that whole time. But it was okay. I couldn't complain.

"Your mom, though... She bitched and moaned that the allowance I provided her wasn't enough. I shoulda realized something was up the moment she took an interest in caring for you, but, I'll be honest, I needed the help. I was on a job site for a week which wasn't no place for a baby. She said you could stay home, and she'd look after you.

"Well, next thing I know, I'm coming home one night to an empty house. Just straight up cleaned out. She moved you off to some apartment I didn't know about. She gets her a lawyer and starts hitting me up for child support. The State always sides with the mother, no matter how piss-poor and deranged they are, so I was shit outta luck.

"I paid up the child support, and yeah, it was more than I could afford. I'm pretty sure it all went to drugs. She'd be blitzed outta her mind for days on end with heroin. Her way of caring for you was to lock you in the bathroom. You lived on the floor, eating dog food."

Isaac shook his head. "This is all bullshit."

"Ain't bullshit, boy."

"I don't remember any of this."

"You were five."

"A five-year-old can remember things, Dad. I think I would remember sitting on the floor of the bathroom eating dog food."

"Would you?"

Isaac didn't move a muscle.

"Hell, I knew your mom was a psychotic whore, but even I didn't believe she was treating you so bad at first. But the cops who found you clued me in."

"You got a police report or anything? Maybe some photos? Proof?"

Walter smirked. "You know I don't. But it don't change the truth. That woman knew how to twist you around her finger. She was a conniving little cunt."

"Watch it, Dad."

"I'll grant her this, she felt bad 'bout how shitty of a mom she was. She'd come outta her stupor, swear she was getting sober, and she'd spoil you rotten. Ain't that what you remember of your mom? Her taking you to the store and letting you buy any toy you want? Then some ice cream later? Eating pizza rolls for breakfast, lunch and dinner? That's all you'd say when you came back to live with me. 'Mom used to...' 'Mom used to...' 'Mom used to...' She used to let you have *this*, she'd let you do *that*. I didn't have the heart to tell you what she really was."

Walter leaned in, finally slowing down so that his next words could truly hit their mark. "That weren't no aneurysm that felled her, though I told you that's what it was. She was a plain, old suicide by overdose. Took so much at one time that her heart just shut down."

Isaac's jaw clenched.

"It just went 'click.'"

Isaac took it in without saying a word.

"You're lucky she was a drama queen who needed attention. She taped a note to her apartment door. Took half a day before some neighbor actually took the time to read it, though. That neighbor called the cops. They busted in. Found you locked in the bathroom. Your mom was dead on the bed. I know you remember some of this. I know it's flashing something in that brain of yours, connecting two and two together. Some old dream of yours that your mind's been chewing over, but just hasn't been able to spit out or swallow down. Ain't it?"

Isaac's dry throat gulped. His eyes blinked. But besides that, he kept his face cold and solid. He merely shook his head. "Nope. Nothing. Doesn't ring a bell."

"I guess that's your survival mechanism at work." Walter looked off with a philosophical look plastered on his face. "Amazing thing, the human body and mind. It's like it goes into energy saving mode. Keeps itself from frying out. For instance, I was worried about those girls, down in the basement, bleeding. I planned to keep 'em down there more than a month, and I ain't never bought a tampon in my life. Didn't intend to. I was perfectly fine to let them wash their shit down that grate with a hose, but there's something about period blood that really yucks me out. But lo-and-behold, you know what? Captive women don't bleed. Body shuts down non-essential systems."

"Women get pregnant in captivity all the time. Which means they're probably menstruating in captivity. Which means, you're probably full of shit again."

Walter shrugged. "Wasn't my experience. From what I saw, them girls stopped getting their periods. Just like your mind stopped remembering. I guess what I'm saying is your brain is like a vagina, boy."

The old man folded his arms and leaned back, waiting for that last dig to really embed itself into his son.

Isaac let out a little laugh. "I bet you thought that was quite an insult. You're going to be disappointed to learn that your son does not share your weird disgust, or anger, or phobia at the concept of vaginas. Yet another example of how my generation has failed to meet your standard of *real* manhood." He crouched forward. "You truly are a loser."

At those words, Walter leaned in. The two men's faces, separated by glass, were just inches apart.

"That's right, disrespect me," Walter said. "You ain't never wanted nothing to do with me. When I took you back and showered you with all the warmth and love I could muster, I thought we might actually have something. Maybe I could form one genuine human fucking bond in this shitty world. But you know what? You're an angsty little shit, and you always were an angsty little shit. I took you back. I raised you. I fed you. I clothed you. I *saved* you. A simple 'thank you' woulda been enough."

Walter's breathing was speeding up. His right hand was now clenching the phone so tightly that his knuckles were losing circulation.

"And what was my payment?" Walter said, his voice rising above the hum of prison conversation. "You spending all your youth mourning some junkie slut. You blamed me for her death. Oh, I've killed people, but no one never gave me cause to do them harm like that skank did. But I never laid a hand on her on account of her carrying my flesh and blood. And still, you hated me."

"Oh, fuck it. I'm done listening to this bullshit. Everything you say is a lie."

The veins began to bulge on Walter's forehead. "I'm telling you the goddamn truth! You built yourself a lie, you made your bed in a lie, and you lived blissfully in that lie. You're the one telling tall tales to feel better."

"Whatever."

"Fuck you, boy."

"I just want the truth. For once in your fucking life, give me some truth."

"I been giving you the truth."

"Really? Then tell me, Dad... The question that started this whole fucking rant of yours."

"What question?"

"The question you're not answering."

"What the fuck are you talking about?"

"How does a one-armed builder swing a sledgehammer?"

"I didn't! Elizabeth did!"

Isaac's jaw hung slightly open. He never expected to get to this point. He had convinced himself that it would be fine, best even, if his dad just spun stories. Give the audience what they want.

But now the pieces were fitting into place.

"Tell me," Isaac said. "I want to hear the rest."

Walter's lower lip rose up and nibbled on his mustache.

Isaac leaned closer. "What happened?"

"I ended it. Well, I had Elizabeth end it."

"Why?"

The old man's face scrunched up as he gazed off, as if trying to determine the answer to that question himself. From the lines on his face, it appeared he knew the answer, but was searching for a better one. Finally, he shrugged. "They just really started to stink."

CHAPTER 32

Smell is a funny thing. You just get used to it.

I can't tell you how many jobs I went on where I stepped into so-and-so's house only to be hit by the worst goddamn smell you can imagine. From my experience, you can tell you got a problem brewing on your property by either a rotten smell or a nasty sound. Those are your first signs. But a lotta people, well, they don't like to call a handyman or contractor at the *first* sign of a problem. They like to wait it out. And then, once they've gotten used to the problem being there, they think that it done fixed itself. But it's not that the smell of some dead animal or a sewage leak got better. They just got used to it. Humans like to think that we're too smart to let ourselves get boiled like a frog, but that's exactly how we are and exactly how we do.

Lemme tell you—problems don't ever just fix themselves. If you hear a squealing in your car engine, well, you didn't fix it by turning on the radio. But that's how people think.

It's only once things get bad that they actually call someone to come in and help. And that someone was often me.

Their toilet would finally back up into their shower and they'd call me to fix the plumbing. Well, more often than not, I'd find out that their sewer line had been backing up into their crawl space for months, filling the underside of their house with their own shit. They must've smelled it back then, but they just ignored it.

The key to keeping a house from falling apart is maintenance, maintenance, maintenance.

And then more maintenance.

You can rig temporary solutions, but you can't just patch over problems. You got mold growing on your bathroom walls? A coat of paint will hide it, but it ain't fixed the underlying problem. There's moisture collecting there somewhere. You either got a leak, or you need to install better ventilation. You gotta be paying attention, and you gotta roll up your sleeves and be willing to do the dirty work.

That's where I failed.

I hung about a hundred air fresheners in the stairwell and along the basement ceiling, trying to mask that wretched stench. I pointed a floor fan out the front door and tried to blast that foulness out. I was masking the problem, but not digging down into the foundational issues.

To be honest, it was a sign of laziness.

The stench from that basement must've been festering for months. I'm sure it was. It had to be. If some salesman stopped by the door, they'd have smelled it at the driveway. It wouldn't surprise me in the slightest to find out that the Perkins family, almost two acres away, got a whiff of it now and again if the wind was just right. I just got used to it is all.

That whole business with the screwdriver in their ears? Well, they became infected. Covered in pus. Bacteria everywhere. But I think, more than anything, the smell wasn't a sign of their bodies decaying as much as it was their minds. They gave up. They stopped trying to live. And once they stopped trying to live, they stopped taking care of themselves.

That dog chow may contain all your necessary vitamins and nutrients, but a human intestine ain't meant to feast on that for too long. They all had either wretched diarrhea or wretched constipation. Real nasty stuff. And no one was bothering to shit at the grate anymore. I guess it didn't help that I removed their hose privileges for a week after their escape attempt, and so, there was nothing to wash it down with.

I think it had only been about six months all in all, which is a fairly short length of time considering how long some folk are kept in captivity. But hey, I was new at this. Anyway, at about the six-month mark, I woke up and suddenly that smell my nose and brain had been suppressing... whew. It had been boring deeper and deeper into my head, and it finally broke through.

Couldn't mask it. Couldn't vent it. Couldn't ignore it.

My house smelled like death.

I climbed outta bed that morning, put my nose to that heater vent, and the wafting whiff of those bodies filtering their way through that grate made me scrunch up my face. I nearly puked right then and there.

Even then, I didn't do nothing about it.

I went about my day. Choked down my breakfast. Read the paper.

That odor clung to it all.

I even tried watching TV, and managed to fall asleep and take a nap. But a foul smell can seep its way into even the deepest dreams. I woke with a start, right there in the recliner.

I made it all the way to dinner that night. Meat and potatoes. But, boy, I had to work that food around my mouth. They say that smell and taste are the closest linked of the senses. Well, every bite tasted like a shit-encrusted corpse.

I had to do something.

So, I set down my knife and fork, and I stood up from the table.

Went to the garage. Got me a respirator, a sack of shop rags, and a sledgehammer. I opened that basement door and carried them all down.

It was time.

When I stepped back into that basement, respirator on my face and sledgehammer in hand, I realized how much I had neglected my toys. They had become too much work.

It was like that dog you used to have.

Buddy.

Oh, you wanted a dog so bad. You thought it would be so much fun. And I thought it would teach you a thing or two about responsibility. When I first brought Buddy home, you were in love. You must've been about twelve or thirteen. I ain't never seen you so happy. Over the moon. You used to read to Buddy. You used to sleep with Buddy. You would curl up next to that beast and watch TV. Hell, you would play fetch for hours, and I mean hours, with that there dog.

I got you that dog because you promised me it was the one thing that could bring a smile to your face. You were a sullen little son-of-a-bitch, so I figured it was worth a shot.

And it made you happy. And you took good care of him, as you promised you would. Our house, and your life, suddenly seemed all that much brighter.

It warmed my heart to see you laugh again, especially after all that shit you had to go through with your mom. The three of us, why, we were a team. You and I never had much to do or talk about, but we could walk Buddy together.

Those were good times. Maybe the best times.

But then, one day, you got lazy.

I don't know when exactly it happened. I wouldn't have let it happen if I knew. But you must've just told yourself, "I don't feel like picking up Buddy's shit today. I'll let it sit there and I'll pick up two piles of shit tomorrow."

Tomorrow came and went.

There were no consequences for your laziness. So you just up and kicked that can down the road.

Leaving Buddy's shit in the backyard for a day became two days became a week became a month. Before I knew it, our entire backyard was dotted with doggy landmines.

At that point, it was too much shit for you to bother picking up at all. Also, you didn't like going back there for fear that you'd step in some of it. Once it became uncomfortable setting foot in our backyard, you just kinda stopped playing with Buddy.

He was spending more time back there alone, looking for something to entertain himself with. This meant he was more likely to pick up fleas, or roll in dirt, or step in his own shit. He started smelling, and he always had that layer of crud on him. And so, you didn't like cuddling with him in front of the TV or in bed no more. The problems just kept snowballing from there.

Didn't take too long before I was coming home from work, it was dark and I was tired, and I'd find that I'd have to deal with all the responsibilities of caring for *your* dog.

I never complained. I loved that dog too.

But eventually, the inevitable happened.

Through your neglect, Buddy dug his way under the back fence. I know you remember that. It was about the time you were graduating high school. You were bummed. I ain't never seen you so sad. You and I spent a week making flyers and driving around the neighborhood, calling out his name. We tried really hard to get him back. That week, with the loss of your dog, was probably the best father-son time you and I ever had.

But he was gone.

I thought back to Buddy when I walked down those steps into the basement that last time. I had neglected my pets. I hadn't maintained the situation properly. They were sitting in their own filth. Perhaps one of them was even going to dig their way out one of these days, like Buddy did.

It was time to clean up my mess.

When I stepped into that basement, they barely moved. The days of them crying and cowering and begging were long gone. Their infected wounds had gone gangrene. They were wasting away. Just pale, scarred shells of humans.

All but Elizabeth, that is.

That ounce of extra care I gave her over the months had made a world of difference. Oh, sure, she didn't look too pretty. But she had more flesh and color in her cheeks than the rest of them combined.

I walked around the perimeter, nudging each one with my foot. If any of them wanted to, they could have grabbed me at this point. Dragged me down. Choked the life out of me, like they tried before. But they didn't have any fight left in them. I'd kick 'em with my foot and they'd curl up into a little ball like one of those roly-poly bugs.

I nudged Chink-Woman. She didn't move at all.

"How long has Chink-Woman been dead?" I called out.

No answer. Not even murmurs. Their ears were long gone. The infections had finished off what the screwdriver started. But it wasn't just that they couldn't hear me. It was as if their little mushy minds couldn't even understand language no more. Or life.

I gave Chink-Woman one hard kick with my boot, just to be sure. She flopped about like a squirrel that's had its neck snapped by a pit-bull.

Then I went over to Elizabeth. I set down the sledge and kneeled by her side.

"Elizabeth, today is the day," I said. "Do you want to leave here?"

Her head gave a faint nod. Maybe it was a muscle spasm or a trick of light, I don't know. But it sure seemed like a nod to me. She was agreeing to join me.

"Very well," I said.

I took the key out of my cardigan pocket and unlocked the padlock that fastened the shackle to her leg. It fell off and clanged on the concrete floor. It was a sharp sound. Made me wince. None of my pets moved at all, though.

"Stand," I said.

But she didn't stand. She sat there. Nothing tethered her to the floor no more. She just couldn't get her legs under her. Or she just didn't care to.

So, I pulled her to her feet. She swayed.

Until recently, she had been exercising. She was a runner when I first met her, and I imagine that she was the kind of person who needed to keep the blood flowing to stay alive. When I used to watch them through the keyhole, she was always doing little stretches or pushups or leg lifts. Even when chained up, she kept her muscles strong and toned. She used to lead the others in those exercises too. Kept them fit. Kept them hopeful.

After the screwdriver thing, that all went away.

I put the sledge in her hands. At first, the weight almost pulled her over, but she corrected pretty quick.

"The trick to a sledge is to start with your hands far apart on the handle," I told her, trying to keep my voice calm and teacher-like. "This helps you hit the target. Then, as you swing, bring your hands together at the end of the handle. This is where the power comes from."

I mimed the motion a bit. I can't tell you how often it pisses me off to see these big, tough Hollywood actors swinging an axe or a sledge in a movie and doing it all wrong. You waste a whole lot of energy when you don't use a tool the way it's meant to be used.

Once I had mimed it a few times, I told her to try it on Average Joe.

She didn't move at first.

I gently reminded her that she had to at least try. It was the only way that this was gonna end.

It seemed as though maybe I was asking a bit too much of her to crack a skull like that, especially of someone who was her friend. The least I could do was give her the common courtesy of not making her *watch* his skull collapse. So, I took one of those shop rags and draped it over Average Joe's face. I felt that should do the trick. I was like Sir Walter Raleigh, keeping my maiden's feet from getting splatter on them.

Average Joe moaned out a soft, "No... No..." as Elizabeth did her best to raise up the sledge. It was adorable, almost childish, the way she had to give all her strength to swinging it over her head. Then she brought it down real good.

When it comes to swinging a sledge or an axe, at a certain point, gravity takes over. It came down hard and—

WHACK!

It smacked right into the concrete next to Average Joe's skull.

"Try again," I said. I tried to keep my voice patient. It was a learning experience for her, after all.

She lifted the sledge and swung it again.

WHACK!

And again it slammed into the concrete.

"You need to have confidence in your swing. Keep your eye on the target. Now try again."

She took a deep breath. Her muscles really struggled to swing that sledge. She was kinda like a new kid on the crew, and I was the foreman simply teaching her how to do her job properly.

And so, up went the sledge again.

Average Joe's face was covered by that shop rag, but he seemed to be coming around to what was happening. His head started shaking. He managed to croak out, "Elizabeth... please..."

CRACK!

Those were his last words.

That hammer head found its way true to that target.

To be honest, I don't even remember what it looked or sounded like. My eyes weren't on Average Joe. My gaze stayed firmly planted on Elizabeth. I must've been beaming. I was so proud. It was a good swing. Better'n most movie stars.

But I couldn't hold up this train. I had to keep things moving.

I went around and laid shop rags over all their faces. I was impressed how much it kept Average Joe's splatter to a minimum. Always a plus. "And now Trixie," I said.

Elizabeth shuffled over, dragging the sledge across the concrete floor.

"Firm and quick."

Trixie managed to mutter, "No... no..."

At least I think that's what she was saying. I could barely hear it.

Elizabeth lined up her swing and—

CRACK!

"That was good," I said. "But it was more cheek than temple. I think you'll need a second round to finish her off. Whenever you're ready."

CRACK!

"Very good. Chink-Man next?"

Elizabeth staggered over to her next spot.

WHACK!

Her swing bounced off the concrete by Chink-Man's head.

"Eye on the target, not on the hammer."

CRACK!

"Very good. Now do Good-Sam."

She shuffled over to her next spot and—

WHACK!

The sledge slammed into the concrete again

I admit that I was getting frustrated that each of these was taking multiple swings. Some of these handy skills are easy to learn but hard to improve. That's what your generation don't get. If you don't know how to do a good, strong, confident swing of a hammer, you're likely to bend the nail or send it in crooked.

It's as if kids are so worried about hitting their thumb that they end up fucking up the swing. But that's neither here nor there. I was determined to help her.

"Follow through."

CRACK!

So much for Good Sam.

"You're getting better. Now see if you can do Hitch in one."

She squared up her shoulders, like I told her.

She spaced her feet for balance, like I told her

She heaved that sledge around her head, up in a perfect arc, like I told her.

Her hands slid together toward the end of the handle, building up all the innate momentum of all the weight of the head. It was beautiful. I couldn't have swung it better myself. A worker on the Transcontinental Railroad couldn't have had a purer swing. It was a sign.

CRACK!

"One hit wonder."

CHAPTER 33

I stood in awe for a while, just beaming at my girl.

Carnage was everywhere.

Blood flowed to the drain. Skull chunks lay about.

Elizabeth swayed on her feet. She didn't seem to mind nothing. She had had a long day and looked a little tired. I figured she'd earned herself a bit of R&R.

"I'll clean up," I said. "You can drop it."

She did exactly as told. The sledge fell from her hand and clanked onto the floor.

I pointed her toward the stairs. "Go on up and hang a right through the kitchen. You'll see the bathroom. I left a towel and some of my son's old clothes for you. Go ahead and draw yourself a bath. Or a shower. No, a bath. I don't want you slipping. Safety first. Help yourself to the soap and shampoo that's already in there. There's a towel and a washcloth hanging on the rack up there too. If you feel like draining the water and doing two, three baths just to get the grime off, go right ahead. I got my work cut out for me down here. I'll be awhile."

I turned to start planning how I was gonna clean up this mess, and I noticed she wasn't moving. Silly me, I hadn't given her permission.

"You may go," I said.

And with that, she ambled toward the door. She held that handrail tight and took one wobbly step after another up them stairs.

"Take your time. Your legs are weak," I called after her. "Holler if you need anything."

She thumped her way on up the stairs and into the kitchen. A moment later, I could hear the sound of water running in the bathroom. She was drawing the bath. Time for me to get to work.

I went on out to the back yard and grabbed the best hose I had. Didn't want to use that little nubbin of a hose that I had given them. Thing couldn't coil worth a damn.

So, first thing's first, I rinsed down those bodies and that floor. This is the reason I installed a drain system in this room in the first place. I could have always made them piss and shit in a bucket, but I wanted this drain for cleanup.

I sprayed down their bodies, trying to wash the blood off the floor and trying to get the smell to go down there with it. It was only somewhat successful. Their heads just kept draining more and more blood. Holy hell, a human body holds a lot of fluid. And, shucks, I had half a dozen to mess with.

After spraying them down, best I could, I trudged out to the garage and grabbed me a couple sacks of kitty litter. Ain't nothing better for eating odor or cleaning up a mess. At least not for the price.

So, I went around, dumping that over all the bodies and all the heads. I figured if I were to let that soak in overnight then I'd be able to shovel it all into garbage sacks and dump it in the yard by morning.

When I was up in the garage, I saw I had a leftover twenty-five-pound bag of agro lime. I figured, what in the heck am I saving this for? Lime disinfects and cuts down on smell, right? I cut the corner off the bag, lifted the whole damn thing on my shoulder, and let all that white powder pour on out over every body and piece of skin I could find. That lime had a real strong scent, but better that than shit, am I right?

And that was that.

I knew I'd have to pound out all that mortar and brick I used to seal up the window, but that was a job for tomorrow. I was tired. Didn't have it in me for this type of work like I used to.

Now, I know what you're thinking. I gave Elizabeth free reign of the house for a solid forty-five minutes. Wasn't I scared that she turned the water on in that tub and then high-tailed it out the front door?

Not on your life. I never had me a doubt.

You know that sinking feeling you get when you're walking down the street toward your car, and you know you parked it here somewhere, and you start thinking, *My God, it must've been stolen or towed or something.* Well, I was kinda surprised that when I walked on into that kitchen and didn't hear nothing, I didn't have that feeling. And when I turned the corner and could see down the hall into the bathroom and couldn't see her? I still wasn't scared.

Now, *that's* trust.

I strolled on up into the bathroom without a single one of my heartbeats ramping up at all. And, lo and behold, sitting on the floor behind the vanity, fully cleaned, dried, and dressed, there she was.

Elizabeth had done as I said and waited patiently.

"Come. I have your room all made up," I said as I offered out my hand. She took it and let me pull her to her feet.

We went down the hall and walked on into your old room. You'd taken most of your stuff with you. All that you had left in that room was three posters. One of Clyde Drexler dunking the ball. One of some babe in a bikini eating a hamburger. And one of an alien with a doobie saying, "Take me to your dealer." Real classy boy I had. It's a small wonder you didn't go to college.

Anyway, I said, "Let me change the sheets. You sit and relax."

She took a seat at your old desk, that big oak one you and I found at that yard sale. Remember when we spent the weekend stripping, sanding and staining it? You wanted more and more coats of finish. We ended up with about ten layers of polyurethane on that desk. You couldn't scratch that thing with a hatchet.

Elizabeth sat real quiet as I changed the sheets.

I wasn't used to the company. I figured I better make some conversation. "What do you think I should do?" I asked. "Bust out that tiny window and hoist them on through into the backyard? We could throw them in a wheelbarrow then and bury them off in the woods. We'd have to dig pretty deep to keep the coyotes from finding them."

I finished tugging the corners of your old red flannel sheets over the mattress. I started shaking the pillows into the pillowcases.

Elizabeth kept staring off. Her eyes seemed to be adjusting to the world outside the basement. I had kept her red purse on that desk, and that's where her eyes finally fell. I wanted to make her feel at home. I wanted her to have something that belonged to her, you know, like giving a kid a teddy bear or something. It told her I cared.

The purse sat there in front of her. She stared at it with this faint look of recollection in her eyes.

"I could also hack up the slab and bury them in the basement," I blabbered on.

She set the purse on her lap while I was busy tucking in the sheet. She opened the purse and pulled out her wallet. Her driver's license fell out right onto her lap. It was in there loose because I had taken it out so I could look up her name and keep tabs on the police search for her. Anyway, she picked the license up and stared at the picture.

"It would be a lot of work to dig the concrete up. But then I wouldn't have to move the bodies. Wouldn't run the risk of someone hiking through the woods and seeing me dig graves. I could dig right under the house then lay concrete over everything. That would keep the critters away."

The bed was finally made. I went over and stood behind her, looking over her shoulder at the driver's license photo in her hand.

T.J. PAYNE

"You go and rest yourself," I said. "I think you're going to be very comfortable here. I'll cook you dinners. I'll do the cleaning. We can watch games together. Maybe we can get a dog. Do you like dogs?"

She gently nodded her head.

"And Christmas is around the corner. That'll be fun. Do you like Christmas?"

Again, she nodded her head as if it were on a swivel.

I put a hand on her shoulder and turned her chair around so that the two of us were facing the mirrored closet door. We stared at that image for a while—her sitting, me standing and resting my hand on her shoulder. We looked like one of those old-timey family portraits. I smiled.

"You were in a bad place. But I got you out. You're safe here."

The room was quiet.

"Elizabeth? Is there something you would like to say to me?"

Her voice was weak, but it had no hesitation. "Thank you," she said.

It was all I ever wanted to hear.

"You're welcome."

CHAPTER 34

Isaac's eyes snapped up.

The words *thank you* bounced around his mind.

Memories from his childhood flooded in.

He thought of the many nights when he was a kid, sitting on the couch, watching a basketball game, as — *DING!* — a timer went off in the kitchen. He thought of his father, weary from a day's labor, rising and shuffling off into the other room, only to return with a plate of steaming pizza rolls. All for Isaac.

He thought back to summer evenings in the backyard. His father grilled steaks on a charcoal barbeque. Never gas. Walter would pile charcoal in the grill, then he would spray lighter fluid on a mound of cotton balls that lay on the concrete patio. Together, Walter and Isaac would shove the cotton balls into the tiny holes evenly spaced around the bottom of the grill. Walter let Isaac choose where to light first.

And he thought of the time his father redid the fence boards that enclosed the backyard. Isaac was ten at the time. He remembered his father giving him the hammer and guiding his hand toward the head of the nail as a demonstration.

"The power comes from the elbow, not the wrist," his father had told him. "Follow through. Be confident in your strike. If you do it right, you should be able to pound that nail all the way in with one blow. Go ahead. Give it a try."

Isaac had lined up his strike and released a confident, powerful swing. Just as his father had predicted, the nail buried itself into the board, all the way up to its head. He remembered turning and grinning proudly at his father.

"One hit wonder," Walter had said as he ruffled his son's hair.

In none of those memories could Isaac picture himself saying two simple words. *Thank you.*

He thought back to these recent conversations with this father:

Would it have killed you to say thank you?

You and your generation don't know the meaning of the word gratitude.

I saved you. A simple "thank you" woulda been enough.

***

Isaac stared through the glass at Walter.

A lifetime of realization hit him.

Walter had stopped talking, seemingly aware that the pieces had finally clicked together in Isaac's mind. The two men looked at each other in silence, both clutching the phone to their ear and waiting for the other to break through the spell.

It was finally Isaac who spoke. "This... this is all about *me*?"

"Don't flatter yourself, boy," Walter scoffed.

"I thought... *everyone* thought that you were grooming them for—"

"I know what people think."

"But this whole time... this whole time you were grooming a... a..."

The corners of Walter's eyes shimmered with the hints of tears.

"A daughter. A child," Isaac finally choked out.

Walter shrugged. "Doesn't really matter now."

"I just don't understand."

"I thought I could create something with Elizabeth. Something you and I never had."

"You tortured her. You tortured them all."

"If I've learned one thing, it's that life is torture."

"It's not the same, and you know it."

"Is it? I gave you everything, boy. I poured my heart into you. Pampered you. Provided for you. Loved you. And you ain't never appreciated me. Never gave me no gratitude. The words *thank you* never managed to slip through those lips of yours. What I couldn't accomplish with you in years, I accomplished with Elizabeth in months."

"But you... you..." Isaac couldn't form the words or the thoughts behind them. He tried to say something. All that came out was, "What happened next?"

"It all got fucked up. Like things usually do." Walter stared off as his eyes glistened in the wistful memory. "I was so close. It was all almost so perfect. It was like that year I built you that Christmas tree lot. You were so happy. You were so grateful. Boy, every time I showed you some new plywood snowman I'd cut and painted, the eyes would bug right outta your skull. Just for a second, you actually loved me.

"And then, when no customers came, I had to watch you come down off of that high. You'd look at me with those sullen eyes of yours, and I could tell you blamed me for God knows what reason. I ponied up good money for ads in all the papers. But the big warehouse stores in Portland had started selling trees for twenty bucks that exact year. They took a loss on those trees just to get the customers in the door. For the first time in the history of fucking Christmas, ain't no one driving out to the boonies, past our house, to cut their own tree. It happened *the year* we set up shop."

"I don't understand."

"Every time I feel my life is about to turn that corner, that I'm about to taste an ounce of the success I've worked so hard for, it gets snapped outta my grasp for the dumbest reason. And it's always shit that's outta my control."

"What are you saying?"

"Stores selling Christmas trees fucked over my chances with *you*. Mirrored closet doors fucked up my time with Elizabeth."

"What?"

CHAPTER 35

I installed those mirrored closet doors back in, well, the 70s? I guess they still use them now, mostly in small apartments and stuff, but it was really the style back in the day. Hell, the thought was that if you just installed mirrors on as many surfaces as possible, it made people feel like you just doubled the square footage of your place.

There was always a part of my mind that wanted to tear it out and get rid of it. I don't care to look at myself much anyway. But those damn things are a real pain to dispose of. You can cut yourself pretty bad if you try to bash one up. You gotta do this whole tape and cardboard thing, and it was just more work than I ever wanted to deal with.

So, those mirrored closet doors stayed up.

Elizabeth sat at your old desk, and I stood behind her. We both looked at ourselves in that mirror.

I had her. She was all mine. Ain't no one ever gave me a lick of love in my whole damn life, but here she was, *thanking me* for saving her.

But I pushed too far. We looked at ourselves, our new family, in that mirror. I called her beautiful. I stroked her hair. I allowed myself to dream what it would be like to finally have a partner, a friend, a daughter who loved and depended on me

She had that red purse of hers in her lap and her driver's license in her hand.

That's what broke her.

She looked down at the photo of a girl who didn't exist no more.

Then she looked in the mirror at a girl I thought was beautiful, but who she probably couldn't recognize.

In truth, her face had become drawn and tight. Her eyes had these deep bags and were a bit sunken. She was always skinny, but now she was all bone. Her skin had become white with a bit of yellow sprinkled in.

I knew she didn't look her best, but I was prepared to nurse her back. She just needed some good food and some good rest in a bed. She was gonna be fine. She was gonna be comfortable. She was gonna be happy.

But something deep in her cracked at the sight of herself. I saw that tear form in her eye. But I convinced myself it was from happiness. She tensed up. But I convinced myself it was just her body adjusting to her new life. I saw her hand reach down into her purse. I told myself she's just going for a lip balm. Maybe a lipstick. Maybe she was trying to make herself pretty again.

Her mouth opened.

She couldn't form words.

A sound started rolling out her mouth. It started soft, like a train whistle in the distance. But then it grew and grew and grew.

Soon, she was howling.

It was an animal's scream. I heard plenty of yelps and hollers down in that basement, but I never heard anything like this. It was a screech, like the kind you hear from an angry dog that just got its leg cut off. A high-pitched squeal that can cut through walls.

Her hand came out of that purse and she clutched that can of pepper spray. It was the same can she tried to use on me when I took her. The same one that I scooped back up into her purse because I didn't want to leave any evidence at the scene.

The same one that I plumb forgot all about.

My defenses were down.

In the basement, she had had every chance to slam that sledgehammer into my kneecap and run away. When I stayed behind to tidy up, she could have gone right out the front door. She didn't. And I trusted her for it. I never expected her to turn on me.

There was a large part of me, and this is true, that felt that whatever anger she was feeling could be tamped down by the purity of a father's love.

But that didn't matter to Elizabeth.

Before I could stop her, she aimed that pepper canister right at my face and unloaded it into my eyes.

I screamed.

I tried to shove her away. But she kept spraying and spraying until there was no spray left.

I couldn't see anymore. I couldn't feel anything.

The stinging, crying pain in my face drowned out all my other senses. The spray had gone directly into my eyes, and now felt like it was burrowing beneath my pupils and into my brain.

In my blindness, I cried out, "Elizabeth! Stop this!"

The best I could do was feel around blindly in that darkness. My arms found her, and so, I wrapped her up and pushed her to the floor. I groped around, trying to find her wrists so I could pin her to the floor until she calmed down.

In that darkness, I heard the purse fall from her lap. Its contents clattered all over the floor. Suddenly, a searing pain shot through my leg. All I could hear was my own voice crying out in agony. I let her go. My hands reached down to my leg, toward that pulsing, rippling fire that shot up and down from knee to hip.

It was a small pocket knife.

I'd gone through that purse a dozen times. I'd set each of those objects out on the desk and studied them, sniffed them, touched them. I'd seen that goddamn knife each and every time. And each and every time, I'd set it back in the purse. Nowhere in my mind did I ever think that she could betray me like this. Not with such a tiny blade. But sure enough, she had plunged that little knife straight into my fucking leg and given it one good twist.

I snapped back to the task at hand. I had to be back in the moment. I had to act quickly. I had to stop that girl before she did any more damage to me, herself, or the life we were going to have together.

My eyes opened for a brief moment to get my bearings. The world was blurry and on fire. The stinging became too great and I had to shut them again. I groped around, looking for her, but she was nowhere to be found.

I dragged myself to my feet and stumbled out into the hallway. I could just make her out through the burning tears that swamped my eyes. She staggered straight through the kitchen and into the living room where she threw herself against the front door. She tried the knob, but the door was locked, of course. For a bit, she clawed at the wood, like some animal. It was as if she lost all knowledge of how to work a door.

It came back to her, though. She tried turning the deadbolt, but boy, was she struggling with it.

My right leg dragged behind me as I marched toward her. She didn't look at me, but she seemed to sense that I was coming. She got frantic. She pushed and tugged on that lock. It was the simplest of levers, the most basic of tools that humans ever invented, and she couldn't slow her mind or hand enough to work it properly.

She finally clicked the deadbolt to the right and tugged on the door. But it didn't open. The weather-stripping on that door always made it catch. You remember, right? You have to push it a bit before you can open it.

As I limped through the kitchen, I could feel her terror and confusion. She had no idea why, after a lifetime of opening and closing doors, this one, the *one* door she needed most to open, was giving her so much fucking trouble.

I entered the living room and reached toward her. Suddenly, through some combination of pushing and tugging, the door swung open.

Like a flash, she was gone. She sprinted faster than those weak legs should have been able to carry her.

I stood in the door and watched her sprint away. I couldn't catch her. Even though she was running barefoot down a gravel road, in a neighborhood she didn't know, I couldn't grab her with only one good leg.

"Help... help... help..." she weakly shouted out to the darkness.

Each time she shouted, her voice found new strength.

I didn't have much time.

As fast as my one-and-a-half legs could move, I stormed back down the hall and into my bedroom. Went to the closet and grabbed that old thirty-ought-six rifle. I put five shells in my pocket and went off in pursuit.

Even in the moonlight, I could see her down the road. She had on one of your old white t-shirts and basketball shorts, and it stood out against that dark backdrop of trees. She didn't have her wits about her. She coulda chucked the shirt and hid in the bushes and I wouldn't have been able to find her 'til morning. By then, it would be too late.

But no, she ran in a straight line down that road.

I called after her, "Elizabeth! Come back!"

She kept on going. She kept on shouting out to the darkness, "Somebody help me!"

I limped after her.

My legs were weak, but I could tell that hers were giving out too. That burst of adrenaline had given her a sizable lead, but now, all that muscle atrophy was settling in. Her lungs and heart couldn't keep up. I sure as hell wasn't moving any faster than before, but I could see the gap between us close. I imagine her mind was screaming at her legs to move faster, but, like when a monster chases you in a bad dream, her legs just couldn't hit that next gear.

I was going to catch her.

We limped down the road, one after the other, curving our way through the bends in that street. I wasn't going to be able to catch her before she reached the highway.

"Elizabeth, please!" I called out. "Don't make me do this."

She didn't pay me no mind. She just kept hollering for help.

What choice did I have?

My eyes blurred. The pepper stung, sure, but those tears were from something deeper—sadness.

I loaded a round in the rifle.

Took aim.

And fired.

It was like a thunder clap on a silent night. That sound bounced around the trees, went all the way up to Heaven, down to Hell, and back again. But Elizabeth ran on. I didn't see where the bullet went, but it hadn't struck her.

I limped on after her, closing the gap ever so slightly as I loaded a second round. I took aim. I fired.

Once again, the bullet vanished into the night, embedding in some tree or the dirt, but not in my dear Elizabeth.

On she ran.

She reached the highway. That road's not particularly well traveled, but I could see one set of headlights approaching. Elizabeth ran straight up the middle of the street, waving her arms and yelling for help.

I fired again. The bullet sailed out, but the night ate it too.

The car screeched to a halt.

Elizabeth ran up and pounded on the window, screaming for help.

I was about twenty yards away now. It was my last chance. I loaded a round and took aim. Elizabeth was just a white blur to me at that distance. I pulled the trigger anyway.

The center of that white blur exploded into a burst of red.

She collapsed on the pavement.

The driver of the car panicked. He wanted to drive off, but he released his clutch too fast and killed the engine. As he fumbled around, trying to restart his car, I limped right up and loaded my last round. I stood five feet from that car window, took aim and...

Bang.

CHAPTER 36

Walter sat silently, looking up and to the left, trying to access some portion of his brain that he apparently didn't have the key to unlock. "I don't remember too much after that. I been kicking it around in my mind, but it's all blurry. Sure, I had pepper in my eyes, but it's not just my vision that was watery, it's the whole thing."

"Somehow you got Elizabeth back to the house," Isaac said. "She was found in the basement with the others."

"Yep. That's right. Don't know how I did it. I must've put her in that guy's car and drove her back home. Then threw her back down in the basement and covered her with lye with the others. I kinda remember burying that guy out in the back yard. Wasn't a good grave. Might've just shoveled some dirt over him. I don't remember."

"Why did you put Elizabeth back in the basement?"

Walter shrugged, "I felt that's where she wanted to be. She chose it over me."

"Do you remember what happened next?"

"Bits and pieces."

"You seem to remember everything else pretty well."

"Ain't that the thing about memory?"

"I think that's the thing about *control*."

Walter nodded, not disagreeing.

"So, how did you end up at the college? There still wasn't any evidence on you. You might have been able to clean up the mess on the road before any cars came by."

Walter took a deep, contemplative pause.

The other inmates and visitors in the room hummed along with their conversations. The door of the visitation room buzzed open and Isaac caught a glimpse of an inmate being allowed a late entrance into the room. Isaac had ignored all the other inmates, all were different shades of the same hardened criminal, but this man caught Isaac's eye.

The inmate was huge, easily the largest man in the prison. His shaved head sat upon a mound of tattooed muscles. But it was his eyes that grabbed Isaac's attention. The man's expression was both empty and purposeful, like a robot on a mission. Isaac noticed the man's gaze locked onto the back of Walter's head.

Perhaps it was just another case of someone ogling at Walter's celebrity status. Isaac remembered how other families and inmates had stolen glances at his father as the old man had been escorted to his seat.

"It had all gone so easy the first time, I guess I felt I could do it again," Walter continued, grabbing Isaac's attention again. "But I was impatient. I wanted to start faster this time."

"That's why you went to the college? To collect more victims?"

Walter looked down at his chest. "Maybe. But I wasn't in a good place. I was angry. Or lonely. I don't know. Part of me was desperate to try again. But part of me just didn't give a fuck at this point. That's a bad combination. I saw a girl unlocking a door. I had a hammer in my hand. I was going to knock her out, force her into my car. Instead, I just bashed her pretty face in. I figured, why start again? Maybe I was just meant to die alone. Maybe it's better that way."

"Dad...?"

Walter looked up at his son. The two met eyes. "Yeah?"

"I'm sorry I wasn't there for you. I'm sorry I never said thank you."

"Well... you're welcome. I did the best I could."

"Dad, I... I don't love you. But I think I understand you a bit better."

Walter smiled sadly. "I guess that's the best I could have hoped for. I'm glad I told you my story. Maybe it'll help you figure out what to do with yourself." Walter sighed. "I've always seen myself in you. Not just the face, but in the way you go about your life. It wouldn't surprise me in the slightest if one day you ended up on this side of the glass."

"You think I'm like you?"

Walter shrugged. "As I said before, the only thing that separates good from evil is restraint."

As Walter and Isaac looked at each other, out of the corner of Isaac's eye, he saw the large inmate walk up behind his father. And then he caught a glimpse of Teddy standing behind the massive man, escorting the man through the room.

Isaac didn't know what to make of it.

The inmate suddenly grabbed Walter's head in one massive hand and slammed Walter's face into the glass partition.

Isaac leapt from his seat as Walter's nose shattered and exploded blood across the glass.

"No!" Isaac called out.

The other visitors jumped. From somewhere, an alarm sounded. People screamed. Guards shouted, "Hands on your head! Hands on your head!"

All the other inmates responded to the orders and placed their hands up. But the large man who had Walter's head in his hand wasn't done. He slammed the side of Walter's head down on the counter.

For an instant, through the blood on the glass, Isaac saw his father's eyes. They were wide. For the first time in his life, Isaac saw his father scared.

"Wait, wait, wait!" Isaac yelled.

The inmate pulled out a four-inch spike. It was a handmade shiv, crafted from what looked like toilet paper compressed together with paper-mache. It didn't look strong. It didn't look threatening. But the man plunged it down hard, spearing directly into Walter's ear.

Walter screamed out.

The man yanked out his shiv and stabbed down again.

And again.

And again.

A flurry of lightning quick stabs, each one penetrating deeper and deeper into Walter's head. Each time the shiv was removed, Walter's ear canal spewed out a gulp of blood, only for the shiv to plunge back in for another round.

Finally satisfied with his work, the inmate stabbed down one final time. He snapped the end off and left the tip of the shiv deeply embedded in Walter's ear. Then he put his hands on his head.

"I'm done, boss," the man calmly stated as he lowered himself to his knees. Guards rushed the inmate. They placed him in a headlock. He gave no resistance.

"Clear the room! Clear the room!" someone shouted.

More guards flooded both sides of the glass wall. They slammed every inmate onto the floor and slapped handcuffs on them.

On the visitor's side of the wall, guards pulled women from their seats and pushed everyone toward the exits.

In the chaos, Isaac saw Teddy wrestle an inmate to the ground. Isaac pounded on the glass. "You did this!" Isaac shouted.

Teddy looked up at him. "Clear the area!"

"You put him in here! This wouldn't have happened in the private room!"

"Get him out of here!" Teddy yelled to the other guards as he pointed at Isaac.

One of the guards grabbed Isaac by the arm and wrenched him away from the glass, pushing him out of the door.

As he left, Isaac looked back over his shoulder.

He couldn't see Walter. His father's body had slid off the counter and now lay somewhere on the floor. All that Isaac could see was the smeared, dripping blood on the glass.

His final image of his old man.

CHAPTER 37

The corridor echoed with chaos. It was a stampede of humanity.

Isaac felt a firm hand on his shoulder, shoving and prodding him forward until he was pushing up against the woman in front of him, and in turn, propelling her forward. The guards shouted commands that were drowned out by the screeches of the visitors.

Somewhere in front of Isaac, children cried and screamed out. One mother lost her grip on her son's hand. The little boy, who couldn't have been more than seven, dropped where he was and curled into a ball on the yellow line on the floor.

Isaac saw the boy too late. He tried to stop, but the guard's hand on his spine shoved him forward and he ran into the little boy, toppling to the ground.

The boy cried out. The guards screamed for everyone to keep moving and clear the hallway. Someone grabbed Isaac's shirt and yanked him to his feet and threw him back into the mob.

The guards herded the entire crowd of screaming, panicked visitors through a narrow doorway and into the main visitor waiting room. The next shift of visitors was waiting patiently in their seats when the doors burst open and they were swarmed by shouting, terrified parents hugging their children close.

Isaac looked behind him one last time at the corridor and yellow line leading to the visitation room. A guard gave him one last shove and then slammed the door in his face. For the forty guests in this room, now only a confused desk clerk was present to keep order. Instead of taking control of the room, she picked up her phone and asked for instructions.

With no one to stop him, Isaac marched right out of the room.

He stepped out of the prison and hurried across the parking area.

He could hear the alarms wind up and begin blaring inside the prison, but he looked at the walls and saw that none of the red lights were flashing. If a lockdown was occurring, it hadn't been fully implemented yet.

Isaac gulped the outside air. He needed to calm himself. He looked at his hands and saw they were shaking. He just wanted to get out of there. To get away. To get that smell of the prison out of his nose and the sight of his dad's ear drum erupting out of his mind.

He jogged to his car, climbed in, and drove away.

As he stopped at the exit check-point, he was still trembling. The guards there peered into his backseat. They made him pop his trunk. They ran a brief mirror-check underneath his car. Even with the alarms sounding and an obvious incident occurring, nobody was stopping him.

The guard gave a signal. The gate arm went up.

For the final time, Isaac drove out of the Willamette Valley Correctional Facility.

He looked in his rearview mirror and saw the gate arm swing closed behind him. And then he saw the red flashing lights that topped the wall begin to spin. A mounted siren wailed across the area. A chain-link fence, topped with razor wire, slid out of the brush and closed off the road behind him.

He turned onto the main street and saw his last glimpse of WAVECLIFF before it disappeared from his view. It took a few more deep breaths before he was calm enough to reach under his seat and pull out his phone.

He dialed a number.

"You've reached Ben Stewart, senior editor at DOPER Magazine, a trustworthy news reporting service," came the voice on the other end. "I'm not available to take your call. Please leave a detailed message."

"Ben. It's Isaac Luce. Big news is breaking, man. Gonna be a lot of interest in The Handyman now. I got that first recording. For the rest of the story, I'm taking bids on interviews with me. I'm the last one to see him alive, man. You'll love the shit he told me. Call me back." Isaac almost hung up the phone, but then, as an additional thought, "And let's finally meet. I'm moving to New York."

He drove in silence for several minutes, winding his way through the streets of Salem, completely in a daze.

A smile crept over his face.

The Handyman was dead. And he, Isaac Luce, a nobody and perpetual loser, was going to get rich.

CHAPTER 38

Most of the guards had cleared out of the visitation room, but Teddy remained. He stood in the corner, trying to appear calm and in control. After all, he was the senior visitation coordinator in the facility—at least for another 12 hours until the *real* senior visitation coordinator returned from vacation.

He tried to act indifferent. He tried to play it cool, as if having a man stabbed multiple times through the ear canal in front of a dozen visiting families was just a fact of life in prison.

But Teddy's heart pounded so hard that he could *feel* his pulse in the veins of his right eye. He wondered if everyone else could see it too, like a Tell-Tale Heart. Maybe his entire right eye was pulsating and would eventually burst.

However, all attention was on the bloody mass of the man on the floor. The two prison EMTs were already hard at work.

They laid Walter on his back. The lead EMT performed a rapid assessment of Walter's vitals. He checked Walter's pulse, breathing, and pupils. The lead EMT issued some orders to his assistant who prepped an IV.

Teddy gulped. An IV? What was with all the rushing? Why didn't they just zip him into a body bag? Was Walter still alive?

The assistant EMT inserted the IV into Walter's arm. They worked with a sense of urgency.

"Pupillary dilatation. Full Cushing's Triad," the lead EMT announced.

Teddy had no idea what any of that meant. He prayed they would just pronounce him dead, cart him away, scrub down the room, erase the visitation logs and be done with all this.

Suddenly, Walter retched. His mouth opened. Vomit bubbled out in a stream of foamy chunks and bile, like a child's volcano made of baking soda and vinegar.

"He's aspirating vomit. Start intubation before he chokes," the lead EMT calmly ordered.

Walter was still *alive*.

He remained unconscious. His airways were blocked by vomit. The foamy bile formed bubbles as Walter struggled to breathe. But he was very much alive.

Teddy made a conscious effort to stay calm. But he realized a few seconds later that he was forgetting to breathe. He forced himself to take a big breath of air. Was it too big? Did everyone notice?

The assistant EMT reached into his bag and pulled out a laryngoscope, a metal device that had a handle and a curved tongue-suppressing blade. The thing looked like a shoehorn.

They inserted the scope into Walter's mouth and over his tongue. The assistant EMT gently pried down, opening Walter's jaw. With help from the lead EMT, they cleared the chunks of vomit from his mouth and inserted a breathing tube down Walter's throat.

Teddy couldn't believe it. They were trying to save this man. *Really* trying. He briefly considered calling them off. Maybe he still had authority in this situation. Maybe he could step over and say, *He's gone, guys. Take a break.* But he could never do it. No one would listen to him.

At that moment, the door opened.

Teddy turned, ready to shoo out whoever this lookie-loo might be. He jerked to a stop when he saw that it wasn't a guard or another doctor. It was a man in a suit. Jeffrey Ortega, the superintendent of the Willamette Valley Correctional Facility. The man in charge.

Superintendent Ortega had worked in prisons his entire adult life, being promoted from guard to supervisor to administrator to assistant superintendent. It was a trajectory that a man like Teddy *should* have been on, but Teddy could never rise above his station. For the past 6 years, Jeffrey Ortega had been WAVECLIFF's superintendent, a title that used to be "warden" only that it was changed for some reason that Teddy didn't know. Probably politics.

He walked past Teddy without even looking at him.

Teddy bowed his head and took a step toward the door, fully intending to leave the scene *before* the superintendent recognized his presence. But as he made his first faint move to slink away, the superintendent's hand shot up and motioned for him to stay exactly where he was. Teddy gulped as he straightened his back and stood against the wall.

The superintendent walked up to the EMTs, allowing them to know he was there, but not getting so close as to crowd their work.

"How is he?" Superintendent Ortega asked.

The lead EMT didn't look up. They were putting the finishing touches on inserting the breathing tube. "Penetrating trauma to the head. Cerebral swelling and bleeding. We're getting him on a breathing tube now."

"And the weapon?"

"Paper-mache shiv," the EMT said, apparently all-too familiar with such weapons. "Looks like it was constructed with toilet paper, water, and flour, probably from the commissary."

The superintendent nodded. He turned and locked eyes on Teddy. His voice stayed calm, but intense. "What was he doing in the general population visiting room?"

Teddy gulped. "It was the only space available."

"Was it?" The superintendent walked over and stood face-to-face with Teddy.

"I, uh, I believe so, sir."

"Not a single private room was available?"

"I... I'll check the records. But he agreed to have his visitation here. I wouldn't have put him here if he didn't."

"And why would that matter?"

"Sir?"

The glare was now settling onto the superintendent's face. He seemed suspicious. And angry. "Why would his preference mean anything? *We* choose where they meet. This facility has private rooms for our high-profile inmates for a reason."

"I, um, I felt our job was to accommodate the comfort of our, um, Death Row inmates. And to, um—"

"You think *your job* is to keep Walter Luce comfortable?"

"No, sir. I—"

"Your *job* was to keep him safe. To keep him alive for a court-ordered, governor-approved execution. Under no circumstances should he have been moved from the special housing unit. Under no circumstances should he have come into physical contact with other inmates. Especially with the history of death threats that have been made against Mr. Luce."

"Yes, sir. It was a mistake, sir."

"Who was the other inmate involved in the attack?"

"Prisoner 51134—"

"Just give me a name."

"Um, it was, um, Richard Nolan, sir."

The superintendent took a deep breath. He seemed to be putting things together and didn't like the way it was looking. "Richard Nolan is also a Death Row inmate, isn't that right, Teddy?"

"Yes, sir."

"And so, that means you brought *two* Death Row inmates out of the SHU and into the general population where they would be in close physical proximity to each other."

"It was a mistake, sir. I apologize. This isn't my usual job."

The superintendent's mouth hung open for a moment. "This isn't your job?"

Teddy didn't respond. He avoided eye contact.

"Were you aware that Richard Nolan has a daughter of the approximate age of Mr. Luce's victims? And that Mr. Nolan had been making death threats against Mr. Luce? In fact, he tried to strangle Mr. Luce in the courtyard about a year ago."

"I was not aware of that, sir."

"Seeing as how you work in the SHU, I'm surprised you did not know the history between these two inmates. Mr. Nolan has been very vocal about his desire to harm or even kill Mr. Luce. Has he not?"

Teddy didn't respond.

"Is this not the reason we've kept Mr. Luce isolated from the other inmates at all times?"

"I, uh, I don't know, sir."

The superintendent looked Teddy up and down. "Did you search Mr. Nolan before he entered the visitation room?"

"Yes, sir."

"And you didn't notice a weapon on his person?"

"No, sir."

"How does that happen?"

"Someone must have handed him the weapon later."

"*Someone* handed him a weapon *later*?" His stare ripped into Teddy.

Teddy looked at the ground. He shifted his weight from leg to leg. His entire face glowed with sweat. He could feel the moisture pooling under his armpits and collecting on his shirt, now wetly sticking to his skin. He hoped it wasn't noticeable.

Across the room, the lead EMT stood. "Sir?"

The superintendent turned to address the situation at hand. "What is it?"

"He's bleeding internally. His head is filling with blood. It needs to be drained. Our infirmary's not equipped for this kind of surgery. I'm also concerned about infection. With weapons like this, the inmate usually smears the tip with feces to force bacteria into the wound. We need to get him on antibiotics immediately."

"You're authorized to transport him to a hospital. Do whatever it takes to keep him alive."

The lead EMT nodded and went back to work. "Ready the collar and backboard."

His assistant pulled a backboard from his cart and set it on the floor beside Walter. They prepared to move him.

The superintendent turned his attention one last time to Teddy. "You are suspended. Someone will escort you from this facility to your car. I am going to personally review all Death Row visitations you authorized and scheduled. You are not to return to your workstation or locker. Your personal items will be collected and returned to you. And you are not to log on to any system computers on your way out. Do you understand me?"

Teddy gulped. "Yes, sir."

"Is there anything you'd like to tell me before I begin my review process?"

Teddy stood rigid. He tried to say something but only squeaked out some unrecognizable sounds. He finally settled for shaking his head.

On the floor in front of him, Walter's body seized up. He spasmed and jerked on the backboard. The EMTs held him down as he had a seizure.

"Get this man to a fucking hospital!" the superintendent shouted.

CHAPTER 39

Isaac exited the freeway and stopped at a light on the onramp that entered Woodburn. The outlet mall was across the freeway to his left, and the Walmart for the locals was to his right. He pulled onto a familiar road that was all motels, gas stations, and fast food—a resting place for weary I-5 travelers.

He'd taken this exit too many times to count, but for once, it all felt different, like returning home after a long trip away. The colors and details didn't necessarily feel brighter or sharper. Just different. New. Isaac figured that he had been sleepwalking through this town ever since his father was arrested. And in truth, he wondered if he'd actually been sleepwalking his whole life.

Never again.

His father's violent and shocking death would send public interest in The Handyman skyrocketing. Isaac was ready to capitalize on it with his recording. He knew Ben would pay top dollar now. He also trusted that Ben would wisely dole out the revelations from the recordings, sustaining public interest for weeks, if not months. Certainly long enough for Isaac to conduct multiple paid interviews.

Perhaps a book deal could be in the works. And where there was a book deal, there would be feature film rights.

What then?

He needed to keep this business moving and evolving. He would take Lauren's idea and license The Handyman name to a series of haunted houses, mazes, and escape rooms. Maybe he could sign a publishing deal where he could write his own series of horror books. He always wanted to be a writer. This way he could expand his brand. He could spin it off into The

Handyman Publishing Company. Then *other* authors could publish serial killer novels and Isaac could collect royalties off their work.

Isaac wondered if he needed an agent or a manager. A lawyer too. Someone to set up his LLC or S-corp, or whatever the hell he needed. Surely Ben could hook him up.

For years, Isaac had jokingly referred to his tool-selling income stream as "Handyman Inc." But that was a business that only resided on murderabilia auction sites on the dark web. Well, today, Isaac was positioned to take Handyman Inc. out of the shadows and turn it into a global empire of monetized murder. He could achieve everything his father strived for and never attained—money, comfort and security.

He turned on the radio and scanned through the channels. The voices that came over his speakers discussed politics. And more politics. Several stations were in Spanish. Even the local stations, the ones transmitting from Portland, Salem, and Eugene, gave rundowns of the day's boring top stories without any mention of the horrific, unplanned, public execution that had just occurred at WAVECLIFF.

The news of The Handyman hadn't broken yet.

Soon the cops would want to interview him.

And then the media.

But for these last precious few minutes, Isaac remained insignificant and anonymous. He knew he needed to get cleaned up. He had to be presentable. He had to practice his story and practice different tones of his delivery. There were all sorts of prep-work that had to be done if he was to stretch his fifteen minutes into a lifetime income stream.

When he parked at his apartment, he simply sat in his car, though.

There was only one thing on his mind. One person he wanted to share his moment with.

He pulled out his phone and texted Lauren.

"Big shit going down. I'm coming into some money. Come hang out at my place and I'll explain. There's a hammer in it for you."

He entered his address and pressed "send."

His eyes stayed fixated on his screen as he sat and waited for a response.

It was 3:15. She'd be done with class by now. Maybe she was hanging out with her friends. Or maybe she was at lacrosse practice. Or maybe, just maybe, she was with some other guy.

Ding!

A new text popped up on his phone.

Lauren had simply replied to him with a picture of herself flashing the camera. In the image, she pulled up her shirt with one hand, showing off her bra, while her other hand gave him a thumbs-up. She had made sure that her face wasn't in frame, but Isaac knew it was her.

And it was hot.

He typed in his reply.

"I love you."

His thumb hovered over the send button. But, at the last moment, he deleted the message and simply replied, *"Ha! See you soon!"*

Then, he climbed out of the car and jogged up the steps to his room.

When he entered his studio apartment, he noticed that it seemed smaller today. Or maybe his expectations on life had simply gotten bigger. He jetted past his photography rig, past his crates of tools, and directly to his closet. He needed a nice shirt, but not *too* nice. Reporters were coming. He had heard somewhere that stripes don't work on TV. This interview would be the first step in launching a career. It would be the screen-shot that everyone would see.

He settled on a black button-up. Not too formal, not too casual. He wasn't some Goth, but he felt the black showcased a darkness. The perfect image for the beginning of his serial killer franchise. "Handyman Productions" he'd call it.

Not since Christmas Land had anything excited him this much.

He went to the mirror and straightened his hair. He debated shaving but decided that the stubble also added to that dark mystique he was going for. As he stared at himself, he began practicing various facial expressions.

How did he plan to portray his reaction to his father's death?

Was he devastated? In shock? Mourning? Righteously satisfied? His voice had to strike just the right tone of being respectful toward the victims while still eliciting sympathy from the audience over the fact that he had just witnessed his own father's bloody murder.

And why was he visiting with his father in the first place? He had to tease the existence of the recordings without revealing their profiteering nature. A narrative quickly formed in Isaac's mind.

When I first heard about the murders, I was shocked. This wasn't the man I knew. This wasn't the man who raised me, who bought me a dog, who built a Christmas tree lot, who liked to watch basketball.

I couldn't comprehend how someone could do something like this. I was distraught. Devastated for those poor families. I wanted to reach out and help them, but I didn't know how. They had already lost everything. But then I realized exactly what I could do.

I visited my father so that I could probe the mind of a madman. I could learn why he did the things he did. I could uncover when and why exactly he veered down the wrong path. I could put a roadblock up on that path. I could start a conversation. With proper knowledge and education, we might be able to get the next Handyman the help he needs. If we can do that, we just might save a life. And if we can save one life, it will all be worth it.

And so, what did you discover? Why did he go down that dark path?

Isaac stared at his reflection. An uncomfortable smile flitted onto his lips, but he quickly wiped it away, knowing that smiles seem disingenuous.

Well, he, um, he was angry. And lonely. And he had a fucking darkness inside him, like so many of us do.

There was a knock at the door.

Isaac panicked. It would either be the police or the local news. In either case, he didn't want them to see his tool-selling enterprise.

Knock knock.

"Just a minute. I'm getting dressed," Isaac called as he hurried to detach the camera from the tripod and shove it in the closet.

Knock knock!

Isaac grabbed a crate of tools and looked around the apartment. There was no good place to hide it. His closet was full. He carried it to the kitchen and shoved it into the pantry.

He hurried back and grabbed the second crate of tools. There was no more room in the pantry. He debated hiding it in the refrigerator, but quickly squashed that idea.

KNOCK KNOCK!

The door shook on its hinges. The person outside pounded so hard that the tremors from the blows shook Isaac's desk. They were slamming their fist into the door. This probably wasn't some reporter. This must be the police. The only way they could knock harder was with a ram.

"Just a minute!"

Isaac dumped the contents of the crate onto the floor and pushed all the tools under his bed. He tugged on his blanket so that it would hang down just enough to cover the tools.

He stood, took a calming breath, and walked to the door.

He opened it.

His eyes went wide with surprise. It wasn't the police or the media.

"Teddy?" he said as he stared at the man at his door.

Teddy had apparently come straight from the prison. He still wore his green uniform pants, but had taken off his beige uniform shirt. And now he stood there in his white undershirt. Or *once*-white undershirt. It was gray with stains and age at this point, thread-bare around the neck and shoulders. A t-shirt that had done its duty but hadn't been allowed to properly retire because there was never the budget for a replacement. And now that poor shirt was drenched in large patches of sweat.

Teddy's whole face shined. He was red, seemingly having run here straight from his car. He nibbled on his lip and shifted the weight on his feet.

"What the fuck do *you* want?" Isaac asked.

"If anyone from the prison contacts you, I think it would be best if you didn't mention our arrangement."

"Fuck you," Isaac said as he moved to slam the door in Teddy's face.

Teddy's massive hand braced the door open. It seemed to require so little effort on his part to hold it against Isaac's will.

"Are you going to tell them?" Teddy said.

"Learn to live with the unknown, asshole."

Isaac again pushed on the door, trying to close it. Teddy easily shoved it wide open with one hand. His other hand pushed Isaac back into his own apartment. Teddy stepped into the room and closed the door behind him.

"What the fuck are you doing?" Isaac shouted, his eyes frantically searching for where he left his phone in case he needed to call the police. He saw the phone on his desk. But he knew it wouldn't look good if the police arrived and found Isaac in a shouting match with his dead father's guard.

"We don't want them investigating our deal," Teddy said as he stepped toward Isaac. He towered over him. He wasn't even trying to intimidate Isaac. It was almost as if he were in a daze and was drifting, physically and mentally, around the room. "I can't have them looking too closely."

"Why? Because you used me to get him out of his cell and into the general population?"

"There's no proof of that."

"You got me to help you assassinate him."

"You can't prove that."

Isaac was done fucking around. He realized that Teddy, like some sort of lost animal, was probably more scared of Isaac than Isaac should be of him. He locked eyes on Teddy and stepped toward him.

"Was it that buyer of yours? Joan? Did she pay for this?"

Teddy looked away.

Isaac persisted. "What the fuck happened in there, Teddy? Did she get tired of waiting for an execution? Did she want him dead so her fucking documentary could sell for more? Well, fuck her and fuck you! I'm selling those recordings myself."

"Don't."

"That's my trade, pal. You give me full control of the recordings and I won't talk to the police about this. You keep your job, I keep the tapes."

"This is my family's livelihood."

"Your family will be fine. Trust me. Just relax. Go home."

Suddenly, Isaac's phone, over on his desk, lit up.

New message.

Isaac turned and walked to his desk. As he reached for his phone, Teddy grabbed him by the shoulder and yanked him back.

"Get your fucking hand off me!" Isaac said as he slapped Teddy's hand away. But as he looked at Teddy's face, he saw that a grimness had begun to settle over the man's features.

Teddy kept one hand up, motioning for Isaac to stay where he was, as he stepped to the desk and picked up Isaac's phone.

"We need to work out our stories."

"Give me my phone, man."

"I can't lose my job."

"You didn't consider that was a possibility when you set this whole thing up? What the fuck did you think would happen? That no one would care?"

Teddy blinked. His head twitched as he tried to work out what exactly he *did* think would happen. "No one *should* care. He shouldn't be allowed to live. He... he's a monster."

"He's famous."

"I did the world a favor."

"He's a celebrity."

The words sank into Teddy. "I'm not going to lose my job over him. My benefits. My pension. You and I, we gotta work out our stories."

"There's nothing to work out, man."

The phone in Teddy's hand lit up again, *another* new message. Teddy looked down at the screen. His head cocked to the side, and his mouth twisted up. He didn't understand what he was looking at.

"Is it the police?" Isaac asked.

Teddy didn't respond. He just stared at the screen, trying to fit puzzle pieces together in his mind.

"Is it a New York number?"

Isaac could see Teddy's knuckles go white as his hand clenched on the phone. The edges of Teddy's mouth turned down and froze into a place of utter shock.

Isaac gulped.

"It's probably my buyer," Isaac said. He could sense that Teddy's mood had darkened. "Look, Teddy, I know I couldn't have gotten in there without you. I'm gonna honor our deal. Fifty-fifty, just like we agreed. It's gonna be a lot of money, I know it. You'll probably lose your job, but this will bridge the gap. Just give me my phone and let me close the deal."

Isaac reached out his hand, but Teddy made no motion to hand over the phone. He kept looking at the screen. It only took small muscle movements on Teddy's face, but his features suddenly transformed from shock to anger.

"Teddy?"

Another message dinged onto the phone.

"Is it New York?"

Finally, Teddy looked up. His eyes dug into Isaac, piercing him with hate. A sinking feeling hit Isaac. His entire body went limp. He suddenly knew what Teddy had seen on the phone, but he prayed that it wasn't true.

"Wh-who is it?" Isaac stammered out.

Tears came to Teddy's eyes.

"Teddy..."

"She's sending you pictures."

"I... I..."

Teddy's face twisted and twitched as he tried to hold back the tears and rage. "How does she even know you?"

A realization seemed to wash over Teddy's face then.

"I did this," he said. "You only know her because of me. I brought you into her life, didn't I? I invited a Luce into our house."

Isaac approached him.

"She's eighteen, Teddy. She can do whatever she wants."

Something within Teddy snapped. He grabbed Isaac by the hair and slammed his head into the wall.

The blow sent Isaac crumpling to the ground. He tried to climb back to his feet. He needed to defend himself. He needed to run away. He needed to call for help. He needed to do something, *anything* other than allow himself to huddle on the floor, vulnerable at the feet of the huffing beast in his apartment.

But as Isaac stood, his legs wobbled. The room was blurry and spinning. His legs gave out and he collapsed back to the ground.

Teddy stepped forward and towered over him.

CHAPTER 40

Superintendent Ortega stood in the prison's primary security suite, watching events unfold on an array of monitors.

WAVECLIFF was on lockdown.

There were pre-existing procedures in place for the transportation of an inmate from the prison to a local hospital. It was a routine occurrence.

But Ortega became paranoid.

In the back of his mind, he was sure that some conspiracy had resulted in his most prized possession getting stabbed through the ear. He would be answering for this for the rest of his career, and that alone made him furious. Through no fault of his own, his upward trajectory had crashed into its ceiling. He had been betrayed.

He saw the betrayal on the face of one of his simpleton officers. But he wondered how much wider the plot was. His mind drifted into vast Hollywood conspiracies.

Was The Handyman some sort of grand chess master who had faked his own murder in order to escape?

Was this Stage One of a much larger and more elaborate plot?

Was The Handyman going to be carted into that ambulance and then snap back to consciousness, rip off his breathing mask, murder all the paramedics, and slip off into the night?

Was this the beginning of twenty years of taunting letters being sent to the police?

Superintendent Ortega was not going to be made a fool of. He was not going to have to explain to the governor and the mass media how The Handyman outsmarted everyone and faked cranial bleeding to escape.

He ordered all his corrections officers to suit up in riot gear. Then, in a quick show of force, they swarmed into the yard and cleared it out, ordering all inmates back to their cells. Any inmate who hesitated, argued, or talked back was forcibly dropped to the ground and restrained. No questions asked.

Ortega watched the inmates herded back to the cellblocks. There was confusion and shouting, but it all proceeded with relative ease.

With the yard cleared, Ortega clicked on his walkie-talkie and ordered his small army to converge on the chow line.

From his observation position in the security suite, he watched as guards burst into the commissary, ordering all the inmates to abandon their meals and line up against the wall. A few protested and were immediately clubbed and placed in head locks.

After they cleared the chow line, Ortega ordered them to proceed to the next cell block and clear the showers.

Then the machine shop.

Then the weight room.

Everyone was herded into cells and locked away. Satisfied that the prison population was under control, Superintendent Ortega ordered every available guard to man the pathway of corridors from the visitation room to the ambulance.

When the full security detail was in place, he hurried from the security suite to the corridor so he could oversee the transfer himself.

Upon arrival, Ortega followed behind as medics jogged Walter's stretcher through the check-points, led by and tailed by a squadron of armed guards. They handcuffed his limp, nearly lifeless arm to the stretcher.

The ambulance idled in the parking area. Police cruisers from Salem PD stood ready for escort duty. When the EMTs loaded Walter's stretcher into the back of the ambulance, three armed police officers piled in beside him.

"This is a trauma system entry. Lights and siren transport," the lead EMT announced as he closed the ambulance doors.

The arm of the main gate swung up.

Superintendent Ortega watched the convoy pull out of the parking lot and speed off down the road. The Handyman had left the prison, perhaps never to return. The superintendent sighed as he turned and walked back inside. There were so many phone calls he had to make, none of which he was looking forward to. First of all, he had to get local police out and searching for Walter's last visitor, his son. There were many questions to ask the young man.

***

Jeffrey Corbin tried to ignore the pain.

After sixth period had gotten out, he and some friends had driven to the old Westview Apartment Building on the east side of Salem. A stone staircase led from the building's parking area up to the main entrance. Along that staircase ran a metal handrail. The rail was Jeffrey's discovery—the perfect angle and length to practice board tricks. Unlike the rails at his high school, *this* rail didn't have knobs welded along its length to prevent kids from grinding their way down it.

Jeffrey and his friends spent the afternoon performing tricks on that rail. Some of the residents grumbled at the noise, glaring occasionally out their windows, but nobody ever confronted them.

After about thirty minutes of trying, Jeffrey finally had a good run. He hopped up on the rail on his skateboard and rode it all the way down, executing the trick to perfection. *Almost.*

The trick went so well that even when he felt his board wobble as it approached the bottom, he was sure he could course-correct. He ended up throwing his weight too far in one direction and he toppled off the rail and off his board. He landed on the stone steps, catching his full body weight with his right arm, which resulted in an audible snapping sound at his wrist.

He didn't want to cry in front of his friends, but the pain spiked through his entire body.

His friends drove him to East Salem General Hospital and waited with him in the emergency room for all of five minutes before they decided it was a better use of their time to leave and do homework. Jeffrey needed his insurance information, and so, knowing she would lecture him anyway, called his mom to come keep him company.

Together they sat in the hard, plastic chairs, reading from their phones and waiting for the doctors to see him.

And yet, the doctors and nurses didn't seem to be seeing *anyone*.

They clustered together in the ER waiting room, expectantly staring out the sliding glass receiving doors.

Jeffrey was annoyed that so many staffers appeared to be available but weren't helping him. He played with his phone for another five minutes until a crackling voice speaking through a walkie-talkie distracted him. He looked up. It wasn't just doctors and nurses talking among themselves as they nervously shifted around. Six armed hospital security officers now flanked the receiving door.

The door opened, and four uniformed cops walked in and joined them. Jeffrey's mom noticed too. "They must be expecting some VIP," she said.

Jeffrey nodded.

"Gee, I wonder if something happened to the governor," she said as she started searching on her phone for information. "Nothing in the news."

Everyone suddenly perked to attention at the sound of a procession of sirens speeding toward the building and rolling to a stop outside the door.

"Clear a path! Clear a path!" someone shouted.

Instinctively, Jeffrey held up his phone and began recording the scene. More police ran in through the doors and joined with the other cops and hospital security to form a human pathway from the ambulance through the lobby. They held back the onlookers, most of whom were hospital staff, as EMTs rolled in a stretcher.

A man lay on the stretcher. Various IVs were connected to his veins, and his face had a breathing mask.

The EMTs passed the man to two nurses, under the guidance of a doctor. "Get him into a CT and clear an operating room!" the doctor shouted.

As they carted him in, the armed escort followed behind. Voices shouted over one another, yelling out vitals, directions, and room numbers. Jeffrey filmed someone say, "Prep for a drain. We may need a craniotomy."

The patient passed directly in front of him. Jeffrey zoomed his phone in on the man's hand—he was handcuffed to his own gurney.

Then he panned over to the man's face.

The breathing mask obscured it, but Jeffrey immediately knew that face. That old, bearded, pale face. He had seen it on the news. One of Jeffrey's buddies had dressed up as that man for Halloween. His friend had carried a sledgehammer through the school hallways until the teachers confiscated it. Everyone knew that face well.

Jeffrey's mom, seemingly mortified that her son would violate someone's medical privacy by filming such a moment, swatted at his shoulder. "Put that away."

"Mom, that's Handyman," he said, a sense of astonishment in his voice.

She looked. Her eyes went wide.

The stretcher and the accompanying security paused at an elevator. As they waited for the doors to open, Jeffrey kept filming. He tried to keep his hand from shaking as he zoomed in with his phone and held the image on that ghastly face. It was now clear that the man's head was wrapped in bloody gauze from an ear wound.

Jeffrey's mom let him film. She didn't say another word.

CHAPTER 41

Joan Larkins paced on Teddy's front step.

In her casual athletic gear, jogging hat, and big sunglasses, she looked like just another middle-aged woman cooling down after a jog. Though it was true that her heartrate had been accelerated all day, it wasn't because of exercise.

Through her earbuds, she listened to the radio as it streamed through her phone. Fifteen minutes ago, one of the local stations reported that an incident had occurred at the Willamette Valley Correctional Facility. The uncorroborated rumor was that it involved The Handyman.

That was all the information Joan needed in order to pack up her Tesla and speed over to Teddy's.

As she paced, she shifted a manila envelope in her hands. It was heavy and slightly unwieldy, having been packed so full that the small metal clasp barely managed to hold the flap closed. The envelope was too big to fit through Teddy's mail slot. She could probably prop it against his front door, and it would be fine, but she hated to do that.

Still, Joan had places to be. She would give Teddy five more minutes.

Although he had promised that he would be able to come home right after the incident, Joan was skeptical. She knew how organizations worked. After a big fuck-up like what she assumed had happened at the prison, it wouldn't matter that Teddy claimed to have a doctor's appointment. He was going to have to stay and answer some questions. If they did allow him to leave, then the police wouldn't be far behind.

Joan certainly didn't want to deal with *that*.

She checked her watch.

Three more minutes and then she would bail.

She *hoped* Teddy would arrive. She wanted to hear all about how it went. She wanted details. Visuals. Graphic visuals.

Did he scream?

Did he cry?

Did he beg?

Was there pain?

Joan had to know.

Her head perked up at a sound. An approaching car kicked up gravel as it sped down the street and skidded to a stop. Just out of Joan's view, she could hear the car door open. Then came a girl's voice.

"Later, masturbator!"

"After while, chunky bile," came the response.

A moment later, a teenage girl strolled down the driveway. The girl wore a lacrosse jersey. Her pulled-back hair had started to grow frizzy from the dried sweat of a long practice session. The girl confidently carried her backpack, her duffle, and her facemask and stick.

Joan immediately liked this girl's swagger.

The girl didn't see Joan standing at the front door. Instead, the girl's eyes focused on Joan's Tesla. She ogled it, both impressed and confused by its presence in her driveway.

Joan stepped out of the shadow of the doorway. "Hello there," she said.

"Uh, hello?" the girl said, jerking to stop. Joan noticed that the girl kept her distance. The girl's eyes seemed to scan the area in attempt to make sense of this stranger.

Joan smiled a friendly, but strained smile. "Are you Lauren?"

"Uh, yeah."

"My name is Joan. I work with your father."

"Okay."

"Teddy thinks the world of you. He tells me you got into Columbia. Congratulations."

"Thanks."

"Are you looking forward to New York? Now that he can afford it?"

"Uh, what?"

"You'll have so much fun. There's an energy and vibrancy to Manhattan that you just can't find anywhere else. I started at a law firm there before I moved back home to Portland. As much as I loved New York, Portland felt like a better place to raise a family."

"Cool."

The two women stared at each other across the short distance. Joan's gaze traveled up and down Lauren. Such a youthful, innocent girl. So much spirit. So alive. The thought made Joan reach up under her sunglasses and wipe away a tear.

"I truly wish you the best, Lauren. Your father loves you so much. Here." Joan held out the large manila envelope. "Will you give this to him?"

Lauren made no motion to take it. "Yeeeeah... uh, I'm not allowed to take gifts from strangers."

Joan smiled. "Smart."

She set the large envelope on the front step of the house.

"Do tell your father that I left this for him. This completes our business." She walked past Lauren toward her car.

Lauren watched her. "Does he have your number, or something?" she asked.

Joan turned and smiled, "Yes, but he won't get through. I'm going on a long vacation. He'll find my phone is off and my offices are closed." She opened her car and climbed in. She started the engine and was about to drive away but hesitated. She rolled down her window. "Lauren?"

Lauren stiffly eyed her.

"You don't trust me, do you?"

Lauren didn't respond.

"It's a good intuition to have. Always listen to it. Never, ever, ever ignore that voice. You'll tell yourself, 'Oh, I'm just being paranoid.' Or, 'I hate to be rude.' Don't. Keep yourself safe. Will you do that? Will you promise me that?"

"Uh, sure. Yeah. Okay."

"Take care, Lauren. Have fun in New York."

Joan rolled up her window.

She slipped her car into reverse and backed her way out of the driveway. She glanced at Lauren one last time before she turned the car around and drove off. Lauren didn't take her eyes off her. *Good girl*, Joan thought.

As Joan drove out of the neighborhood and turned onto the main highway, she wondered how long it would take a girl like Lauren to look inside that envelope. Was Lauren trustworthy? Was she the kind of girl who would skim a few thousand dollars before presenting the rest of the bundle to her father?

Joan bet that Lauren *would* look inside the envelope. Nothing wrong with a teenage girl being naturally inquisitive. Better than being a timid, dutiful damsel. But, ultimately, she felt that Lauren would deliver the entire bundle, untampered, to her father. That's what Elizabeth would have done. And Joan liked to think that she saw a bit of Elizabeth in Lauren. Although, Joan tended to see a bit of Elizabeth in *every* good person she met. She wasn't sure if this habit was a way to keep Elizabeth's spirit alive, or a way for Joan to be haunted by The Handyman, and what he took, forever.

As she drove off down Interstate 5, toward whatever city she happened to end at, she wondered if tonight she would manage to fall asleep without thinking of The Handyman.

It was over.

She had gotten as much revenge as she could have. And yet, she was troubled by the fact that she felt nothing. No relief. No satisfaction. Just weariness.

The anticipation of her plan had energized her and given her purpose. It took time to cultivate Teddy and wait for their window. It took time to liquidate her modest fortune so that she could slip away at this moment. All of that planning had distracted her mind from the wretched, throbbing sorrow that usually filled it. But now there was nothing.

There was enough cash in the car to last her for the rest of her life. She was untraceable. Her options were endless.

Maybe she would drive to her ex-husband in Scottsdale. She could brag to him about what she did. After all, Elizabeth was *his* daughter too.

Nah. Fuck that guy.

Maybe she would tell that media. It would be a grand story of a mother's revenge.

Nah. Fuck those guys.

She didn't want to gloat. She didn't want credit. She just wanted her Elizabeth back.

Maybe she would drive down to Mexico and blow a shit-ton of money in one of those resort towns where she planned to take Elizabeth as a college graduation present. She could tan all day and dance all night, just as she planned. Maybe if she completed that experience, and made that memory, she would finally feel that she was in a place where she could say goodbye.

If not, then she could still take a handful of pills and swim out into the ocean at night.

Joan smiled. That sounded like a good Plan B.

Second best plan she'd had in years.

CHAPTER 42

Isaac lay on the floor. His vision was blurry. The room swam around him as if his senses had gone unmoored. His hand touched the side of his head where a sharp pain pulsated from. It took him a moment to make sense of the texture he was feeling. Slime mixed with grit.

Then he realized, he was bleeding from his head. Teddy had slammed him into the wall so hard that he must have busted through some of the drywall, the dust of which had mixed with the blood in his hair.

Isaac pulled himself into a sitting position against the wall.

Somewhere, through his ringing ears, he could make out the faint voice of Teddy mumbling to himself. Isaac concentrated on the sound of that voice, trying to use it as a lighthouse upon which he could bring his vision and hearing back into focus.

Teddy, it seemed, was now pacing in the kitchen area of Isaac's studio apartment. The man was muttering to himself, shaking his head and waving his hands like a crazy person in the street.

"You slept with my daughter... You slept with my daughter..." He kept repeating the words, seemingly trying to make sense of them.

Isaac focused his gaze and found his bearings. He sat against the wall, next to his bed. Teddy wasn't paying any attention to him. Isaac could call for help. Where was his phone?

He looked around. Not on the desk. Not on the floor. Then he saw— Isaac's phone was the only thing keeping Teddy occupied. Over in the kitchen area, the big man's massive hand was clenched tight around Isaac's phone. He seemed to be swiping through photos and texts, disintegrating inside as he found more and more evidence of Isaac and Lauren's relationship. Even through Isaac's hazy vision, he could see the man's shoulders slouch and the veins pop from his neck as his teeth ground into themselves.

Isaac knew he needed an escape. His gaze settled on his door. It was closed, but it was only ten feet away.

Teddy was preoccupied.

Isaac could make it.

"She wouldn't... She said she was with Becky... They were studying... She wouldn't lie... She wouldn't do this... She wouldn't sleep with you... She would *never* sleep with someone like you..." Teddy muttered.

It was now or never. Isaac quietly slumped down to the ground. On his hands and knees, he began crawling across the carpet toward his door.

But then, Teddy stopped mumbling. His footsteps ceased their pacing. A quiet fell over the apartment. Isaac quickened his pace. He made it to the door. All he needed was to reach up, fling open the door, and find the strength to run out.

Teddy spoke. His voice now calm and loud, as if he had just gained complete confidence in his understanding of everything that had occurred.

"You used her," Teddy said.

Isaac turned to face him as Teddy stepped from the kitchen area. There wasn't anger in his frame anymore, just purpose. He calmly strode up to Isaac and towered over him.

Isaac put his hands up. "No. No, Teddy, I—"

"You raped her."

"I swear to you, I didn't."

"That's why she lied to me. She was ashamed. She was scared of you."

"Teddy..."

"I watched you, Isaac. When you were talking to your father. The whole time, I didn't watch him at all. I watched *you*. I don't know why I watched you. I guess I don't find men like Walter very interesting. I see them all the time. I spend all day with them. But you. I found you very interesting. You were on the edge of your seat. You were holding your breath. You were turned on."

"I wasn't. I hate him."

"You were so proud of him. You wanted to be just like him. He saw that. I saw it too. He was nothing to you until he did all this."

"It's not like that, Teddy."

"You're a psychopath. Just like your old man."

"I'm not, Teddy. I'm not."

Teddy nodded, firmly set on his answer. "Yes. You are. You are a psychopath. That's why you can sell his story. You can sell his tools. Because you don't care. You don't feel bad for those people down there."

"I do. I really do."

"You make money off of them. Their pain is worth money to you."

The calm in Teddy's voice unnerved Isaac. He tried to stay calm himself but heard his own voice wavering as he spoke. "I-I've made mistakes."

"You're selfish."

"Yes. Yes, I'm selfish."

"You only care about what you want."

"Yes."

"And isn't that the sign of a psychopath? Not thinking of others? Only of yourself. Only caring about getting the things you want."

"I-I don't know."

"And you wanted my daughter. Like how your old man wanted those kids. You listened to his stories and you got off on them. You wanted your own." The calm left Teddy's voice. His voice and body started quivering as the rage built in him again. "You took my daughter. You raped my daughter."

"No, I didn't."

"You raped my daughter!"

"No, wait—"

"You raped my daughter!!!"

Teddy ripped the laptop off Isaac's desk.

Isaac put his hands up. "Wait... wait..."

Teddy slammed the laptop into the side of Isaac's face. Isaac's head whacked into the floor.

"You're sick! Your whole family's sick!" Teddy yelled as he kicked Isaac hard in the ribs. He pulled back his leg and kicked him again. Then he bent onto his knees, reeled back his fist and punched Isaac in the face.

Isaac's only defense was to curl into a ball and try to absorb the hits. "No! No! Please!" he cried out.

In his small, dark place, he could feel Teddy's massive blows slam into his body. Teddy didn't seem to be aiming. He was too furious to aim. Over and over, he reeled back his right fist and pounded down into Isaac's flesh.

Isaac felt the hammering on his shoulder. And then it moved down to his back. Teddy wasn't attacking him out of any strategy. He seemed to just want to hurt Isaac.

Suddenly, one of Teddy's punches made contact with Isaac's midsection, and Isaac was sure he heard a snap. At that moment, a pain shot through Isaac's body, and he released a cry of anguish.

The scream seemed to startle Teddy. He stopped his attack.

Teddy leaned back. He climbed to his feet and stood there silently.

Isaac struggled to maintain consciousness. He squirmed his body up against the side of his bed, trying maybe to crawl underneath it. It seemed like the only safe place he could find. He moaned as he grasped at the carpet to pull himself away from Teddy.

He reached under his bed.

"This isn't me," Teddy said, his voice hollow and distant. "This isn't the kind of thing I do. I don't know why I made that deal with Joan. I don't know why I made that deal with you. This isn't me. I never break the rules. I've never punched a man before. This isn't me."

There was a long pause.

Isaac reached under his bed, trying to pull his crushed body away from his attacker.

"I think your family is cursed. I think its evilness is like a virus. It infected me somehow. It got inside me. It made me a different person. I think you're infected too."

There was another pause. Isaac saw Teddy step over and stand beside the bed, looking down at him.

"Isaac, look at me."

Isaac took a breath. He pulled himself into a sitting position, leaning his back against the edge of the bed. He looked up at Teddy.

"What will I do with you now?" Teddy said.

The two men stared at each other.

Teddy broke eye contact first. He looked down, noticing something touching his shoe, something underneath the bed. Something metal. He lifted back the edge of the hanging blanket. He reached down and grabbed the tool that lay there. It was a socket wrench. But the handle was long. Two-feet long.

Isaac watched as Teddy felt the wrench's weight. He gripped it in his hand as if it were a club. A sad realization seemed to wash over him as he held it. He nodded his head, accepting the inevitable. "This is for the best. The world is a better place today."

He straightened his back as he held the wrench.

"Was this your father's wrench?" Teddy asked. "Or is this just something you bought?" He gripped the wrench in both hands and raised it above his head, preparing to swing it down at Isaac's face.

"It's not a wrench," Isaac said. "It's a breaker bar. That long handle gives it leverage and torque. You use it to crack a nut that's been rusted on."

"I see."

"Some people just put a pipe over the handle of a normal wrench. Gives them the extension and serves the same purpose. A real handyman might use a pipe in a pinch, but he would probably own an actual breaker bar. Like that one."

"Good to know."

"The trick to a breaker bar is to use even pressure," Isaac said between his uneven, pained breaths. His hand, meanwhile, groped around under the bed. "Amateurs try to just rely on their arm strength. But that creates a jerkiness. If you got a real tough nut to crack, you wanna use your whole body. Your legs, your back, your arms. All working in a nice fluid motion, like rowing a boat. You gotta commit."

Teddy looked down on him. "You really are The Handyman's son."

"I guess some things rub off."

"Goodbye, Isaac."

Teddy raised the bar above Isaac's head.

In a swift move, Isaac's hand emerged from beneath the bed. He was clutching the handle of a long screwdriver. He threw all his weight behind it as he stabbed the screwdriver through Teddy's shoe. Deep into the center of his foot.

Teddy let out an anguished scream as he fell to the ground. The breaker bar tumbled from his grasp onto the floor.

Isaac lunged for the bar, clambering over the top of Teddy to get to it. They wrestled on the floor, each straining to reach the tool.

A beefy arm wrapped itself around Isaac's neck and tightened on his throat, constricting around Isaac's airway. He gasped and flailed, but Teddy only squeezed tighter. Panic set in. The bar lay momentarily forgotten as Isaac's sole focus in life became the fight to get air back in his lungs.

He could feel Teddy repositioning his body to reach over and grab hold of the bar. Isaac's legs kicked out. His arms flung around. His mind, already woozy from earlier, became fuzzy. His vision seemed to iris into a strange tunnel, the black fringes of which grew ever darker, advancing on the last bits of light.

And in that darkness, something took hold of Isaac. There was no conscious thought-process or memory recall behind it, but something within him awoke with words his father said.

Grab the pinkie.

Even without vision, oxygen, or any other senses, Isaac reached out. His hand wrapped around whatever it could find to grab onto. With all his strength, he gave a yank. The loud snap of a bone being forcibly pulled from its joint, and ripped until it doubled back, rewarded his efforts. It was soon accompanied by Teddy's horrendous shout of excruciating pain.

The boa constrictor of an arm unwound itself from Isaac's throat.

One gulp of air was all that he required for his vision to snap back. He freed himself from Teddy's grasp, sprang to his feet, and stomped down hard on Teddy's hand that was clutching the bar.

Isaac wrenched the bar free from his grasp, and in one clean, smooth swing, bashed it into Teddy's head.

A look of surprise flashed over Teddy's face as the fight left him. He looked up at Isaac but seemed to be unable to focus his eyes.

Isaac stood over him, raising the bar.

Teddy managed to croak out, "Wait... wait, Isaac..."

CHAPTER 43

Isaac limped down the apartment steps.

He crossed the parking area toward his car.

His shirt was splattered with blood. His face was cut and bruised. Each breath he took, each time his rib cage expanded and contracted, sent a wave of pain through his body. But he marched on with a grim determination to get out of there, to leave the scene. He was walking toward the setting sun and he could barely see anything through his swollen eyelids.

"Isaac?"

Someone was talking to him. There was concern in the tenor of the voice. It was a woman's voice. Isaac's woozy mind initially assumed it was his mother, come to care for him. To hug him. To tell him it's all right. That all the nasty things his father had said about her were lies, and that she truly did love him and care for him and that everything in his life was ruined by the old man.

"What happened to you?"

That wasn't his mother. He recognized this voice.

Holding his hand up to block the sun's glare, he squinted as the speaker came into focus. Lauren was standing by his car. Her eyes were wide, and her mouth was limp in confusion and concern.

"What are you doing here?" he asked.

"You... you told me to come. Your dad's all over the news. What... what happened to you?"

"We have to get out of here," he said as he marched toward her.

"Why? What happened?"

"Later." He grabbed her by the arm and tugged her toward the door of his car.

Lauren frantically glanced around, trying to make sense of everything. "That's Dad's car," she said. "Is he here?"

Isaac opened the door to the backseat of his car and gave her a little shove, trying to force her in. She locked her knees.

"Whose blood is this?" she asked, pointing to Isaac's red-stained shirt.

"It's mine. Come on." He gave another shove.

Lauren braced herself. From where Isaac was grabbing her arm, he could feel her muscles tighten in defiance.

"Where's my dad?" she said, her voice becoming stern.

"It doesn't matter. Let's go!"

"What have you done?"

"Get in the car, Lauren!"

She ripped her arm away from his grip. "What the fuck is going on?"

"I love you." He didn't mean to say it, but the words spilled out of his mouth with all the elegance of a gag reflex. He saw Lauren's face transform from confusion to fear. Her eyes darted around, looking for room to maneuver, but he was blocking her against his open car.

"Let me go," she finally said.

"Please. Don't leave me."

"Fuck you, Isaac! What the fuck have you done to my dad, you fucking psycho?"

Isaac grabbed her arm and shoved her toward the open car door. "Get in the car."

"No! Help! Somebody help!"

He yanked her hair so hard that she lost her balance.

He forcibly shoved her into the car.

She kicked and flailed.

Isaac threw himself on top of her, using as much of his weight as possible to hold her in place. She scraped and clawed at him, but he couldn't feel anything anymore. Not outside his body and not inside. All he could feel was the overwhelming urge to have her limp and silent.

"Stop it! Stop it! Stop it!" he shouted.

She screamed, as loud as she could, "Help! Help!"

His hands grabbed her by the neck and clenched tight.

"Don't you fucking leave me. You'll do as I fucking say," he said.

Isaac could hear some back corner of his brain screaming for him to stop. But the sound of that internal scream didn't form words, only noise. An animalistic noise that was rejecting what was happening. The longer he held his hands around Lauren's throat, the less defined that noise became, and the more other thoughts drowned it out.

A rational voice began to speak inside Isaac's head.

It started off low, but quickly overcame the screaming noise. This voice was practical. This voice was didn't want Isaac to get caught. It made plans. *I need to find some way to tie her up. And then I can take her somewhere away from here. But where? A motel room? Do I have enough cash? A credit card could be traced. Maybe I can drive into the woods. Find a campground. Let Lauren calm down and then express my love to her. Win her over. If she rejects me, I'll deal with the consequences then. I can't let her leave me. I've let too many people leave me. It's my fault that I'm alone.*

That voice, that planning and rationalizing voice, grew in volume. It processed thoughts with amazing speed, developing plans, scenarios, and alternative plans. Within second fragments, that voice was troubleshooting every potential pitfall and trap in Isaac's ability to whisk Lauren away and make a perfect life with her, away from the media. Away from the police. Away from his father.

His father...

The voice found time to rewind and replay the entire conversation he had had with his father. Little spikes of detail flashed into Isaac's brain.

He wished he had a U-lock to secure Lauren's neck to the door handle. He wished he had a basement prepared where he could chain her up. He wished... he wished... he wished...

But the voice told him he didn't need any of that. Elizabeth had never loved Walter, but Lauren *did* love Isaac.

She loved him, right? Had she said that? It didn't matter. He felt it.

The voice showed Isaac images of their night at the cemetery. Of them fucking. Of her *loving* him.

And then more images flashed into his mind. Of her chained up. On the bed. He pushed those thoughts away. It wasn't like that. *He* wasn't like that. He didn't have those genes. Those impulses. He could find true, genuine love in this world. He wouldn't be alone any longer.

An image flashed in his mind.

His father.

Elizabeth.

Lovingly positioned together at Isaac's childhood desk. Looking at their reflection in the mirrored closet doors. So close to success.

The image distorted.

Something wasn't right.

A thought ran through Isaac's mind.

Mirrored closet doors... Mirrored closet doors...

He looked up, catching his own reflection in the car's rearview mirror. As he gazed at that reflection, his mind suddenly snapped back to clarity. He wasn't sure how much time had elapsed, perhaps only seconds, but a million thoughts had raced through his head in that time and now they all came screeching to a halt.

He threw his hands back, releasing his grip on Lauren's throat.

She took heaving breaths, gasping for air and filling her lungs.

Terrified, Isaac scrambled to back away from her, desperate to get *himself* and his own arms out of range of being able to grab her again.

He tumbled from the car and landed with a thump on the pavement. Even that felt too close for comfort. He scurried backwards another few feet.

"I'm sorry. I'm so so sorry," he said. He looked at his hands. They trembled terribly. He couldn't control them, he couldn't calm them. He had to remind himself to breathe.

Lauren pulled herself into a sitting position and huddled in the car as far away from Isaac as possible.

Their eyes met briefly.

He had to look away. "It wasn't me. Or it was. I don't know. I don't know who I am. He... he fucked with my mind. With what it meant to be a man. What it took to get what I wanted. I... I... I don't know. That's no excuse." The words weren't coming out cleanly, but he continued stuttering his way forward. "I... I'm sorry."

He sat on the pavement. Then he forced his head up so that Lauren could see his face. "I idolized him," he said. "I always did. I wanted *him* to like *me*."

Lauren continued to huddle against the door. She kept her eyes on him, but her hand fumbled for the lock. She popped it and then pulled on the handle.

Isaac made no motion to stop her.

His voice drifted from his lips, leaden and empty. "Your dad's tied up in my apartment. Unit 204. He's beat pretty bad. He broke my phone, so I was going to drive myself to the hospital. He's alive." Isaac took a deep breath. "I assaulted you. When you press charges, the police can find me at my father's house."

He tried to stand, but his ribs hurt too much. He had to place his hands on the pavement and push himself up off the ground. The movement startled Lauren. She suddenly threw open the door, leapt from the car, and sprinted off across the parking lot as fast as she could.

Isaac barely even glanced up at her as she fled.

Each step shot razor blades through Isaac's body. He marveled at how his body had been able to numb the pain while he was violently attacking Teddy and Lauren, but now that he was done, it felt as if someone had turned open a spigot on his entire nervous system.

With great effort, he walked around his car, slamming the various doors. Then he climbed into the driver's seat and started the engine.

CHAPTER 44

The offices of the Defenders of Public Enlightenment and Recreation Magazine (aka, DOPER Mag) were located in a large, open warehouse space in Brooklyn. The primary decorations on the walls and ceilings were the building's own exposed steel girders and rivets. After centuries of office spaces obscuring the skeletons of buildings—making warehouses look like anything *but* a warehouse—now it was hip to make an office look as functionally out-of-date as possible.

Any decorations or fixtures that DOPER added were of a wrought-iron steam-punk design, adding to the ironic future-of-the-past appearance.

The only deviation from this decorating rule was the ceiling mounted flat-screen TVs—all tuned to various news channels—that encircled the entire office.

Ben sat in his desk in the middle of the open office and pushed "redial" on his phone. It rang. And rang. He glanced up at the TVs. Two of the twenty-four-hour news stations had cut away to stories about The Handyman being in critical condition after an attack at the prison.

A voice came on Ben's phone. "Hey, it's Isaac. Leave a message and I'll—"

Ben hung up. He bit his lip.

An intern clutching a phone, his hand covering the receiver, rushed over to Ben's desk.

"His parents are about to sign the license deal," the intern said.

"To who?"

"I, uh, they won't say. It's one of the networks."

"*Networks* or cable?"

"Um, I... I don't know."

Ben snatched up his phone again and pressed redial.

"Just stall them a couple minutes, will ya?" Ben said.

"They say we need to get our bid in now or we'll lose out," the intern said.

"Stall them."

The intern's eyes went wide. This wasn't part of his job description. "Uh, I... how would you like me to do that?"

"Look, I got a guy I'm pretty sure can get us something better. I don't want to have to pay for the same fucking material twice. Stall them."

The intern gulped. He removed his hand from the receiver and spoke into the phone. "Hi. We're very interested in your footage. I just spoke with my supervisor and he needs to clear some things through accounting..."

Ben turned his attention back to his own phone.

The voicemail picked up again. "Hey, it's Isaac. Leave a message and I'll call you back."

Beep!

"Isaac, it's Ben. Where the fuck are you, bro? There's a feeding frenzy out there for all things Handyman and Handyman-related. I really need to know what you got and what you want for it. And I need to know, like, five minutes ago. Don't freeze me out, bro. Don't go selling stuff without talking to your old friend, Ben, first. Okay? I've always done right by you, and you'll always get a fair price here. Call me back."

Ben hung up. He leaned back and stared up at the TV screens.

The intern returned. Ben noticed that he wasn't cupping a phone in his hand.

"Is it gone?" Ben asked.

The intern nodded.

"Did you find out who bought it?"

"Um, WNN. I think."

Ben glanced up at one of the TVs. A blaring graphic exploded across the screen, announcing "WNN EXCLUSIVE!"

Ben stood and walked closer to the screen so he could hear.

The WNN anchor announced, "Breaking news out of the Willamette Valley Correctional Facility in Oregon. Officials there have confirmed that serial killer Walter Luce, better known as The Handyman, was violently attacked by a fellow inmate. Unconfirmed reports claim that the other inmate—who is also on Death Row but whose identity has yet to be confirmed—stabbed Mr. Luce through the ear with a sharp object. Mr. Luce was transferred to a local hospital. Details are forthcoming, but WNN has obtained this exclusive footage. We warn you, these images might be disturbing."

The picture transitioned to the video that the teenager in the ER lobby filmed of paramedics rushing Walter into the hospital.

Ben watched the video with an analytic eye. "Good shot of his face there," he said mostly to himself. "I like how the angle is such that you can see the ear, or at least the bloody gauze on it. That red really pops. The most interesting part is how much fucking security they got here. We got prison guards, police, hospital security... Jesus Christ. He's a seventy-year-old unconscious man. Do they think he's gonna rip out of those restraints and start biting people's faces? Still, it's a good final shot. It makes him look scary and important. We can draft off this with our own stuff. How much did they pay?"

He glanced over at the intern whose eyes went wide again. *Me? Are you talking to me?*

Ben shrugged. "Doesn't matter."

He strolled over to the refrigerator by the snack table in the center of the office. He pulled out a sparkling water, cracked it open, and held it up to the screen.

"To The Handyman," he announced to himself before taking a swig.

He stood there, drinking his fizzing water and thinking up copy for all the different headlines he could run on this story for the next few months.

Hopefully he had enough content to carry this through until the next serial killer, or school shooter, or crazy spree killer.

He wasn't too worried. There was always another killer on the horizon. "You're missing out, Isaac," he said out loud to no one in particular.

CHAPTER 45

I climbed out of my car and walked up that well-worn driveway.

I was back at my father's house.

The chain-link fence blocked my path. My ribs screamed in pain and I had a numbness in my right leg that was making me limp. I couldn't remember what caused that. Teddy must've hit me hard enough on that leg to damage muscle.

In any case, there was no way I was going to be able to will my body to climb over that fence. I thought about giving up, turning around, and driving to a hospital, which probably should have been my top priority considering how broken my body was.

But I knew I wouldn't have the opportunity to see the house again if I did. At best, the county would probably bulldoze it to the ground soon. At worst, it would become a shrine to my dad. And then the county would bulldoze it anyway. To turn back now meant allowing his story to stand, exactly as he told it. Exactly as he wanted it. His story of murder and power.

But it wasn't his story anymore.

This was the day I intended to start *my* story.

My life.

I really fucked up my story recently. But, as my dad exemplified, it's never too late to rewrite your narrative.

I was reminded of a corny motivational poster in my high school guidance counselor's office. It read, "Today is the first fucking day of the rest of your fucking life." Or something like that.

In order to carpe-my-fucking-diem, I needed to put the old man to rest. I needed to know one final truth. I needed one tiny detail.

And it was in that house.

So, I limped my way around the length of that fenced perimeter, looking for some sort of gap I could slip between without hurting myself.

It was a beautiful day. The cloud cover had moved in at some point, making it cool and overcast.

Not the normal, Oregon, dreary overcast, either. It was that weird, bright overcast. The kind of clouds that when you look out the window, you think you won't need sunglasses for the day. At first glance, it's dark and gloomy. Then you go outside and, somehow, you find yourself squinting. You can't see the sun, but it's there, and it's brightening up the world. Those are the days when kids get sunburned if they're not careful.

I wandered around into the backyard.

The fence ran along our old concrete patio.

It seemed that when the county fenced off the property, they didn't want to go through the effort of driving the posts into the concrete. They also didn't want to have the expense of extending the fence *around* the patio. And so, right about where Dad and I used to light the charcoals for the grill, the fence-posts stood on stabilizing legs on top of the concrete.

I could move these.

With a great deal of effort—my left hand was struggling to grip things—I nudged the post aside enough for me to slip through.

This portion of the backyard hadn't changed much since I was a kid. Over in the corner where the concrete pad reached the basement window, I knew I could find my handprints in the concrete. I was about seven or eight when Dad had me leave those impressions. I didn't want to see them, though. Nothing about this house gave me nostalgia or longing anymore. Those handprints may as well have been from a stranger. At this point, they were someone *else's* childhood memory.

I looked around for a way in. I didn't think I could hoist myself through the living room window like before. And the front door was well sealed. The sliding glass door that led to the backyard had long since been shattered and covered in plywood.

But when I walked over to it, I was happy to discover that someone had ripped the plywood out from where it had been nailed to the frame and then just set it back over the hole. It was probably done by high schoolers who wanted easy future access.

Even sliding that plywood to the side caused me pain in muscles I didn't even know the body possessed. I didn't understand how the body was all connected. Gripping things caused pain in my chest. Lifting felt like someone jabbing a ball-point pen into my side.

Pain is fucking weird.

I stepped into the kitchen. There was nothing I wanted to see here. Nothing worth noting. I avoided looking at the basement door as I walked past it. There was nothing more to be said about that place.

My destination was my bedroom.

I stepped in and looked around. My head spun slightly, partly because I was probably still working my way through a concussion. But it might have also been the weight of so many realizations hitting me. Everything I thought I remembered was true. And everything my dad said— well, at least *some* things my dad said—were outright lies.

Just to make sure, I walked over to the closet.

Exactly as I thought, on the wall beside the closet door were my childhood height markings.

Isaac—Age 7
Isaac—Age 8
Isaac—Age 9

I leaned against the hollow core door to make sure it was real.

Then I turned and walked out of the room.

A few steps across the hall and I was standing in my dad's room. Although lacking furniture, the size and layout were exactly as I remembered.

It was the biggest room in the house, but that didn't say much. It didn't have a master bath or a walk-in closet. The house was much too old for such things, although my dad long fantasized about adding them. Like so many other fanciful projects of his, he never did.

The closets in Dad's room were the same size as mine, but they were positioned in a funky place. The old hinged doors that came with the house required a radius of space to open, which limited the kinds of furniture that can fit in a small room like this.

Long story short, sometime in the eighties, my dad installed sliding mirrored closet doors in his bedroom.

And only his bedroom.

Which meant that when Elizabeth saw herself in the mirror and had her breakdown, it wasn't from the desk in my room. Not the kiddie room for Dad to groom his long-lost child. It was from the bed in Dad's room.

He brought her to *his* room.

He had her on *his* bed.

I used to say that Ted Bundy was my favorite serial killer. It's kind of a fucked-up thing to say, but I don't think I'm alone in that statement. I thought he was a badass. He was smart and suave, and everything that I want to be, yet am not. But at his core, the man was a rapist. He not only raped his victims while they were alive, he would have sex with their corpses, sometimes weeks after they decayed in their graves in the woods of the Pacific Northwest. There's nothing badass about that.

John Wayne Gacy and Jeffrey Dahmer too.

There's nothing deep about these guys.

Ed Kemper.

There's nothing to idolize.

Leonard Lake and Charles Ng.

There's no grand purpose.

Richard Ramirez.

There's just hate and anger.

There're just guys who are fucked up.

Elizabeth escaped from my father's bedroom. Chances are that he either raped her or intended to rape her. This wasn't about grooming a daughter or starting a family. It wasn't about teaching me a lesson in respect. It wasn't about righting the wrongs of his life. It was about him. It was always about him. He hurt people because he could. Because he wanted to.

I walked out of the room, down the hallway, through the kitchen, out the sliding glass door, and back around to my car.

Standing there, looking back at the house, I wondered what I would do next. Selling murderabilia always felt dirty, but now it felt gross. What was left? It might take some time, but I could probably find a job. I was reasonably smart and well-spoken. Until an hour ago, I was also in decent physical shape.

We'll see.

Most of all, I knew I needed to leave Woodburn. I needed to leave Oregon. I had friends in major cities up and down the West Coast. I was going to leave here. I was going to find work. I was going to make a life for myself.

I climbed into my car and backed out of the driveway.

This one last time, I allowed myself to think about my father and contemplate who he was and why he did the things he did.

My dad was a handyman. And like a good handyman, he knew the value of troubleshooting. To troubleshoot, you isolate one component and test it. Just as he would test every individual circuit or plug to find a solution, he tested me. He probed until he found my weaknesses.

Sometimes, however, all that troubleshooting just fucks up the system more. Was my mom really a horrible person?

I honestly didn't know.

Did my dad truly love me?

I honestly didn't know.

The lies had twisted themselves around my head and choked off the oxygen that truth so desperately needs to survive.

I didn't even know why he lied so much.

Maybe he actually didn't know why himself. I could say that he lied to protect his self-image, or maybe garner sympathy from an ungrateful son, but those answers require a level of planning and self-awareness that I'm not sure he was capable of.

Or maybe he always was capable of such perversions of the truth, and that the real con was that he had me believing he was being simple and honest with his lies.

I honestly didn't know.

As I neared the highway, I saw a police cruiser racing toward me. Its lights were flashing, but its siren was off. It had to be for me. No siren meant that they considered me a flight risk and were trying to sneak up on me.

I pulled to the shoulder.

The cruiser came up behind me. Its lights continued flashing, but the officer stayed in the car, probably jotting a note or reporting back to HQ.

It didn't matter.

I had assaulted Lauren. I hurt her. I tried to abduct her by force. If the world was just, I should face punishment for it. I'll probably spend time in jail. I'll probably get a felony or two or three on my record. That'll make finding a job hard. It'll make starting a life hard. Pulling out of this might be as challenging or more challenging than anything my father had to overcome. But, at that moment, I determined I would face the consequences for my actions and rise above. I would live my best life. I wasn't going to let the world beat me. Not like it beat my father.

Did the world beat my father?

Or did he just use that as an excuse?

I honestly didn't know.

Why did my father do what he did?

Maybe he was lonely.

Maybe he was lashing out.

Maybe he wanted to feel powerful.

Maybe he felt that infamy was the antidote to a forgettable life.

Maybe he was creating a new family, one that would never abandon him.

Maybe he wanted to fuck young women.

Maybe he wanted to hurt the young men that young women habitually chose over him.

Or maybe he was just a fucking psychopath.

A loser. A hateful, pathetic loser.

And maybe he's not worth analyzing beyond that.

EPILOGUE

The surgeons huddled around the table.

The whirls of drills cutting through bone filled the room. They worked with calm intensity.

Walter lay beneath them, unconscious.

His eyes fluttered.

One final memory seeped through what remained of his brain.

He sat in his kitchen, enjoying his after-lunch coffee. The little afternoon caffeine kick kept him from napping and thus helped him have a decent night's sleep. It was a small ritual that he came to cherish. No matter how hot the Oregon summers became, Walter enjoyed his steaming cup of afternoon coffee.

The front door opened.

Walter's eyes glanced up. His lips stretched into a smile as Isaac walked in.

"Dad? Why aren't you at work?" Isaac asked, not out of surprise, but more as a conversation.

"I figured I could take my son's eighteenth birthday off."

"Oh. Cool."

The two looked at each other. Neither had much else to say. Walter took the moment to study his son's face. People always commented that the two looked alike, but Walter didn't see it. The boy had his mom's eyes, and there wasn't much left to the face after that. On top of that, Isaac had been trying to grow out a beard for the past year or so. Walter had long looked forward to the day when he could lather up his son's face with shaving cream and teach him to use a straight edge. But the boy could only manage a nasty teenage mustache. He could get by with a twenty-dollar electric razor for the rest of his life.

T.J. PAYNE

So much for *that* bonding experience, Walter thought.

"I, uh, gotta load up my stuff," Isaac said, shifting his weight from one foot to the other. "So I can, you know, return Ryan's truck."

The boy was moving into a friend's apartment. He would have to pay rent, which he probably couldn't afford because he only seemed to want or be qualified for minimum wage jobs. To Walter's mind, it was yet another foolish choice Isaac was making. But what could one expect? College should have been the boy's out. It should have propelled the boy out of the sickening tide pool of do-nothing that the Luce clan had been mired in for generations. Union jobs were supposed to be the escape, but those were dried up now. The boy would amount to nothing, and so would Walter's legacy. Oh well. Such is life in this house.

"Fine, fine. Oh—" Walter slid an envelope across the table. "Happy birthday."

His eyes sparkled as he watched his curious son step toward the table and pick up the envelope. Isaac opened it and pulled out its contents. The boy's eyes lit up.

"Tickets to Game Three?" Isaac shouted.

Walter nodded. But that was only Phase One of the surprise. Walter knew the boy would recognize what this gift was, but he would have to read it a bit closer to realize how *expensive* this gift was.

"Lower level?"

Walter nodded again. "Go Blazers."

"Oh my god. Oh my god. Holy shit, Dad. These are—"

"Two rows behind the bench. The players can hear you fart."

Isaac smiled. "I'll hold it in during free throws."

"Happy birthday."

"Thanks, Dad."

Isaac pulled out his wallet and shoved the tickets inside. "Do you mind if I take Ryan? I owe him for letting me borrow the truck and all."

Walter took a sip of his coffee, his smile stretched on his otherwise stoic face. "I was going to spend the day mending the fence anyway." He rotated slightly and stared out the window.

"What if Buddy tries to get back through the hole?"

"It's been a week. That dog's gone."

"But—"

"Don't get attached to things, boy."

With that, Walter stood and plodded toward the sliding glass door, carrying his coffee out of the house.

He walked down to the patio.

For several minutes, he just stood there, shutting his eyes and soaking in the rare Oregon sun. He heard the front door open and close a few times as Isaac lugged boxes, luggage, a desktop computer, and an old TV out to the truck.

Walter, of course, also owned a pickup. And he was glad the boy never asked to borrow it.

After he heard the front door slam closed one final time, and the pickup's engine start, Walter finally set down his coffee.

He picked up a toolbox he had set aside for the job. He walked out across the backyard toward the fence. He needed some lumber for the job and he always kept scrap wood in a pile, covered in a tarp, near the side of the yard. It was all the leftover wood from any job he ever performed.

He walked over, pulled back the tarp, and selected the boards he would use. That fence was twenty years old. He knew he would need to sink at least three new four-by-fours for the uprights. Then he would need to pour concrete. It was a pain-in-the-ass job and he had been putting it off for years.

As he selected his lumber, a fly circled his face. The fly's soft buzzing grew louder then softer then louder again as it orbited him. Walter swatted it away and tried to ignore its angry hum. Flies and other insects were a common nuisance in the many ditches and crawl spaces in which he found himself working every day.

The fly swooped around and came to a landing on his mustache. Walter could feel its tiny legs poking among the hairs on his lip. He swatted it away again. At which point, the fly seemed to multiply. Three flies... no wait, four... maybe as many as ten were taking off and landing on his back, his arms, and his head.

And then it clicked for him. He knew where the flies were coming from.

He looked at a sheet of plywood that lay flat on the ground. He reached over and slid the sheet away, revealing a large, gaping pit in the earth. As the plywood moved, a swarm of flies belched out of the pit. Like an angry cloud, the flies flowed up, out and around the yard.

Walter swatted them away, shielded his eyes, and glanced down into the hole in the earth. There lay Buddy. Right where Walter had left him. It had been only a week ago when Walter had stepped into one pile of his shit too many. It always infuriated him. Dog shit had a way of adhering and compacting into every crevice of the tread of a shoe. When he had felt that slimy sludge of a fresh turd compress under his foot, and then smelled its scent waft up, a rage bubbled up within him. He took out that rage on the nearest creature.

He hoped the boy never found out what he did. That would be embarrassing. Shameful even. Besides, it was a one-time act of anger. Walter was sure it would never happen again now that he had gotten it out of his system.

Poor Buddy, though, Walter thought.

Although, the more he looked down at the dog's body, the more he realized that he felt nothing at the sight. Just emptiness. The same feeling he had about the boy moving out.

Walter calmly climbed back to his feet and dusted himself off. Whistling softly, not a care in the world, he slid the plywood sheet back over the pit, grabbed some of the boards he intended to use, and walked toward his fence project. He would fill in that pit some other time.

It was a beautiful day for Oregon. The kind of cool, sunny weekend day that would make any man proud to be out in their backyard, working with his hands. A perfect day.

He sang softly to himself as he walked.

"With a knick-knack, paddy-whack, give a dog a bone. This old man came rolling home."

That memory was the final thought that went through Walter's mind as he lay on the operating table. It was a memory that popped into his mind many times as he sat in his cell on Death Row. He used to wonder if it was a good memory or a bad one. Was he capable of determining the difference anymore?

He had spent hours, days even, debating what it meant about his own psychological makeup. How did he truly *feel* about that moment?

He wasn't able to ponder it too much today, though.

His head filled with blood and choked his brain to death.

Walter Luce was pronounced dead at 6:32 p.m.

THE END

Thank you for reading! If you enjoyed *In My Father's Basement*, I invite you to check out my other books:

Intercepts: a horror novel

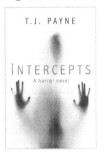

Joe works for a company that performs human experimentation. His work just followed him home.

Named one of the best horror books of all time by *Cosmopolitan*.

The Venue: a wedding novel

Amy never expected to be invited to Caleb's wedding. And now, she doesn't expect to get out alive.

"Rollicking dark, twisted fun!"

ACKNOWLEDGEMENTS

Writing is neither an easy nor a quick process. I could never have finished this novel without the support of several individuals. First of all, I'd like to thank my mom. Few people could so deftly handle the balancing act of unconditional encouragement and constructive criticism. She has always pushed me to follow my dreams and become a better writer in the process. I know that the unpleasant tale in *In My Father's Basement* is not any sort of story that she is attracted to, and yet, she dedicated so many hours to reading and rereading the manuscript for errors while always offering the best of advice. Thank you, Mom.

I'd also like to thank my wife. I could not have accomplished anything without her love and support. She fills my life with so much joy and happiness. My writing descends into some dark places, but because of her love, I never have to fear that I won't be able to find my way back.

Thank you to both my brothers. They are genuinely good guys who have always supported my creative endeavors and taught me valuable lessons about family in the process. One of them also taught me that inmates spread feces on their shivs for infections. The more you know!

And finally, I'd like to acknowledge my father, a kind, good-humored man who is nothing like the monster in this book. Although, they do have one thing in common. My father made sure that all his boys learned their way around a hand tool, and that we all knew the value of an honest day's work. Dad, you may not be the inspiration for Walter, but you're an inspiration for me.

Made in the USA
Middletown, DE
22 June 2023

33223845R00166